VAMPIRE: THE MASQUERADE

CLAN NOVEL:
ANTHOLOGY

I0630741

Edited by Stewart Wieck

WORLD OF DARKNESS

www.worldofdarkness.com

Table of Contents

Embarkation

Kathleen Ryan

Thursday, 10 February 1916, 10:42 PM
The docks
Alexandria, Egypt

Erich Vegel leapt from his taxi before the driver could stop.

"*Effendi!* My fare!"

"In good time, my man—in good time." Vegel snatched his bag off the luggage carrier and fumbled for his wallet. His fingers closed on a thick coin-purse, full of local money. He smiled and drew it out. "For you," he told the cabby, "for your good wives, for your family—" The Setite folded cash and case together into the astonished man's hands. "Take it! Save me the price of changing it. *Bahksheeshl*"

"*Shukran*," said the Egyptian, staring at the madman.

Erich didn't notice. He had already started running.

———

The *Ellen Tucker* slept quietly in her berth, hoarding strength for her next voyage. Passengers trickled up her gangplanks, porters and cases in tow, and the stewards greeted them cordially. There were widows among the guests; the wounded were not few. The *Ellen*, her officers and her crew were suitably subdued—no champagne flowed, no band played, no streamers crowded the air. The docks could not help being noisy, and as the convoy prepared to leave the clamor grew—

but each sound was businesslike, impersonal, and so the whole seemed hushed.

When Erich hurtled into sight, heads turned. Though strongly built and rather short, the Setite was a spindly and awkward-looking sprinter. His legs wound up and let fly like a child's tin toy might. His arms were trying to do the same, which would at least have balanced the motion below—but his baggage got in the way. The heavy leather grip bogged down his right shoulder, and his left hand, holding a white linen jacket, flailed the cloth about like a flag of shamefully pacifist truce.

Vegel careened toward the ship, and a steward stepped out to help him.

"*Ellen Tucker*, sir?"

"Yes!" Vegel sped by the porters and the waiting queue, past the luggage vans and into the dimmer reaches of the pier. He caught sight of bundled cargo and veered toward it. Out of sight of the British garrison's soldiers, out of earshot of the customs men and the merchants, in the midst of the sailors and the dockworkers, there were two men standing, supervising careful hands to net and hoist a set of small crates.

One, clearly the foreman, was a sunburnt, grizzled giant in very cheap American clothes. His eyes flickered over the newcomer, then turned back to the loading.

The second watcher, looking like a dwarf beside his companion, was a black man in Moslem garb. His robes and kaffieyeh were well-made and clean, and the band around his headdress glinted a little with gold. He handed a sheaf of yellowed papers to the foreman. With his chin, he pointed toward the fast-approaching and disheveled European, and said something under his breath—something funny, to judge by the grins that sprouted on the Arabs around him.

Vegel recognized him instantly, and staggered to a halt. His hat flew off at the sudden stop, and his pocketwatch tumbled from his vest. Erich stooped to pick them up, conscious of the poor figure he was cutting, just when he had hoped to impress. He gathered his goods together, as well as his wits. Donning his straw panama once again, he looked frankly into the eyes of the man he had come to meet

"*Bismallah*." said Vegel brightly. "Hesha abn Yusuf?"

"*Bismallah*. I am Hesha."

"Thank goodness I found you, sir." Erich smiled disarmingly, continuing, "I took the train from Cairo as soon as I heard you were leaving."

Hesha pursed his lips and seemed to study his words. "Why?"

The younger Setite glanced around. "I had hoped to speak with you in private, sir."

The African shrugged. "Speak Latin," answered Hesha in that language. "These men are not familiar with it."

"I shall," Erich replied, feeling proud of himself for finding a short 'yesso quickly. He had been literate in Latin since he was old enough to have a tutor, and literate Latin handicapped short speech.

"Well?" Hesha's abrupt tone cut off the schoolboy mood. "Who are you?"

"Vegel." He heard the disappointment in his own voice. He hadn't expected Hesha to forget. The 'Prophet' had such a reputation for memory—for excruciating detail—among people who ought to know. That famed talent for scholarship was one of the prime reasons he, Vegel, had asked his sire for leave—had packed in an hour, while the others of his nest looked on in disbelief—had jumped on the express to get here before the tide turned—

"My name is Erich Vegel," he explained formally. "I must apologize for not having introduced myself immediately." Feeling very Austrian, he bowed and clicked his heels. "We have met before now, sir, although it was quite a long time ago.

1 suppose that I had hoped you might remember me...at the time, you see..." he ran down, felt a fool for hesitating, and carried on: "I was given to understand that I was chosen to serve by your specific recommendation, sir."

Hesha made no reply; he scrutinized his visitor coolly. The water lapped hollowly against the hull of the *Ellen Tucker*, and it seemed to Vegel that the waves washed his confidence away. What do you want, Erich Vegel?"

The Prophet's voice and expression were intimidating, unwelcoming. Erich had thought his die was cast—his Rubicon crossed, in fact, for he tended to think in quotations—when he bought his rail ticket in Cairo. It seemed he was wrong—surely going on with this *here* was the real risk. Nonetheless, he summoned his courage and answered, "I want to go with you, sir."

"Go where?"

"Aren't you sailing for Baltimore tonight?"

"I am. But what takes you to Baltimore?" Hesha paused. "Erich Vegel—" he rolled the sounds across his tongue—"Vegel. In Damascus."

"Yes," cried the younger man, relieved.

"But Damascus wasn't so very long ago—have you completed your education?"

Erich nodded eagerly. "Yes, sir. I've been finished for some years now, and I was granted—" he smiled, but there was no better way he could think of to put it—"1 was granted an end to my apprenticeship and the beginnings of my journey work last night. So you see, I can go where I like and choose my own duties. And I want to work with you."

"For me," said Hesha slowly.

Erich hesitated. "For you," he replied shortly.

The elder Setite frowned. "You give in very easily."

Erich paled.

"Obviously, you cannot offer strength of character." Hesha up ended a crate and sat on it, studying his petitioner. "What do you offer?"

"I am an archaeologist."

"As am I."

"I speak and write more than twenty languages."

"That is useful," said Hesha, "but only if you understand some that I do not."

Shorn of his professions, Erich began to inventory his hobbies. "I can draw, and I am a photographer. I have kept up-to-date on the wireless, and I know how to drive an automobile."

"I might have a use for those abilities," said Hesha doubtfully. "Now tell me why you want this."

"I want to learn from you."

"You have not learned from your teachers?"

"Yes. Of course 1 have. But they can't tell me what one needs to know outside—" Vegel fumbled for expression, and found a solid cliche to fall back on—"the ivory tower. I understand that fieldwork can't be taught in the classroom. What I need to know now can't be had in an elder's havens, or from my brethren in the nest."

Hesha said nothing, but seemed to invite further explanation.

"I shouldn't simply observe, however. I would help. 1 want to accomplish things."

"And the temple here does nothing?"

"No, it does—but it doesn't do what you do—"

"What do I do?" interrupted the older creature. Erich opened his mouth to speak, then snapped it shut. This argument was leading nowhere. If he mentioned the man's scholarship, he could feel it leading back to the teachers at the temple. If he touched on Hesha's famous expeditions, he would probably be told to go find his own—and Egypt was far better ground for that than America. He thought back to his sire's words the night they'd heard that the so-called Prophet was returning to Cairo.

Son of a bitch. Hesha's come home—what? Oh, yes, you met him, didn't you, boy—playing with the Turks, wasn't he? Subversive old sod. Brought down two houses that year. Still Cainites around who can't hold their heads up 'cause of that little affair. Watch him wreck us here. Imagine he'll put his fingers in Surich's pies.

And Surich won't do a damn thing about it! Neither will his precious pet priests! Hesha fought them over the chapel in the Valley of the Kings, right on their turf, and won, boy. He won. Wouldn't tell any of us how he knew the shrine was trapped, but there it was, sure enough, and his way in was the only safe one that kept the body from being destroyed. Son of a bitch has vision. Shame he won't take a temple, but if his intuition won't let him, it won't, and after Bombay no one cares to wrestle with him over that.

Never you mind about Bombay, boy. Enough for you to know the man has a calling. What do you mean, is it a true calling? Don't ask such stupid questions. How the hell would I know if it's true? If he won't say who's talking to him or what name of Set he serves, the rest of us can hardly prove he's listening to an impostor! Now shut up and finish your sketches. They're good enough. I think we can work them into place before dawn.

Erich struggled for words. What he really wanted to know was what Hesha thought he himself was doing. He was notorious for being right without reason. He was revered for his faith, though what he believed was anyone's guess. Somehow, he was subversive among the crooked, and Erich longed to follow that.

But the younger man would have felt ridiculous asking to be a disciple, even had he known he wanted that. He came close when he answered: "You do what needs to be done."

"But you don't know what that is." Hesha laughed. "Your foresight and your will are well matched, apparently."

Erich let the insult go—if he could get away without losing any more face, he would.

"However, I like your temper," said Hesha. He drew breath as though preparing to speak at length. "Suppose I let you travel with me, Vegel. Do you really want to be a Hun in America just now?"

Erich's confidence soared. He could prove himself on this point, at least; disguises were one of his strengths. "Who are you calling a dirty Hun?" he snapped, in a magnificent Brooklyn accent.

Hesha raised an eyebrow. "What school?"

"P.S. 106."

"Very good."

"I made it up."

"I know." Hesha folded his hands together. "What parish?"

A pause. "I—"

"You used an accent common among the Irish immigrants. If you were playing your part well enough, you would have known the name of your church faster than you knew your school. You're not ready."

"How could I find that out here?" retorted Erich.

Wearily, Hesha stood and began walking back to his cargo. "You could," he began, "have used a milder accent—one less subject to identification. You might have invented a persona without easily traceable features. You could have modeled your fiction on a real identity." He stopped and fixed his gaze on Vegel. "Or might have decided not to show off. It is not easy being a Hun here among the British," said Hesha, mimicking Vegel's scholastic Latin. "Or perhaps, 'I have practiced disguising my accent. You might have dealt with the race issue, and asked, 'Do you really want to be a black in America just now?'

"Simpler still," he finished, "'I don't mind the ill-feeling the war has created against my countrymen.'"

Erich stood stunned and speechless. His pride stung him. He felt himself staring stupidly; he wrenched his eyes away from Hesha's and watched the stevedores wrangling their burdens into the hold.

"Work with me," said Hesha, "and you would be known." If the words held the faintest hope, the slightest opening for debate, the tone destroyed it. "You would be marked among our own by my reputation. The Camarilla and the Sabbat would brand you Setite, and you would never again have a real chance to work in secrecy or safety. Do you honestly think you could survive that?"

Erich scratched his brows, considering. He had lost his chance; he might as well keep talking. "My sire asked me the same question last night. I didn't know what to say. I boarded the train anyway."

"So, you did," admitted Hesha, speculatively. He pulled something brown and square from beneath his gallabiyah, inspected it a moment, and then held it out to Vegel. "Tickets," he explained. "First-class passage through New York."

Erich goggled.

"American passport belonging to Eric Wells. Captain, United States Army. You have shellshock, Captain, and become extremely agitated if asked about your service." Hesha smiled. "And now that I have heard your accent, I think you may need to have had your throat gassed out as well." He placed the brown leather folder in his junior's unresisting hand.

"Whisper, Captain," he instructed. Whispering himself, he said, "If I weren't going to take you on, I never would have let you find me."

Erich Vegel stumbled happily toward the gangplank, and the *Ellen Tucker* blew her horn — ready to sail at last.

Selfless

Kathleen Ryan

Sunday, 4 October 1987, 9:31 PM
Amid the nightlife
Calcutta, India

"Thief!"

Khalil scuttled nervously into the shadows as the cry went up. He felt the alarm spread through the crowd.

"Help! Police!"

The euros drew closer to each other. The rich Hindus—the ones who only played in this district—put a hand on their money and craned their necks to watch. Doors on balconies swung cautiously open, and brightly colored, silken ladies leaned out of the upper rooms. The dull eyes of the police on the corner flashed into unlikely alertness.

Khalil's gaze flickered ahead of the cops and found the chaos in the crowd. He breathed a sigh of relief. Not him, not this time.

"Stop her!"

She was just a girl, a scrawny, bony little thing who moved like a monkey—gracelessly, but without the slightest regard for gravity. She scrambled up, through, and over a street-hawker's stall. She vaulted onto the back of a nervous donkey behind it and danced away, using the heads of angry citizens as stepping-stones to the main street. Khalil cheered silently. The boulevard would be loud, busy, and bizarrely lit this time of night, perfect for a run. On the other side, there were at least fifty dark alleys—fifty for a man his size. For a slip of a girl like that, there might be a hundred.

He turned and looked toward the cafe his marks had been drinking in. Gone, of course. The kid had stirred up a hell of a hornet's nest. Probably wouldn't be any loose wallets worth having, not for hours...better to go over to—

A throaty scream tore through his thoughts. He looked up, and it seemed as though everyone looked up with him, just as startled. A *man...no*, a *horn*... Tires squealed into the deeper note—and just as the listeners braced for it, the crash came. The mob surged toward the boulevard to get a better view, and Khalil let them carry him along. He slithered through to the sidewalk and found a wall to stand against.

His little urchin was down, sprawling in the mud beside the wrecked cars. Wild luck had kept her from being caught between them, but she'd been hit. He could see it in her face and in the way her bare, brown legs kicked the air. She rolled and brought her feet under her, pulled herself upright on a fender and started off again.

The cops were too fast for her now that her breath had been knocked away. Khalil muttered a curse and stood on tiptoe to see past the crowd.

A corpulent tourist shoved past the bystanders and snatched a bulging camera bag off the girl's shoulders. He squawked out his grievances to the world at large. One cop listened, making neat notes in his book. The other man half-dragged, half-carried the child to the sidewalk and wrestled the little thing—half his weight—into her shiny, new, steel bracelets. Khalil heard (or more likely imagined) the terrible click as the first cuff caught in its ratchet. The girl's head flew up. She howled obscenities at the law, and Khalil jumped.

Cousin! he thought. He very nearly shouted it. He hadn't heard such words out of anyone (living) in ages...gutter-harsh

Rom vileness no decent gypsy family would let their daughter speak, but sweet to his ears. The girl happened to turn his way. She seemed to look right at him, despite the shadows and the throng. Her baby face contorted with defiance, and she bucked her head into the cop's chin. Khalil stepped forward, entirely on impulse. He couldn't hope to fight two policemen in a crowd like this (And *who needs to?* he sneered) and he hadn't much skill (At this, he reassured himself, *just* yet). So, it would have to be, he decided, looking up, a *very* small change....

Red—green.

Stop—go. Simple.

A truck, small but heavily loaded, plowed through two compact cars as they crept into the intersection. The horrified workman at the wheel slammed on his brakes heavily—too heavily—and began to skid. His cab clipped a sports car on the nose and shattered its plastic moldings. His trailer fishtailed into a bus, tearing it in half and throwing passengers onto the raw, wet pavement. The back half of the bus sped on over the bodies and sparked its raw metal edge along the curb for twelve more yards. The front half careened into a first-floor restaurant and began billowing thick, oily smoke.

Khalil chuckled. *That ought to do it*, he thought.

The crowd, yelling (and crying) at the top of its lungs, was pushing to see the accident better (and to get away). The cops had to struggle against the tide. The *shilmulo* crossed his fingers and started toward the thief, the tourist, and the policemen—

One of the cops raised a fist to strike. Khalil leapt forward, trying to get through what was fast becoming a riot. Smoke drifted across his eyes (*Only smoke!* he told his tingling nerves), and he caught mere glimpses of the scene: The gypsy dodging the blow—the look on the tourist's face as the girl twisted her arm out of the law's ham-handed grip—the other officer leaving to deal with the accident—the kick the gypsy got in on the remaining cop's shorts. The tourist brushed by, trying to follow the officer through the crowd, shouting about the attack, shouting threats, shouting nothing as he lost his footing in the crush and fell beneath trampling feet. At last, Khalil gained the sidewalk and a clear view, expecting to see no one but the cop, crumpled over his tender parts.

The little thief had more trouble than he thought.

The cops had snapped the other cuff around a stair rail, and that rail wasn't flimsy, ornamental aluminum set with cheap screws into sandy cement. It was heavy iron pipe welded on itself, sunk deep into municipal concrete. Rusty, yes, but not nearly enough. The policeman was already back on his feet. The lucky bastard had fallen too far away for the girl to kick again, and the pain in his gut hadn't improved his temper.

Khalil sprinted through the crowd without stopping to think. He barged straight into the small, calm clearing which the uniform, and the fight, had managed to make around the cop. Bloodshot, angry mortal eyes locked with his own clear, startled, lifeless ones, and Khalil, not usually gifted with foresight, saw his own future quite clearly. The officer, six feet tall, built like a bulldozer, protected by a helmet, gloves, and huge boots, wielding a nightstick—and possibly carrying a gun—was about to thrash him within an inch of his proverbial life. Too late, he wished he had thought before he ran, minded his own business, lain low, let bad enough alone—wished for a plan, a cheat, a buddy, a weapon, a trick:

The *shilmulo* bared his teeth and claws and prayed the human wasn't too mad to notice.

Khalil gained a half second's astonishment with the maneuver. He used all of it to snatch the nightstick away and sap the big bruiser between the helmet and the nape of the neck. The cop sagged. Feeling surprised at himself and unusually chivalrous, Khalil kept the weapon ready with his right hand and fumbled for the railing with the other.

"What the fuck are you doing, you little moron?" he demanded. "Tagging a tourist *here!* Idiot! Who taught you? Blind, deaf, dumb dung beetles? Go home until you learn better. As soon as I get you out of these, you disappear, but good, and you don't show your scrawny ass this side of the—" His fingers snagged the cuff and gave it a tug. It came sliding into view — easily and quickly—attached to nothing and no one but the pipe. Khalil stared at it stupidly.

A pebble dropped on his bare left toe.

He looked up. He could see only her face, smirking down sweetly from the roof's edge. For a moment, she seemed to smile for real—with just a touch of gratitude—and then she was gone.

"Bitch!" Khalil yelled, throwing down the nightstick. He stamped a foot helplessly. "See if I ever help another—"

The man at his feet moaned slightly. Khalil kicked him in the ribs and stalked away.

———————

Khalil doesn't dream.

He's spared the nightmares. He's spared memory chasing him down glossy, echoing hallways that corner back on themselves.

Khalil was never one for introspection.

The boy's dreams spanned spiced meat wrapped in bread, a full belly, and a few coppers to buy betel nut with. The youth thought only of others—the man on the corner with the cane and the gun—the girl in the next street with the full hips and full breasts and full lips. The adult hardly rose above a pocket, a tumble, a purse, a bottle...a petty theft and its petty reward limping along behind it.

When the voice invaded Khalil's own private skull, he had to learn to think out of sheer self-defense. With a little help from his—

What should we call them? Not friends, because he has none. Not enemies, because if he were important enough to have any, they would wipe him out in an instant…and any enemies incapable of wiping him out would be so short-lived that the term hardly suits them.

No, the word is definitely victims.

With a little help from his victims, he has crawled…generally on his belly…toward self-awareness. It's still not something he strives for. His haven of the day is guaranteed free from Freud, from what you needed to learn in kindergarten, from page-a-day philosophy, from the joy of, from Mars and Venus doing dainties at the laundromat. When Venus meets this one, she's not taking twelve steps to anywhere but the backseat, the alley, the whorehouse, the crackpipe, the ER, the morgue….

So, he doesn't think about it. Ever.

———

A few years later, two hours before dawn
The same part of town, but past the bright lights
Calcutta, India

Khalil stood in the doorway of a cheap bar he'd had business in, waiting for the opportunity to leave without being noticed. When his little urchin came into sight, he recognized her immediately. She wasn't so little, nor so young as he'd thought. No—*of course, she's mortal. It's been what? A year? Three? She is older….* Without looking at him, she passed by, picking her way carefully among the trash and sewage in the street. Khalil leaned out to watch her go. She turned the corner, swaying gracefully….

"Damn her." She was out at night again, even deeper into this filthy district than the first time they'd met. There were no tourists here—deadbeats, yes—crooks, whores, and sharpers, certainly—Khalil and his kin, often. The *shilmulo* beat his hand on brick, spun on his heels and dove inside. He hopped across broken bottles and bodies, sprang out the back just four feet from her, and stood there, glaring.

She stopped short. She blinked bright brown eyes, and then started to walk around him.

"I thought I told you to stay out of here," he barked.

"It's none of your business, freak," she retorted, but her glance dropped to the ground, and he could feel her fear.

Damn. Tough mouth on her, anyway. He tried to reach her with his voice. "Come on, little sister," he said softly. "We'll go someplace safer, all right?" Khalil put a hand on her shoulder. His fingers left ruddy brown marks on her sky-blue shirt, and he could feel the warmth of her body straight through the thin material. "This ain't the kind of place a pretty baby like you ought to hang out in." He took her wrist, and she didn't pull away or holler.

Got her! The *shilmulo* felt a touch of pride. This was a *good* thing he was doing. He wished someone had steered him away when he was her age. *I might still be alive today*, he thought briefly—moving on before any of the impossibilities involved could occur to him.

On the other hand, was he going to be able to reach the camps and get back before sunup? *Shit.* Virtue was going to cramp his style. Annoyance all but snuffed the spark of altruism, and Khalil tightened his grip.

"You're going home," he told her sharply, irritated by the time lost here and the time he'd lose escorting her out. He half-turned to close the back door of the bar behind him.

There was no warning, only one sharp breath at his ear. Her wrist twisted half out of his grasp before he knew it.

Khalil was faster than the cop had been. He might even have been expecting it, half-consciously. He whirled around and locked both hands on the girl's bony arm. She bared her teeth angrily, doubled up her other hand in a tiny, ridiculous fist, and hit him square and hard beneath the breastbone—

But she was the one who gasped, not him. His chest and shirt were dry and cold in the middle of squalid summer.

She gaped at him, realizing there was something wrong—not comprehending what it was. Khalil, watching her, felt a little lost. The gulf between them was huge, and it was all in her eyes. He remembered one of the reasons he didn't roam the camps anymore. He had grown sick, long ago, of seeing *that* look on faces like his mother's.

And then—what was so much worse—the girl's expression changed. Now it was one of understanding. She knew precisely what she was standing next to. He swore at himself. She was real, full-blood Rom, all right. She could have smelled a curse in a pigsty.

Khalil took a quick look to either side. No one was watching them yet. He pushed the child down the alley beside the bar, clapping a hand over her mouth to keep her quiet. He twisted her arm behind her shoulder blade, near the point of breaking—what would that matter now, after all? She fought, a little, and managed to open her jaws far enough to bite his index finger. Khalil pulled free, but lost the tip of the nail to her sharp teeth. He moved behind her for more control—the saliva made a tricky grip—and kept shoving.

His bare foot fumbled over a slippery patch. Khalil realized, too late, that with her in front he couldn't see where they were going. He stumbled. Tripping, he lost hold on her face. She didn't bother to scream, but did a backflip, instead—over and around her own arm. The *shilmulo* landed on his chin, enraged, and disgusted. He'd lost control of the wrist, of the situation, of the girl....

He heard her feet pounding away, faintly, through the trash. *Good.* Running home, where a girl like that ought to be.

Hell, maybe he'd scared her enough. Khalil wiped the muck off his beard and got to his feet. It would be worth it if she learned to keep out.

Khalil slunk down the alley and looked in on the bar. No change there.

The image of his own grandmother, telling stories by the fire, rose in front of him. All the women used to come to listen to her. And girls, as well, just like this one. He smiled. This baby would probably spin a good yam tonight to her own grandmother—

Who would believe her—

Who might, maybe, know what to do about it—

Khalil bolted the door and did a little running away of his own.

Midnight in spring, perhaps five years later
Worse places
Calcutta, India

When he saw her the third time, she was older still—shockingly older—walking quite slowly down a very wrong street. Khalil marveled. The body on her...the brass of her...the sheer, flaming *idiocy*...every courtesan in this ghetto should have her pimp, her owner's bodyguard, a john—at the very least, a wicked old woman, full of knives, as an escort.

The more he watched her, the angrier he got. *Her protector*, he fumed, *ought to be more careful.* He glanced toward the gaping door of the nearest building: a brothel. She was dressed too well to belong to that fat bastard who ran the place, but...

Khalil stepped out of the shadows. His girl—this woman— stopped. Khalil's eyes narrowed. He approached her, she let him, and he scowled. Whoever it was, they hadn't trained her well. *She ought to run. She ought to bolt for her keeper's door. She should never, ever, let a man just walk up to her in the street, staring at her like I am....*

He was within arm's reach now. "Moron," he snarled. "Run home before someone happens to you." He tried to put the demon in his eyes, and found her challenging him with hers — bold, dark, daring, dead eyes, dead enough for an ancient, street*bred, drugged*out whore or a —

His hand, fast as fire, reached out to her jaw. He felt for her artery. He couldn't find it by pulse.

Khalil recoiled in disgust. This called for serious consideration. It might take a while. He took another look at her face, more surprised by his own shock than at her condition. *Of course.* A creature like this girl, out for trouble in a witchy, rotten neighborhood like this, was sure to find it. And he'd warned her. He'd damn well told her so...perhaps not in so many words...but she had obviously come back to the ghetto and found an even bigger bastard than himself.

All the while, she simply stood there, waiting, while he readjusted. When he stepped up toward her again, she watched him coolly. As he paced around her, wary, she turned with him and didn't try to break his mood. Finally, minutes later, Khalil was ready to speak, ready to find a quiet corner with her somewhere and ask all the usual questions. She seemed to sense that, too. Her hands relaxed and dropped to her sides.

Footsteps began behind Khalil and came steadily and rapidly up to them. The *shilmulo*, still not sure whether he was the only one on this block, turned to face the interloper. It was an oily man wearing green, the proprietor of the sex shop across the way. The look on his face wasn't that of an angry owner come to reclaim his property (and thrash the wayward buyer). His expression was more...acquisitive. Khalil hesitated. Should he stay to help her fight or leave her to it? He had just chosen the better part of valor (and had a nasty barb ready on his tongue as a parting shot to her) when the panderer spoke.

"How much?" he rasped.

Khalil hardly blinked. There was good silk in the bastard's clothes and gold on his grimy fingers. "By the night or the hour?"

The woman opened her mouth to speak. The *shilmulo* got a hand across it and clamped it shut. Tm older than you, little girl," he said in Rom, "and if you cross me, I can make sure you never see another night." To his shock, she stopped resisting. He took his hand away, very slowly, remembering his torn nail and watching for the bite.

ᵂI take sixty percent," she whispered back. Now Khalil blinked. He was thoroughly puzzled—and paralyzed with admiration.

The green man jabbed at the girl's thin veil. He checked her pupils for narcotics, felt for padding…and other things…beneath her dress. She endured the humiliations without another word.

"Drugged?" demanded the broker suspiciously.

Khalil shook his head no.

"I don't rent girls, I buy. What do you want for her?" Khalil named a shockingly high sum, the pimp a shockingly low one. Gradually the numbers drew together. In half an hour's time, the green man snapped his fingers. Khalil held her until they came—six of them—grinned at his customer, and strutted away like a sated tiger. The inner door of the bordello opened, and the men carried his girl away into its rot-scented darkness.

———

Four hours later, that same morning
In an alley slightly to the west
Calcutta, India

Khalil crouched uneasily in a junk heap. Not as a tiger—that act had lasted exactly so long as he was still in sight of the flesh peddlers—no, he crouched more like a fretful dog, restlessly watching the stained walls of the whorehouse.

He wasn't sure what he should do. She was inside and had been for hours. Probably she was tied up in there, somewhere. She might even have had visitors already. Imagining that, he leered…but hollowly. She might have been beaten. She might be locked in a room with a window. He shook his head. If there were windows, the mortal girls would claw their way out of their cells. But under a skylight, or a cheap plastic roof with cracks in it…any leech would be just as fried.

It was going on for dawn already.

Of course, *he* had the money. He had counted it seven times already. The temptation to leave was strong, yet he stayed. It wasn't honor, nor chivalry that kept him there—or at any rate, not much of either. And he felt that any girl who was willing to go in *there* and do *that* must be trash, anyway…unless that were how she fed. Khalil leered again at that image.

It was really his curiosity that kept him waiting. How was she going to get out? How and when was she going to come and get her share of the money? If she didn't see him here, tonight, then how (and this was worrisome to a *shilmulo* who counted on his privacy to keep the prince's ill-humored goons from the door) did she expect to find him afterwards?

Khalil felt, however, that he was waiting out of noble intentions—casing the joint for a break-out, if the girl seemed to need it. A rescue. *That window, up there…dry rotted*, may be… supposing he were going to risk it, could he get from here to the side wall without the look-out man catching sight of him? If he managed that, he could be up the side and onto a flattish section of the roof. From there, he might be able to—

A man—not one of the customers—unmistakably an enforcer—stomped out of the front door. Khalil abandoned his vaguely brave plans and hid. He told himself he was merely scoping the bastard out, waiting for an opportunity. To his surprise, he found one. The doorman accosted a passerby and began speaking in sharp and emphatic tones. When the unlucky stranger began to back away, the thug followed him.

Khalil crept around his trash heap and up to the wall he liked. He hopped onto a rickety crate, gained his balance, and felt for a handhold in the crumbling mortar. *There...and there*...now the feet, on that row of bricks, and then both hands in the gutter...

He heard a slight rustling above him, to his right. A bare and slender leg swung over the side of the broken roof-tiles. In another moment, she was hanging next to him. "Drop lightly, or they'll hear you inside," she mouthed. Khalil eased himself down and bent to let her land on his back instead of on the crate's hollow, noisy boards. She pointed out an alley between two wrecked shops. They slunk off together through the maze of back streets.

They instant they stopped, she held her hand out.

Khalil did a double take, came to his senses, and dug up the cash. Over an oil drum, he counted it out. His quick fingers made a mistake, not in her favor, and on purpose. She said nothing, and shortly a second note went astray, and a third. By the finish, his share was the closer to sixty. He put a hand out to push her pile across the makeshift table, hesitated, and drew back. Without meeting her eyes, he fished the errant bills from his stack and added them to hers.

When he looked up, expecting angry accusations, she grinned and asked, "What's your name?" with genuine interest.

"Khalil Ravana."

"Ravana?" The girl chuckled. "Sure, you're Ravana."

"What?"

"Nothing." She still seemed amused, but he couldn't see the joke. "Mind if I just call you Khalil?"

"Fine," he snapped, affronted. "And who the hell are you?"

"Daini." She added proudly, "Of one name only."

She picked up her money and tucked it into a fold of her dress. Khalil couldn't make out where it went, though not for lack of looking. "Thanks for haggling. Makes a difference; I've never gotten this much before." Daini put her fist down on the oil drum and something clanked on the rusty steel. "His ring. Your cut of the inside haul."

Khalil picked it up. "You do this often?"

"Yes—and no." She shrugged, and looked east. "Mostly I just pick them up and roll them, or get kidnapped and clean out their rooms. Never been sold into slavery before." Her mouth twitched. "More money in it," she added speculatively. "Meet me in the silversmith's street tonight, about an hour after sunset?"

"I'll be there," answered Khalil, and they split up to deal with dawn alone.

———

In a month, they were friends, the way only the *shilmulo* can be. She tricked him into kissing a bandicoot—twice. He cut a slit up the back of her dress in the middle of a mosque. They rooted out undead scandals together, and caused quite a few themselves, just for fun.

In two months, they were partners. Daini had her looks and could act, beautifully, no matter what the part. She played seductress, victim, blackmailer, and the innocent backwoods girl to perfection. Khalil had less range but boasted more experience. He was convincing as the heavy in the classic cons, the husband in the badger game, and the seller in the slave dodge that was fast becoming their favorite scheme.

In four months, they lured a prancing social club of Camarilla vampires into the scaly depths of the river and framed a pack of Sabbat for doing it. Khalil suggested they spend the days bunked down together—just for a while, just for safety.

In seven months, Khalil didn't bother to rationalize the arrangement. It was simply right to wake up next to her every evening. He found out that she liked the theatre and started taking her to shows. Daini bought him a new shirt and a pair of real shoes. They played with bright crowds of actors and dancers almost as often as they cut purses and picked pockets. They made monkeys of the slavers every two weeks or so, and when the opportunity arose, they freed whole houses full of prostitutes—just to annoy the bosses, Khalil said, and confuse them as to which woman was escaping so often....

In ten months, Khalil started planning for the future.

Near dawn, in the last days of winter
Among the red lights
Calcutta, India

Khalil sat atop a pile of old tires and threw stones at the rats. Around the comer, a boombox blared out the latest movie soundtrack, all twanging strings and ululating voices. The song was an old one, a stage classic redone. He'd heard it live less than a month ago, over in the theatre district. He'd taken her there for a bit of fun, and after they'd dealt with the *artiste fop* they'd come to play with, they'd lounged on the rooftops and talked. They could hear the shows drifting up from the stage doors. After hours, more strident, drunken acts followed, and stranger cries had reached them from the boarding house on the comer. Forty or fifty years ago, its "furnished rooms" had been a cover for less legal activities—a very rich, upscale version of the places he and Daini were knocking over already. He wondered, vaguely, if it were still in business, and how much his partner would bring in on the high-class market.

Khalil brained an enormous, mangy bandicoot and tried to decide whether the rodent was too vile to feed from. He picked up another rock and tried for more rats. *Hell, if she'll drink one. I'll drink one.* It would be kind of nice to have dinner waiting for her when she came out. *Homey.* A love theme swirled out of the cheap speakers. Khalil grinned and snuck a peek at the door she was supposed to leave the 'massage parlor. *Should be out any minute...*

The radio station announced itself and told the city the time. Khalil pursed his lips. *Should have been out an hour ago.* They'd be pushing dawn soon. The apartment on this side of the bridge wasn't as easy to get to, unseen, as their main digs, but there wouldn't be time to reach the other if she was inside too much longer—

The door opened suddenly. Daini lurched out of it and landed, hard, on her knees. Two bottles and a knife flew out after her, smashed and clinked on the opposite wall. She rushed past his hiding place at top speed, snatching at his arm, pulling him after her down the alley. They ran all the way home.

She fell asleep before he could get an explanation.

Next evening
The apartment by the river
Calcutta, India

Khalil woke from black, dreamless death and was happy. Hair-like silken feathers spilled across his pillow—her hair—and her small, cold hands were holding his, just as when they had tumbled down to rest. Then—as every morning—he had waited until her eyes closed before he slept. Now he watched those same eyes open, stare—as every evening, she stared—into space, somewhere beyond him—and slowly focus, softly, on his own.

Daini reached out and touched his cheek. Her expression was serious—almost grim. She stroked his hair gently...thoughtfully. She seemed to Khalil to be looking for something in his face, and so he kept quiet. His questions about the night before went unasked. The new idea, about the cathouse in the theatre district, died on his lips. *Time for that later. Time for anything later...*

There was a little tug at his temple. He looked across his nose—she'd coiled her fingers around a lock of his hair, and her long nails were tangling in the strands. He laughed out loud, and Daini made a irritated grimace at him. A claw slid out— hers. Before he could say a word, she sliced the hair away, took it to her lips, and kissed it.

"For luck," she said, and started braiding.

"Why do you need luck? What happened last night?"

"Nothing."

"Like hell."

"Nothing," she insisted. Her fingers worked busily on the braid. After a pause—long and empty—she went on: "I went to the boss bitch's office and snatched her jewelry. Only the door to the hall was barred and padlocked, so I had to cut through one of the bedrooms to get out. Must have been fifty candles in there. Around the table where they...well, these two must have had a thing about candles. I lost it. And I don't remember a goddamn thing until I ran out the back and saw you."

"Shit," Khalil remarked.

"Yeah." Daini wound the finished braid into a knot and tucked it into her blouse. "Lost the gold along the way somewhere."

"Candles."

"Yeah."

"Coincidence, right? They couldn't have known—guessed about you?"

"Of course not."

"You just be careful, girl." Khalil sat up and reached for his shoes. "Anyone see you?"

"Hell yes. Said it was a bedroom, didn't I? Even if he was too busy, she must have noticed. Probably the most interesting thing that's happened in there in years."

Forty-six minutes till sunrise, three weeks later
On a street of run-down theatres
Calcutta, India

Khalil put a palm on the cracked facade of the old rooming house. *God, let me be right!* There had been a door here...forty, fifty years ago... if he could trust his memory, it was right about—here. Under pressure, the stucco caved in. *Only paint and plaster. Cheap job. Stroke of luck. Time we had one.*

He'd sold Daini at about eleven the night before, and the money had been more than twice what they'd ever managed in the slums. She'd gone off, struggling artistically (though not well enough to arouse alarm) and hurling oaths at him. Khalil had waited, chatting with the madam in the front parlor, for as long as he dared. He asked casual questions about the kinds of wares the old whore might like him to bring next time, and listened for his partner's swearing. The madam suggested a few traits: eye color, native language, height, and Khalil heard, coded in Daini's curses, details of the layout, the exits, the guards. The madam brought the interview to a close and showed the *shilmulo* the door, and Khalil lost Daini's stream of words on the way out.

He couldn't hear her from the street. He hadn't expected to; if every woman held in that vile pit could be heard on the outside, more questions might (*only* might) be asked. But the hours (more of them than usual, more than ever before) had passed by without a sign of or from Daini, and Khalil—still nervous from the candle incident—had decided he wasn't going to wait any more.

Khalil flaked the plaster away and tore at the boards beneath. Someone, years ago, had decided to block up these stairs—probably when the neighborhood first went bad, when they needed to keep the guests from coming and going as they chose, and began funneling the customers through the lobby. He poked a hole in the inner wall and peeked inside. He saw lightless black and smelled mildew; at a guess, he decided, the owners had shut the stairs in from both ends. Khalil rammed out an opening big enough to climb through, and raced up the creaky steps.

An old door at the top opened easily. The plaster wall beyond was even more fragile than the one at the bottom. Khalil broke it down in half a minute. The balcony the stairs gave onto was empty, which was lucky—and had no other exits, which was not. The *shilmulo* racked his brain. Four more doors *had* led off of this patio, but he couldn't remember exactly where they'd been. Time was slipping by…

Khalil cursed and stepped forward. He vaulted onto the balcony rail and looked at the floor above. There was a window, barred but open, in jumping distance. He could grab at it and swing along to the next ledge or go up to the roof. He ran catlike along the balustrade—leapt for the bars—felt them give, sickeningly, as his weight strained the powdery masonry— fought for handholds on the window ledge itself—

And caught a glimpse of what lay on the other side.

One enormous thug sat on a folding chair by the door. His attention was riveted to an old iron bed which took up half the room. It was an ugly, ancient, iron thing, rusting through its flaky white paint, and Daini was cuffed through it to rings set in the wall. She was twisting her hands in her fetters, blood on her wrists from the tight steel. Khalil shook his head, confused. She'd never had trouble with shackles, rope, steel cuffs, plastic cuffs—damned if he knew how, but she could *always* slip through the tightest of them. If these were really that bad, she could pull free by main force. It would hurt, she would lose a lot of skin, probably, but blood would take care of that. What in hell was she waiting for?

The guard moved slightly, warningly, and Khalil saw the gun. He didn't recognize the make, but the end of the barrel was very large and the whole thing was built like an elephant gun. It was pointed directly at Daini's head.

Unless the thing shot flames, it wouldn't destroy her in one go, but she would be blind, possibly deaf, with no skin on her hands. The guard might get his second round in while she wrestled with the ankle cuffs. Others could come up from the floors below and bring more firepower with them....

Khalil kicked his feet against the wall, and the bars wiggled in their moorings. *One good shock,* he thought, and looked down—three and a half floors down—to broken, unforgiving cement. *Damn.* He jammed his left elbow half through the bars, let go the ledge with the right hand and very carefully pulled a knife from his belt. Damn, *damn,* damn. Steel met mortar—tink, *tink*—the guard would have to notice—chipping away at the sand and lime—*tink, tink, tink*—Khalil hoped Daini would hear it, too—*tink, tink*—

Khalil pulled himself up and peeked over the top. The guard wasn't even looking. *Damn!* He dropped, wrenching his left shoulder, and started again—*tink, tink*—louder this time, and checked again. The guard started, jumped, locked eyes with him. The gun barrel swung up, not covering Daini anymore—covering him. *Shit!* Khalil cursed success this time, and tried to let go of the bars.

He knew his hands were wrecked before he remembered hearing the blast. He was falling as the echoes rang through the alley…or the second shot went off. He couldn't tell; he was hit from behind before the noise stopped. *Roof*, he realized dully. Khalil lay a moment, floating on pain. He started to open his eyes, and heard:

THUNG—khhhgg—clankgkgk.

Suddenly his chest hurt more than his back. He was being attacked—how the hell? Another blow landed. Someone knew how to hit…like steel…no, of course: The bars had just fallen on him. Iron bars dropped from a height of fifty feet on his ribs. He forced an eye open and discovered that the other wouldn't budge at all. His right hand (where was it?) could move, and he explored the ground for a moment. The roof's edge met his groping fingers. Khalil rolled cautiously in the other direction and didn't fall off the side.

THUD—shsss—unnhhh.

Someone was on the roof with him. The *shilmulo* curled into a defensive little huddle. Daini wouldn't, couldn't be free yet. He waited for the gun to go off.

"It's me."

Too soon. Impossible. Or perhaps he had blacked out. It didn't matter; she was there. Wet fingers touched his face, and Khalil smelled blood. His wounds made him hungry; he licked at the smell. Cooling human blood filled his mouth…and there was a taste of another *shilmulo*, as well. Daini's blood.

She pulled her hand away. "Damn it! Don't do that. Stop!"

Khalil tried to use what he'd drunk to open both eyes and focus. The flesh knitted slowly; he felt hungrier than ever. It seemed to take a year, but finally he could see.

Daini had no skin on her hands. Her face was scorched. She'd been shot and her face was scorched. There were gashes and bloodless tunnels in her skin—trails left by shot or shrapnel.

"It's all right. I already—" he hesitated over the words—"1 don't feel any different." He was surprised to find himself telling the truth. He tried to grin and reassure her. "It's only one, not binding. It ain't the end of the world, sweetheart."

Daini shook her head. "It's not the same thing." She picked up his hands, examined them carefully, and rubbed her thumb across a lump. With a careful claw, she sliced his palm open and cut out the piece of rock buried in it. After a moment, she put her mouth to the wound and drank. "There," she told him, "now we're..." Unexpectedly, she ran down.

"Now we're even," finished Khalil. He pulled himself up by her shoulder, and Daini smiled bleakly.

Harsh voices, screams, and gun barrels popped out the barless window, and the two *shilmulo* helped each other scramble through the raining lead, off the roof, and out into the streets. They found a filthy but windowless hotel room and a clean, but unlucky, hotel guest, and hid with them from the sun.

———

Sundown, three days later
In a small apartment
Calcutta, India

Daini said it as soon as she woke up. "They're on to us." She turned over to face Khalil, who shrugged.

"Yeah. I know. That was always in the cards."

"What do we do now?"

Khalil rolled his eyes at her. Wasn't it obvious? "We do what I always do. We pack up and move on."

"Cut and run?" Her voice was skeptical, scornful. "Through the wilderness? I like my skin more than that."

"There are ways to get through." He considered a few, and added, "I invented most of them."

"Huh." Daini knew him well enough to winnow out his lies without throwing away the facts. "But you've been gathering moss here since I was so high. What makes you think any of your tricks still work? Things change."

"Nothing changes that much."

"Cocky son of a bitch, aren't you? Besides, how many years have you been doing that for? You find a place, you bum through it, and you go...but you don't ever have anything," she touched the necklace at her throat, "or a safe place, like this, to rest. Or anyone...allies, or friends, or..." Her hand crept out to his. "Or someone close."

Khalil frowned. "Bullshit. I take whatever I want with me. I make *new* safe places—I'd have to, anyway. There's a reason we've had three apartments here, sweetheart."

"Yeah. You're a thumb-fingered clod who can't pick a politician's pocket." Daini laughed, then looked out of the sides of her eyes at the pillow. "I can't leave, Khalil."

He smirked. *Sure. The reluctant maiden act, from this one! Fuckin' amazing...* "You can do anything you damn well feel like, you lovely lying harlot, and don't you dare go all shy on me. I've been behind the scenes of *that* performance."

Khalil winked and rolled off the mattress, reaching for her bag.

"Seriously, what do you want to take?" He pulled open the wardrobe and rummaged through the saris clipped inside. "This blue one? You'll take just one or two to get yourself started with. The style will probably be different wherever we go, so we'll buy a whole new lot when we set ourselves up." He paused, absorbed in the selection. He considered a dark pink thing and a gold-tone blouse to go with it, "I've got a friend in New Delhi, runs a smuggler's rest—and there's this scam I've had planned for years—pay him back for a trick he pulled in the early seventies—he'd know me a mile off so I never tried it, but he won't know you—" he turned around, grinning from ear to ear.

Daini sat on the edge of the bed, looking up at him through trembling eyelashes. Khalil stared, stammered, and began snatching up the discarded scarves and baubles.

"No. Hey...we can bring all of this along if that's what you want. I'm used to traveling light, alone, but—" he tried to brush the dust off a bright green dress and tore it on the door hinge instead.

Her gaze lowered, came up again slowly, ruefully. Khalil felt a hot, embarrassed flush creep up his face.

Whatever his mistake was, it was bigger than pawing through her clothes....

"We—" Khalil stammered—"we don't have to go to Delhi. We could do Bombay. It's a good town...there's ex-Soviet mobsters running around...but more money, you know, to make up for the extra danger." He stopped himself. "Bhopal. Let's just go see Bhopal. No tricks—no work, anyway. If the game is sea—if the game is boring you.

"Daini?"

She twitched her shoulders and looked straight at him. "I'm not going anywhere, Khalil." Continuing sadly, determinedly, apologetically, she said, "I never will."

Khalil's brow creased in stubborn lines. He opened his mouth to speak, but she rushed her next words, loudly, hotly, over his:

"I'm not free."

Khalil, numb, froze. He said nothing, showed nothing, felt nothing—The saris fell to the floor. Jewelry clattered on silk.

"Not free," he murmured stupidly.

His face broke. He grabbed her by the shoulders, shook her—"1 *told* you to stay out. I *told* you to go home." Wordless sounds of rage escaped him—and of despair. "You *had* to keep coming to that goddamn rat's nest!" His nails sank into her arms, and she winced. "Bitch! Why didn't you tell me?" he demanded, and sobbed as he spoke. "Daini!"

Khalil scooped her up as if to steal her and fell on the bed. "Daini, why?" His arms wound round her, and he rocked her back and forth. "Who is it? What can we do?" he whispered frantically.

Just as suddenly, he stopped.

"No," he decided. "No. Tell me—tell me when, first? Khalil didn't know why he asked, but it seemed the question that would bring the least pain. "When did this happen?"

"Before I met you?" She sounded as if she were crying. "Good advice, love, but years too late."

He let it sink in, cursing the world for cruelty.

"Now. Tell me how." He paused a moment, and a horrible suspicion crawled through him. "You're not *bound*, are you?"

"No." He thought he heard a catch in her voice, and he felt sure when she said it again: "No."

"Gods. That's it, isn't it?"

She shook her head. Khalil pushed Daini out of his arms, stood up, and turned his back on her.

An hour later, Khalil stood at the window, staring into the boards as though they were glass, as though he could see the night through them. He could smell blood—hers—and didn't care, wasn't hungry, didn't wonder why blood wasn't, (for this moment only) so important.

A *real Rom doesn't get caught*, he fumed, ignoring facts freely. A *real Rom goes wherever and whenever the hell they want.*

A *shilmulo would cut her own throat, stake herself, stare at the sun rather than knuckle under to some cheapass tyrant.* Khalil clenched a shaky fist. Tyrants stack decks. Daini had never had a chance. His gaze flickered toward her.

She had been crying. The red smell was her bloody tears, soaking into the blanket.

The *shilmulo*—the real, free *shilmulo*—sat down on the windowsill. Fuck *it*, he thought, and snapped out: "What can we do?"

"Nothing," Daini raised her eyes. "We're not going to do a goddamn thing. I got myself into it, I'll get myself out."

Khalil saw hope and jumped on it. "Then there is a way out."

She shook her head. "Fuck off. You wanted to help, you could have said it an hour ago."

"Daini—"

"Damn it, I don't want you in this. Understand?" She sat up and leaned forward. After a moment, she added softly, "Don't want you risking—" She bit her lip. "I can't ask you to—"

He was angry again. "You're not asking! Let me help. I'll do anything. I swear, I'll do anything. I—I love you."

Daini jumped up. "No!" She backed away. "Don't love me. Stay away from me." Her hand reached the doorknob; she twisted out, shaking her head. "Don't," she said again, and ran away.

Khalil waited. She was just scrapping. They had had little fights. She had always come back, he had always come back, *she* would come back now. If she thought for a second that *he* would stoop to chasing her—apologizing to her—worrying about her—

Well, then she was right, wasn't she?

Feeling surly, whipped, vengeful, and protective all at once, Khalil wrenched the legs off a chair and went out to shadow his ladylove to her master's lair, whittling all the way.

Later that night

In a pit
Calcutta, India

Khalil followed warily down a half-lit, airless tunnel. He put each of his feet down, carefully, into Daini's tracks, and tested the ground before trusting his weight on it. His heart was still in the rescue, but his mind rang with fear.

When she had fled into a condemned building, he had felt confident. When the trail led down into basement and sewer, he had doubts. When he found the open grating and the ruins — ruins he had never heard of in years of swapping tales about this city — his ideas of wresting his girl from her captor began to fade.

What hopes he'd had had sprung from the admission that she *could* be released. Khalil had imagined a sire his own age — a little older — a crooked, angry son of a bitch keeping an innocent girl under his thumb with lies and blood.

This place looked more like the haunt of an elder.

Khalil rounded a comer and slowed. Daini wasn't running anymore; she stood, holding her side, gazing at the stones before her. She set her lamp down and stepped forward. As she passed through the light he saw her face, twisted in fear and hope, studying a reddish lump high in the wall. She jumped at it once — twice — it was clearly out of her reach — but he was a foot taller. Khalil darted forward, leapt for the red spot on the wall, and plucked down the prize.

It was a fist-sized lump of rust-colored clay, and it fell apart in his fingers. Long, dark strands — hair? — stuck out of the broken edges.

Tm sorry," Khalil whispered. "I didn't mean to break it," he explained, turning to Daini.

"No — no — that was what you were supposed to do. You freed me."

Khalil shrugged, proud and embarrassed. He felt uncomfortable as the conquering hero; he felt crowded; he felt as though they were being watched.

"Pity," she muttered.

He couldn't have heard her right. His ears seemed to be buzzing. "What?"

"I'm sorry for you—really I am." Daini turned and began to walk away. He leapt forward and pulled her to a halt.

"What?" Khalil was stung. "You're sorry for me?"

She laughed. "Terribly. You've kissed your third bandicoot, boy."

"What?"

"Learn a new word, darling, you're wearing that one out. Oh—don't look at me like that. I apologize. You're not ready for sarcasm yet, I know, but…the play is over. You said you'd been behind the scenes for my act—you hadn't been. But now you are."

Khalil's skin crawled. Someone was coming up behind him. He turned on the intruder, stake ready—and found empty air. "What's happening?" he demanded.

"In plain words, I'm free and you're not. You can feel him already, I think, but I'm afraid it's going to get worse, darling. Try not to hurt yourself while you get used to—it. To him. He'll start explaining it soon enough, I'm sure."

Khalil tried to rush her and found his feet unwilling tools. He grabbed at a wall to steady himself. Gritty powder came away in his hand. He let go and fell. Recovering, he dusted what he thought was mortar from his hands—and took a second look at the masonry. It wasn't mortar—it was stone coming to pieces. The rock had crumbled, was so *old* that it could crumble.

Oh my god. "Who are you?"

She shrugged. "You know me. A beggar girl, a thief, a harlot…" Her eyes seemed to see past him again, as they had every night on waking, and she went on: "Queen. Demoness.

One-time consort to the Prince of all Rakshasa..." Her gaze hardened, returned to him. "Just Daini. That's still my name. It's the only name I've ever had. Once upon a time, it would have meant something to any *shilmulo* I met...to *every shilmulo* I met—and you don't even know who Ravana is." She spoke all this grandly, triumphantly, poised like the monarch she claimed to be.

Khalil's jaw dropped.

Daini laughed at him in the tones of the beggar girl he loved.

He seized on that. "You were a child. I saw you living."

Her lips twitched contemptuously. "Do you always believe what you see?"

"I loved you," he accused.

Daini looked away. "Yes, I know. And I am grateful. So, try not to be angry, sweetheart. I've been a servant for a very long time, and I am tired—" she paused a moment—"and I saw a way out, and I took it. You'll do the same thing when your time comes."

"The hell I will!"

"In hell you will, dear. In hell you will." She studied him, and nodded. "May I go?"

"No!" He caught her arm.

"I wasn't speaking to you." Daini turned her head as though listening. "Well then. Thank you—" her words dripped venom—"for nothing, and may Ravana eat your heart if you're wrong.

"As for you," she said, smiling sweetly up at the *shilmulo's* face. "Khalil. I want to say goodbye," she licked her lips and frowned thoughtfully, "but I've never been good at saying it, so I won't. I don't expect you'll remember if I do, anyway. Let go, please." He hardly heard her, and did nothing. "Of my dress, sweetheart. Let go."

"But—"

The silk seemed to slip from his grasp. "Best to let me go before I fade away," she advised. "Think how silly you'll look holding empty air."

Her illusion faded farther. "When you forget me," she began, walking toward him—walking through him, so that her ghostly mouth spoke from inside his head—"When you forget me, remember this. It's all I'll be able to give you unless I wake: From one dead, collect blood, hair, a nail, and a promise. Make a seal of them, bring it and the victim here, and have him break the token I made for you."

What is she saying? The voice was dark, and for Khalil it filled the room; there was nothing else.

"I can say what I like now, Hazimel. I'm free, you son of a bitch."

Daini's ticklish presence vanished, and Khalil knew that she was gone. He slumped to the dirt floor and buried his head in his hands.

––––––––––

Well, rat, what did she tell you? Did she offer up my weakness? Did she claim to want to help? Did she give you hidden knowledge to bargain for your life? Did she give you the secret to breaking free?

Did she say she cared?

It will not matter. I will make it go away.

You will think me vindictive. If you knew more, you might suspect jealousy. Yes. My bride in your arms for a year. I assure you, I am beyond that. I merely want to keep her safe. I gave her up to preserve her; I will not let the loose mind of a whelp like you reveal her to the King.

Of course, you will forget that, too...I might as well explain this to the walls.

Quiet, now. I am going to begin.

––––––––––

Khalil doesn't think about it. Ever.

He can't.

Hazimel is satisfied that the illusions of time and night and loneliness he replaced her with have taken root. Wherever Daini rests (he knows, but he dare not even think it, for fear his thoughts are watched), she hasn't stirred since he let her go...

She seems content to sleep.

...and when Khalil rebels, he rebels as Hazimel plans. When he tries to break free, he breaks what stands in his master's way. When he runs away, he goes where the elder chooses—toward the Sabbat, away from Calcutta, into Chicago, under the streets.

Khalil doesn't seem to remember, and Hazimel is content to play his games.

But sometimes—more often now that he has left New York behind him—Khalil hears a voice behind his master's. Not quite drowned by the commands and the pain, there is a woman speaking:

Nail.

Token.

Blood.

Break.

All the words are there, but disordered.

Meaningless.

It has never yet occurred to Khalil to put them together.

Turning the Face

Bruce Baugh

Monday, 10 August 1992, 8:11 PM
Santa Barbara, California

This is the story of the beginning of my damnation and the beginning of my redemption.

I began to lose my will nine years ago, and I lost the sun exactly five years, one month, and three days ago. I remember it, you see. But maybe that's a little ahead of things. What happened to me begins with the phone call, not the rooftop.

I'm one of those people who's pretty good in both the humanities and the sciences. C.P. Snow's "Two Cultures" problem was never a big deal for me: I can work with techies and academicians alike. Since I've always had the impulse to know as much as I could about everything, I ended up settling into library science as a field. I figured that, although I wouldn't get to do much of my own research, I'd have the fun of knowing about all the work going on around me, and help others in their investigations. And in some ways, I really prefer to dabble rather than to settle down and do just one thing all the time.

When I got my master's, the University of California at Santa Barbara made me a very juicy offer to oversee the technical reference department there. I'd just graduated from the University of Toronto, and I was ready for some warmer winters. Six years went by in very comfortable fashion. To my surprise, 1 did get to do original work, too; I made the cover of

Discover in 1992 (okay, it was a little inset picture, but still) for my papers on adaptive user interfaces. Southern California is a weird place in some ways and Santa Barbara weirder than some parts of SoCal, but I had a good time by and large. My staff was good, and the professors liked the extent to which I made their lives easier.

So, I gradually came to think of myself as settled. I finally managed to get a good apartment a little bit out of downtown Santa Barbara, away from the noisy slum zone that is student housing for UCSB. Roommates came and went for a while. Then I started doing freelance consulting about database problems on the side and didn't need the extra income. My cats and lizards and I went through the cycle of years pretty calmly, enjoying the brief rainy season and enduring the long hot summer with the help of an especially efficient experimental air-conditioning system one of my engineering-department clients rigged up.

The Pacific coast north of the LA. sprawl is a fairly narrow strip of useful land between the sea and the mountains. The mountains aren't all that high—just a few thousand feet, most of the time—but they're rugged and covered in dense scrub. You can go from beach to gully cut foothills in just a few miles, or even less. This is part of what's made Santa Barbara so attractive to rich folks all century: You get great upslope views in lots of places.

Santa Barbara's city fathers being what they are, the city's done its best to keep the boring old working classes who make things work out of sight. Cheaper housing tends to nestle out of sight from the swells, whether it's just back from the shore behind low coastal hills or tucked into out-of-the-way canyons. I was very lucky indeed to have found a place just before the neighborhood right upslope started going from rundown apartments to condos. We'd somehow managed to avoid a couple of buyout efforts, and kept on living relatively frugally (by local standards).

People who haven't been here think of the coast running north-south, but it doesn't always. There's a big promontory between Los Angeles and San Jose, and Santa Barbara's on it. The beach is actually due south of anyplace you're likely to be standing; it gradually curves to run southeast as you head toward L.A., but all through this county, you go east or west to run parallel to the shore.

My little canyon faces southwest, so that I get a marvelous view of sunset over the Channel Islands if I walk up to the end of our cul-de-sac and scramble partway up the steep slope toward the low end of the condo development. There's a pair of eucalyptus trees, more than a century old, that frame the view past where the cul-de-sac meets the boulevard, down slopes stripped to mud by a landslide each rainy season, past a couple of run-down old oil-storage tanks, and then suddenly into beauty. There's a swath of marshland that's never been developed, so it has a very complex mix of water grasses and bog-loving plants where the herons come to nest after the rains. The westernmost Channel Islands lie almost in a straight line with the line of the cul-de-sac, and their rocky summits shine in the sunset glow reflected off the sea.

At least that's how I remember it.

My life began to end nine years ago. I was watching the sunset from my porch. The view wasn't as good there, but I'd been out bicycling in the hills with friends on the weekend, and I was sore. Even with part of the view clipped by my neighbors' houses and a rise on this side of the street, it was gorgeous. The sea was stirred up, agitated by the distaff end of a storm somewhere toward Hawaii. Sunlight glittered on countless wave crests far out from the shore as well as on the big breakers cast up onto sand and rocks. The last rays of twilight shone through the breakers' crests, a sight that 1 almost never see. I wished I'd had my camera handy.

A few minutes later, the telephone in my apartment rang. I strolled in, checked caller ID, and didn't recognize the name: RANULFSON ENG. Engineering, presumably, which meant that it was probably a would-be client. I tried never to pass up a good opportunity for money, so I cleared my throat and answered.

The voice on the other end was heavily accented — something Scandinavian, but I wasn't informed enough to distinguish between the possibilities — and deep bass. "Mr. Walinsky, I was referred to you by associates in the Los Angeles metropolitan area. I represent an international conglomerate interested in centralizing certain data-management functions in that area. We wish to contract out some elements of our data systems design and implementation. Would you wish to discuss this further?"

I would wish, of course. 1 soon established that I was speaking to Mr. Ranulfson himself, though I got the impression that his firm was itself a front for operations elsewhere. That sort of thing doesn't make me happy, but after a few projects for businesses relocating from Hong Kong, I'd gotten used to directorates not just interlocking but layered like so many crazed weasels dipped in slow-acting superglue. We arranged to meet at a temporary office in L.A. on the following weekend. Ranulfson asked if it would be inconvenient to meet at 9 PM, so that he could keep on schedule with European operations. I like a late start anyway, so this suited me just fine.

Before heading down to Hilvaquez Transitional Offices in Santa Monica, I naturally did some research at the library into Ranulfson. Things looked pretty straightforward on the surface: firm founded in the aftermath of World War II by a bunch of demobilized Swedish and Norwegian soldiers in conjunction with some distant American cousins they'd met during the occupation of Germany; held privately ever since; senior staff recruited from the founders' families. Isaac Ranulfson had run the firm since 1982, keeping it profitable and growing slightly. Behind that straightforward facade there was a nightmarish mess of possible connections, traded directorships, hints of family ties, and so on. Old European money takes some very devious routes to avoid attention from modem governments...and by "modem" I mean everything this side of Napoleon. Still, as long as the checks cleared and the work itself was worthwhile, that wouldn't be my problem, but the IRS', and I was glad to leave them to it.

The only person in the office when I arrived was Ranulfson. There were two desks in the entrance lobby, both piled high with file folders and six-line telephones. A short hall led to three glass-fronted offices, two of which had desks also piled with files. The third was empty of everything except taken-up swaths of carpet. At the end of the hall there was a conference room, offering a third-floor view of generic L.A. cityscape. Ranulfson let me in and escorted me to the conference room.

He was tall and very blond. Something like six and a half feet tall, with very long blond hair drawn back into a ponytail. His eyelashes and goatee were almost white, and his eyes were a very pale, watery blue. He wore a plain gray suit, whose severe lines emphasized his lean and angular build. His shoes were gray, too; nothing about him glinted or reflected, it was all matte surfaces. The deep bass voice was startling against that backdrop. "Come in, Mr. Walinsky. I apologize for this temporary state of affairs."

"No problem, I assure you, Mr. Ranulfson. I've worked in living rooms as well as board rooms."

So, we sat down and discussed things. It appeared gradually that what Ranulfson planned for L.A. was a series of rapacious acquisitions on behalf of firms associated with his. Ranulfson had a particular interest in architectural and transportation firms based on criteria that I wasn't at all clear on, but which seemed obvious to *him*. He wanted to gather up available information on the target firms and their personnel so as to help plan a campaign of recruitment and takeover.

That sounded unpleasant. But there were interesting technical challenges in the work. Ranulfson made it clear that he wanted an especially accessible interface, since some of the senior managers who'd be involved were largely computer illiterate. Interface design is a special pleasure of mine, and taken with the money Ranulfson offered, it was just too good to pass up.

I wish that damnation smelled a bit more obvious, or something. I might have chosen it anyway, but I'd have liked to know, to have had the chance. My rescuer keeps silent when I tell her such things.

———

Wednesday, 17 March 1993, 9:03 PM
Ranulfson-Yngve Development Associates
Stockholm, Sweden

Simply figuring out the structure of the system I'd be creating took seven months, including two required trips to Stockholm to meet with Ranulfson's partners. They paid everything, but I used up both vacation and sick time from UCSB to get it done. (They paid me enough to make it all right, but I made it clear that they couldn't count on this as a regular matter. They smiled and made perfunctory apologies in their flawless slow English.)

Something happened to me on the second trip. I know *now* what it was, but I didn't then, or for years afterward.

I was actually ready to quit when I got onto the plane for the first leg of my trip: I was tired and stressed and not altogether happy with the way work was going. I wanted to wrap up dealing with the elegant but creepy Ranulfson, not to mention his uncomfortable associates. They stared a bit too long. Their offices, located in a manor outside town, were filled with paintings and sculptures from all over Europe in the last seven hundred years, and every so often one of the associates would go into a trance while looking at a piece. They were almost too immaculately groomed, as if they never did anything except wait in their offices for visitors like me; I was reminded of trapdoor spiders and burrowing lizards back in Santa Barbara.

As we'd done before, we met shortly after local sunset. I gave an hour's worth of presentation, then we took a break for dinner. Many of them ate sparingly or not at all, and I wondered if they might have some wasting disease they glossed over with the perfect appearances. I'd known colleagues in the library who had AIDS, and one of them went through a similar stage of life-losing elegance on his way to hospitalization. That wasn't it, but Ranulfson's partners were more like that than anything else I could think of.

After dinner, they brought out a thick wine to serve with dessert. For a moment it looked almost like blood pouring into my glass. I looked up, startled, but found Ranulfson smiling slightly at me. I was dizzy for a moment. When I looked back down, it was clearly wine after all, simply with more sediment than usual. I felt a peculiar confidence in the back of my mind, a sharp sureness that all was well despite my reservations. So, I drank.

As I continued my presentation, I felt a tectonic shift in my attitude. My complaints all remained, but now they were balanced out by a sudden sympathy for these gaunt engineers and managers. I wanted to find out what would happen next, and decided to stick with it.

————————

Wednesday, 22 June 1993, 9:15 PM
Ranulfson Engineering
Century City, California

Back in California, I only made one more trip to L.A. before the phase's conclusion. By then there was a small but permanent Ranulfson office in Century City, with a nice view over downtown. Mostly I worked in my own apartment, poking at a variety of arrangements and sending off demo discs by airmail. I did meet with more associates of Ranulfson's, though; they made half a dozen visits either to my home or to my office at UCSB.

"They are the Haqims," Ranulfson told me in a phone call. "They are not part of our alliance, but they sometimes assist us in particular tasks. In this case they are doing surveillance of some of our prospective targets for acquisition. Please assist them by reviewing your currently available profile data and supplying them with a copy of your current compilation. It may be that they will acquire a copy of the finished work, but if so, we will negotiate separate payment for you from them."

I expected Middle Easterners from the name. It sounded Arabic, at least, although I knew that there can be some surprising phonemes among Baltic and Scandinavian names as well. Sure enough, the Haqims who visited me that autumn and winter proved to be as blond as Ranulfson and his crew. They spoke much better English, and moved with a remarkable grace. Not many businesspeople do, all that yuppie emphasis on fitness notwithstanding. These three men and two women didn't just look fit, they looked *elegant*, in complete control of themselves. I never saw one of them stumble, nor any of them drop something. On at least a couple of occasions one of them caught me on the edge of a stumble, too, hoisting me back upright with one strong hand.

Only one of the men and one of the women ever spoke to me. The rest watched the proceedings and took part in my tutorials, but silently. None of them eyer gave me first names, either. They were apparently all Mr. Haqim and Ms. Haqim. I suspected that they might belong to some weird cult, but that was Ranulfson's concern, not mine. I showed them what my employer wanted me to, and they faded off into the night in their tan limousines.

The last woman touched me on the shoulder. Nobody else in the office reacted, but I distinctly heard her say, "Outside, one hour from now." I looked up. She nodded on her way on out. Ranulfson was looking right at us, but didn't seem to actually see our little exchange. Certainly nothing he said then or later suggested he was aware of it.

An hour later, I told Ranulfson that I needed to go get some papers from my car. He nodded in a distracted manner, engrossed in some phone call, and waved me on out. I felt an urge to go down to the sidewalk, making at least that much of my story true. When I got outside, I found two of the Ms. Haqims there. One was talking into a payphone. The little snippets of sound I caught didn't match the motions her lips made. I wondered if I were hallucinating.

The second Ms. Haqim motioned me to a bus bench and sat down beside me. "Let me look at you," she said. For a long time, she stared at me, absolutely motionless, not even breathing. "Your soul becomes dark," she told me at last.

"It does? But..."

"Do you not see the circle of your life contract?"

"No, I don't. I see opportunity here. I'm making good money, doing work I like. I'm learning a lot about business."

She made a short choppy sound that might have been a laugh. "Allah told Muhammed, 'Do you not see that Allah created the heavens and the earth with truth? I occupy a lie, most of the time, but every once in a while I try to honor the words as well as what I tell myself the spirit is. So let me tell you true things."

I don't remember much of the next half-hour. A fog seemed to swirl around us, muffling the sounds of traffic and the city's night life. The Haqim's voice proceeded at a constant alto pitch. It seemed a thing separate from her, a fountain of meaning and warning for me. It spoke of assassins and leeches and parasites on the soul of humanity and of a mountain full of those waiting for truth and of the last night of the world. It told me of cabals older than my country and of a war between ancient powers.

In the end, I know, I told her this: "No."

Whatever it was she offered, I didn't want it. The fog swirled into my mind, blotting out details and leaving me only with the knowledge that I'd been offered a choice I rejected.

As I returned to the office, Ranulfson finished his phone call. Business resumed.

Friday, 24 December 1993, 6:58 PM
Sheraton Santa Barbara
Santa Barbara, California

Finally, just before Christmas that year, I was finished with everything Ranulfson had contracted for. He came up to Santa Barbara for our final review, taking a suite in the Sheraton on the waterfront and inviting me to dinner. "I have requested that my associates send the ingredients you so much enjoyed on your last trip to Stockholm, and contracted a local chef to prepare a meal for us." It was as good as last time, and as we sipped an after-dinner glass of that remarkable wine, I found myself filled with enthusiasm for the venture. Ranulfson smiled for the first time in my experience as he listened to me gush about how much I enjoyed it all and wanted to work for him again. "Perhaps you shall," he told me.

He pronounced himself very pleased with the work. My final payment was in cash, rather to my surprise: Ranulfson drew out a thick wad of hundred-dollar bills and counted them out. He also supplied one of those armored cases to keep them in until I could deposit the money. I felt skeptical, but that sense of admiration swirled up again and I decided to enjoy the unexpected treat. We spoke of inconsequential matters, along with his firm's prospects for the new year, until sometime well after midnight. Finally, he noticed my increasingly frequent yawns, and sent me home in a cab. He picked up the tab for that, too.

The new year started quietly. I began having some problems in my day job. Nothing major, but increasingly I found myself no longer satisfied by the challenges it offered. I wanted to do more work on the Ranulfson project. 1 wanted to see those interesting, exotic people again, and I just plain wanted to be around Ranulfson. Understand, this was not some repressed sexual yearning coming out. It was a different sort of fascination. His presence, the suggestion of old, complex thoughts behind the quiet blue eyes, the glamour of wealth used in subtle ways, all attracted me.

My spring performance review was the most disappointing since I started at UCSB. They still needed me, and I still did good work for them, but the department and I both knew that the creative edge was gone. I was going through the motions too much of the time, fobbing more work off on my assistants. Now, they flourished. It was clear by the end of the spring quarter that, if I wanted to resign, I'd be able to recommend a first-rate replacement from within the ranks. Nobody outright suggested that I do this, but talk of what might happen *if* I resigned became more frequent. The campus newspaper mocked me in an editorial, along with other "dragging" staff members, and my assistants didn't really rush to my defense.

I decided to arrange a sabbatical for the next academic year. The ostensible justification was further work on interface-related papers for the journals. I don't think many of the directors were fooled by my rationales, but they went along (I think) for the sake of avoiding a scandal or nuisance. My workload got parceled out through the rest of the technical reference section, and at the end of the spring quarter I cleared out my office so that they could use it as overflow meeting space. In my heart I knew that I wouldn't be back.

The UCSB library is, at nine stories, one of the tallest buildings on campus. The middle six floors of the south side feature big curving windows, tinted against the glare, with thick, low chairs and couches so that patrons can sit and look out to sea. Most of the library, like most of the campus, is ugly concrete modernist junk, but around these windows some artistic soul managed to arrange tiles in patterns reminiscent of Aztec or Mayan designs. Oil derricks dominate the eastern half of the view—and I've long thought that had something to do with the ease of fund*raising for environmentalist causes—but even so it's a constantly remarkable spectacle. The campus sits on a bluff; a little creek trickles down through marshland to a cut in the sea cliffs, offering a glimpse of the beaches beyond.

In recent years, various student art projects have gone up in the marsh and channel, and I was very fond of the pastel whirligigs and the driftwood mobiles hung from nearly invisible brushed metal frameworks. On this, the last day of my work, a stiff offshore breeze made the mobiles dance, suggesting to me the skeleton puppets on show at Cinco de Mayo. I felt like bones or logs tugged by rhythms I could not see or understand. The thought came sharply and suddenly. I don't normally think of myself in such metaphorical terms, let alone self-pitying ones. But I contrasted my wandering lost sense to Ranulfson's demeanor and even more to the polished self-containment of the Haqims, and felt adrift.

I turned away, ambled to my car, and drove away with the sense that some door in my mind had closed without me ever seeing it.

The summer passed in a haze. That's another thing people don't realize about Southern California: the coast is foggy. Wet ocean air meets dry interior air, and the water draws together just offshore and inland. It's not uncommon for even midsummer mornings to begin with thick pea-soup fog, though it usually bums off quickly. It was a wet summer that year, with the irregularities in the offshore current, and most mornings were foggy. Some evenings the fog would pile up not long after sunset. I felt like that all the time inside. I got no useful work done beyond two quick articles and a couple of outlines. My mind wandered, circling back again and again to the Ranulfson work. My friends wondered if I'd taken up sedative abuse, but no, it was all in my head. At least I thought then that it was.

Monday, 4 July 1994, 11:58 PM
Santa Barbara, California

Then came the call. It was almost midnight, and I was sitting in my living room doing nothing in particular. I picked it up on the first ring, not even noticing the caller-ID information until after I heard that wonderful deep voice again: "Mr. Walinsky. Do I intrude?"

"No, no, not at all, Mr. Ranulfson. I was just thinking about your project, and wondering how it's going." "I'm sure you were. Such is the nature of things. As it happens, we have encountered a few setbacks, and I wonder if I could see you at our office again this weekend? Perhaps if you were prepared for a stay of not more than two nights, so as to allow an extended working period?"

My heart beat faster. (I remember that throb, and miss it.) "Certainly. In fact, since it's a holiday for the university, I could be down tomorrow, if that would be any help."

"No, thank you for your enthusiasm. The weekend, please. The receptionist will be looking for you." He hung up. I sat there some more, watching the phone, thinking that perhaps I might begin to come to life again.

I don't remember the intervening days at all. I must have done something in that time, but not a scrap of it remains. The next thing I remember is being on the freeway, singing along with the radio as I drove. I mocked the traffic jams of weekend vacationers; they were all heading out of the city, while I joined a select few (relatively speaking) heading in.

The firm had made reservations for me in a hotel a block away from the office. I checked in, showered, and changed to good slacks and a comfortable shirt. Ranulfson had never insisted on much formality, but I wanted to make a good impression. In my shoulder bag I packed a couple of spare shirts and a basic grooming kit; I knew what long-haul coding could be like.

There was indeed a receptionist on duty. He was a dour, dark man, who reminded me of some supporting character actor from Mafia movies. He didn't speak when I came in, just motioned me to the third office. It now had a name plate for Ranulfson and elegant furnishings in ebony and redwood. (That was a bit of flash for the knowledgeable crowd. Redwood is brittle as anything, and must be worked very, very carefully to get anything larger than a shingle out of it without major cracking and splintering.) Ranulfson himself stood by the door and ushered me in. I scarcely heard the lock click behind me.

There were *Los Angeles Times* front pages framed and hung on the wall opposite the door. "Take a look at them," Ranulfson told me, "and tell me what is the significance of them."

So, I stepped up and peered. It took me many minutes to figure out that each page contained a small story about violence, generally murder, associated with one of the businesses in my database. Here was a music club in Santa Monica; here an accounting firm and chiropractic clinic that shared a building in Hollywood; here a high-end custom tool shop over in San Bernardino. Nobody who hadn't studied the files as I had would recognize the pattern, but to me it was clear. They were using my information to help plan some sort of mob violence.

I turned around to find Ranulfson standing directly behind me. I hadn't heard him approach. He held a crystal goblet in his right hand, and a razor blade in his left. I saw that a cut ran along his right forearm. The goblet was full of blood. Nothing else has that distinctive reek. I stared at him, wondering what I'd fallen into.

"Drink, Mr. Walinsky."

I wanted to refuse. I really did. I'm sure that I did. But my body acted on its own imperatives. There was no hesitation in my arm as it took the goblet and raised it to my lips, nor in my throat as it drained it down. Something in me could not deny Ranulfson's instruction despite my fear and revulsion. My body was his to command, not mine. I suspected that if he ordered me to swallow the razor blade, I'd do that just as readily.

The blood poured into me. It was vile: dark and clotted, as though it had been stagnating inside his arm. (Was there something wrong with him that I hadn't noticed?) But as it poured into me, I felt a peculiar warmth. I felt stronger, as though muscles that had been asleep within me now woke up. Above all, I felt a devotion to Ranulfson that I cannot properly describe. I've been in love, and I've seen children bonded to loving parents, and none of that begins to compare. I felt that I could not bear to be apart from him, and that nothing he could ask of me would be wrong.

All the while, mind, I knew that this man had ordered me to drink his own blood and somehow made me want to do it. I *knew* that this was an abhorrent situation and that I was the prey of some sort of monster such as I'd never dreamed existed. And yet none of that mattered. He was the monster I adored and wanted to serve. The monster watched traces of conflicting emotions pass across my face, studying me with the sort of detached curiosity I might apply to a rare manuscript or a bug. There was nothing in his gaze to suggest that I had any human value to him; this was a craftsman evaluating a tool, with no moral significance beyond its utility. That knowledge both horrified me and drove me into a deeper frenzy of yearning to prove useful.

It's hard for me even to think about the years that followed. You could have seen me on the streets of Los Angeles and never guessed that I was a slave. I dressed well. I was better groomed than I'd ever been, thanks to Ranulfson's taking me to upscale salons. I stayed in the hotel, but moved to a long-term suite with all the trimmings. Outwardly, my life was the stuff of near-celebrity status, with immense wealth bent to the task of keeping me comfortable.

Inside my mind, the dark blood coiled like serpents. Any thought I had of acting in a way that might conceivably displease Ranulfson perished immediately under the crush of countering desires. It was literally impossible for me to entertain a thought of insubordination for longer than it took me to realize that that was what the thought was. Did my master need me to work at night and sleep during the day? Then I would, and I'd use all the pharmacopoeia necessary to make it happen. Did my master need me to acquire information by abusing connections established on previous consultation work? Then I would. I would do it all.

1 resigned from the university almost immediately. I don't actually remember what I wrote; I just remember Ranulfson's eyes seeming to glint as he told me I should resign, and then there's a blur, like I was writing through tears. Whatever it was, it worked. The university's confirmation came back almost immediately and in very stiff terms. They shipped my remaining papers to the hotel; I think that the "receptionist" Ranulfson had selected disposed of them, but I'm not sure.

The months passed. I learned the truth of what Ranulfson was up to. He was a vampire, part of some ancient society of vampires. They were engaged in a conflict of sorts with the vampires of Los Angeles, who rejected the society. (Good for the locals, 1 thought, until the blood serpents slung that thought dead.) Each of the businesses 1 helped Ranulfson target was controlled or used in some way by the anarchistic locals, and Ranulfson's coterie was out to sweep them up and turn the city into a fief and pasture for their own use. Apparently Ranulfson and his associates belonged to a group better known for being artists, and they were executing this commercial assault partly to show the principle of art in economics. That's what they told me, and of course when my master said it, I believed it.

Within a couple of months, I wasn't just laboring all night, every night, to help gather data for my master. During the day, I performed chores of other sorts with the receptionist. It was ghoulish work. We sometimes kidnapped derelicts or children for my master to suck the blood out of. Sometimes we escorted him to fancy clubs so that he could choose his own victims. Whenever a note of revulsion rose in my mind, that dark blood crushed it again. Sometimes we disposed of bodies by dumping them in out-of-the-way comers of the city.

I don't know who the receptionist was. He was always just "the other one" in my master's instructions. Maybe he had once been a decent enough fellow, and the blood had taken all that away from him. Maybe he was born to a life of crime, and this was nothing unusual for him. I don't know. He worked as diligently as I did, and when allowed his liberty went places that I didn't. Then we'd both feel the compulsion to report to Ranulfson, and the cycle of chores would begin again.

I met the Haqims again. The same five, I think, or at least ones who looked just the same. (I knew by then that some vampires can change their appearance, and for all I knew their entire bodies were like suits or masks put on for the occasion.) One of the women looked into my eyes for a long time one evening while we waited for Ranulfson to return from a detour created by brush fires along the coast highway. She spoke a word or two in what sounded like Arabic, though for all I know it was Enochian or the language of Atlantis. Then Ranulfson came, they stood silently together for a moment, and the Haqims left. The next evening's papers held stories of "gang violence" around more targets, with unusually violent deaths and no signs of robbery.

Friday, 7 June 1996, 11:02 PM
Century City, California

Things changed again five years, one month, and three days ago. It was a hot summer night, I recall, and the receptionist and 1 were sitting on the roof of the office building in the wee hours of the morning. There'd been fires in the San Gabriel mountains earlier in the week; smoke still lingered along with the smog, and there was a dusting of ash in sheltered comers. The receptionist and I didn't talk, we just idly wiped bloodstains off the leather smocks we wore for some chores.

The stairwell door banged open. Ranulfson staggered out, onto the roof. You must understand that I had never seen him stagger at any time. On the rare occasions I saw him fight, he moved with superhuman speed and savage determination, and even when wounded he merely slowed his pace some until he could force that dark blood into the wound and heal it up again. When tired, likewise, he slowed but never became ungraceful. This was unprecedented. Scary. My master weakened, and any threat to the master must be dealt with at once.

"You, down. Guard." He gestured to the receptionist. "You. Stay." That was to me. He drew up into a crouch against the low wall at the edge of the roof. Once the receptionist had gone, Ranulfson spoke again. "Bad times, Walinsky. Something destroyed the other three." He'd been out on a hunt with three other members of the coterie that night, I knew. "I do not know what it was, except that it was fast and fanged and reeked of blood. It drew blood out of me at a distance, and that is a trick I've only heard about the wizards doing."

"What can we do, then?"

"You would do anything at all to protect me, wouldn't you?"

"Of course I would."

"Of course you would. Very well. It is time for you to die."

"You're going to use my body as a barricade?" This time the blood serpent didn't quite sting down all the thought. I knew that I would do it if he commanded it, but I was aware for the first time in half a year of a sustained frisson of fear at what might come next.

"In a sense. I am going to make you undead. You must take up the work that the lost three can no longer perform. We need another in the coterie who understands the situation and the city."

"Then do whatever it is."

"I will. Be still."

How to describe the process of dying? I saw him lurch toward me, and without conscious thought I sat down cross-legged, so that he wouldn't have to reach up so far. He paused just for a moment, murmured something that 1 think was "a good tool," and crawled alongside me. I couldn't see him, but I felt his fangs rest lightly on my neck, then pierce the skin.

For a moment, hot agony flared in me. Then a bliss unlike anything I'd ever known. This wasn't the weird compulsion laid on me by the blood so far: this joy ran through all of me, breaking down the barriers between loathing and delight, flooding them together in an emotion for which there are no mortal words.

Then I died.

I felt myself grow weak. The beat of my heart faded. Warmth withdrew from my limbs, from my head, from my skin, into a little kindling in the heart, and then ceased. There was deep, dark calm within me for an endless moment. I felt my brain cool as the last of my voluntary muscles slipped into quiescence. I was at peace.

Then I became undead.

Wet fire poured between my lips. I knew the taste, Ranulfson's blood, but it seemed stronger now. It carried a power no longer masked by my own vitality. I could taste the dust of ages, the eternal hunger that drove him as it had driven the vampire who did this to him, on back into history. I sensed myself as part of a dark procession across the emptiness of night, marching from unknown damnation at the beginning to awaiting eternal punishment for this abomination. I felt within myself that blood serpent begin to move again, now whispering with my own voice. I felt my blood stir again with a semblance of life, forcing itself into places where living blood had never gone, turning my whole body into one vast chamber filled with the thing that was more than blood.

I opened my eyes to find Ranulfson now sitting in front of me, watching me carefully. "Yes," he said. "This is what it is. This is what we are."

In my ears, the blood that was more than blood hummed quietly, like a dynamo ready to unleash unsuspected power. I stood, and felt myself possessed of that grace I'd seen in the others. How simple, when there is no vitality to interfere with the will. How simple, when there is nothing of the grace that is humanity, only the polished perfection of cursed hunger and pride, I thought, recalling snippets of verse from across the centuries about hubris and the balance of flesh and soul. No more, for me. No balance, only darkness and drive.

So, another trip downward began. We found the thing in the night—one of the local vampires swollen with poorly controlled sorcery—and destroyed it. Ranulfson trained me in my new powers, the speed, the sight, the presence, the uses of the blood. I learned quickly. Others in his coterie were impressed, though they always spoke of me as a child in the blood.

Not long after my death and transformation, the whole scheme fell apart. Vampires from Asia arrived with plans of their own, with far better execution than ours. In short order we were fleeing for our own sakes, abandoning property and wealth as distractions behind us. We survivors gathered in Santa Barbara, in a mansion owned by a successful novelist to whom Ranulfson fed blood just as he had to me while I still lived. The author could no more betray the coterie than I could have. We settled in and began plotting revenge.

It was a stupid notion, of course. We were a handful. Our opponents were more, organized, driven by shared beliefs, and vastly more effective than our little lot. In short order they'd established something like a shadow government for the region, what they called a mandarinate, and they brought the anarchists together and gave them instruction in more effective behavior. Ranulfson and his brethren had dreamed of presenting Los Angeles under their control to their sect, their Camarilla. Now it wouldn't happen. Instead, the coterie would need to destroy what signs of their activities they could to avoid the embarrassment that comes to over-confident fools once exposed.

I thought little about this. For me, the years were a long night of revulsion. I would have liked to walk into sun or fire and end it all, but Ranulfson made sure that the blood serpent within wouldn't let me. Instead, 1 preyed on others as a human leech, doing my little part to take what I once admired and return only desolation. It seemed to me no great consolation that my victims wouldn't remember: Losing one's past is itself a violation, no matter how others may rationalize it. It is not for any of us to take away the right of memory, even the memory of pain, and yet that was the essence of my existence now. I did not wish to prey, but prey I would.

In due season I killed. It was inevitable. Ranulfson and his coterie sank into a quagmire of self-indulgent resentments. The others created new vampires like me, and commanded us to seek out and slay people (living and undead) they imagined had helped in the great defeat. I cannot say who was guilty and who wasn't; powers of mind control make all testimony suspect, and in any event we young ones had no authority to spare, only to destroy. So, I watched ambitious mortal men and women join centuries-old creatures of the night in a final death. My heart shriveled, night by night.

When I was a child, my parents and I had gone to the La Brea tar pits. It scared me. The statues of mastodons and sabertooth tigers sinking into the tar were all too vivid for my fantasy-prone mind, and I saw myself in nightmares for a long time thereafter, sinking along with those magnificent creatures. Now I felt my heart sink into an abyss that made the tar seem light and comforting. I understood now how Ranulfson could use me and others as he did: We simply weren't anything to him. And night by night, people were becoming less to me, because they had to if I was to survive, and I didn't have the option of rebelling to destroy myself.

———————

Friday, 10 August 2001, 3:37 AM
Santa Barbara, California

One evening, not long after sunset, I was alone in the mansion. Alone apart from the bound novelist and his bound servants, that is; the other vampires were out on various errands. The phone rang. I answered. "This is Ms. Haqim," the cool female voice said in its accentless, flat English. "Is Mr. Ranulfson in?"

"No, I'm sorry, he's out for the evening. This is Mr. Walinsky. May I take a message?"

I felt a brief buzzing in the phone, and in my head. "Mr. Walinsky. I remember you, the young man who used to be a librarian. Does your heart still tingle with grief, or have you accepted your condition?"

If I'd been breathing, I would have held my breath. As it was, I simply stood very still.

"Mr. Walinsky," she persisted. "Are you there? Do you understand my question?"

"I am here. I understand. But I cannot answer." I gasped out this last, feeling the blood serpent strike and strike again in an effort to keep me from even acknowledging that there might be an issue there.

"Ah. I see. Very well. We will speak again. In the meantime, you will say nothing of this call to Mr. Ranulfson."

"Can I refuse to tell him?"

"You can, if you are very careful. Goodbye, Mr. Walinsky, until we speak again."

That night was very long.

The following night, I woke with the sense that 1 really ought to speak alone with Ranulfson about the situation. I'd tried keeping silent, but it wore on me like chains, like the tar creeping up around my waist, sucking me down. I babbled something more or less incoherent, which made him raise a questioning eyebrow, but he agreed to step out into the vast backyard with me.

We sat on a bench by a small decorative pond. I tried to speak, and failed. Soon enough he realized what was going on. "You are under a compulsion, Mr. Walinsky. But we will take as much time as necessary to work through it and let you speak what you must to your master."

Behind him, the bushes stirred in absolute silence. A woman stepped through a narrow little opening. She let a branch snap back, and it made no sound. I looked at her, but could not speak. She had a strange appearance. Her features reminded me of the Lebanese families who lived down the block where I grew up, but her skin was a dusky black unlike any mortal skin tone. I recognized her eyes. They were the eyes that had peered into mine twice before, above the mouth that said an unfamiliar word, back in the offices now lost to us, and a warning on the sidewalk before that.

Ranulfson never saw her coming. She wore a simple gray jumpsuit. From one pocket she drew a long knife. As I watched, speechless, she sliced through Ranulfson's neck. His head fell; before it even hit the ground, she'd drawn a stake and rammed it through his heart.

How can I describe what happened next? The blood serpent poured into me years before suddenly coiled and died. I did not return to life, but all at once my will was again my own. I could choose to perish, if I wanted. I could choose anything at all. "Thank you," I whispered.

She sat on the bench, casually pushing off Ranulfson's corpse as it crumbled into dust. "Let me tell you why I did that. It's important that someone know."

I don't really understand the tale she told me. Vampires in the Middle East, some great struggle between ancients who all claim to know the mind of their progenitor, a vampire who proclaims himself master of all the assassins and scholars and viziers and demands their absolute loyalty. "For a year," she said, "I wrestled in solitude. Almost solitude." She paused. "That is not a story to tell now. 1 wrestled, as I say. My heart has always yearned to serve both Allah and Haqim, the father of all things and the father of my kind. I have not found these duties to war against each other, because Allah's words speak of duty and how one may serve the commandments when one must do things otherwise prohibited to believers. Do you understand?"

"No," I said.

"I thought not. Never mind, just listen." She continued, telling me how her own father-vampire had commanded her to give up Allah, and how she had refused. "So I went to the cave, and I pondered on Allah's words. He said to Muhammed, 'It is not righteousness that ye turn your faces to the East and the West; but righteous is he who believeth in Allah and the Last Day and the angels and the Scripture and the prophets; and giveth wealth, for love of Him, to kinsfolk and to orphans and the needy and the wayfarer and to those who ask, and to set slaves free; and observeth proper worship and payeth the poor-due. I thought about how my would-be master wanted to make us slaves, and about how Allah loves those who set slaves free. So, I set myself free, and returned to the world."

She looked at me with the most compassionate eyes I've ever seen. "You were a slave."

"Yes."

"You needed me."

"Yes."

"I remembered you. Deep in your eyes, there was a little shout that said that this was not what you wanted. Many slaves of the blood do seek it out, you know. There are always men and women who dream of power, of holding slaves and taking and never giving. You didn't seem to be one of those. You were tricked, Ranulfson said, and he was proud of it."

"He did?" I was surprised.

"Oh, yes. He didn't precisely realize it, but we—the Children of Haqim, that is—seldom take contracts until we understand our employer as well as his targets. We maneuvered him into telling us more than he may have realized. So, when it was time to set slaves free, I decided to start with you."

I was speechless for a long time. She just watched me. Finally, it occurred to me to ask, "What about the others you were with?"

A crease of pain ran across her brow. "They...chose to remain slaves."

"Did you destroy them?"

"Not yet. Perhaps never. Punishment is a worthy task for Allah's servants, too, but I would prefer to begin with liberty. There are enough prisons of one sort and other in the world. So." She paused. "Tell me. What will you do now?"

"I haven't the faintest idea."

She smiled. "Liberty takes more work than bondage." The smile faded like shadows after sunset. "I will watch, and see what you and the other freed slaves do. You will be a testament to me and to the other Children of Haqim, to show us whether the words of Allah remain for us or whether we are no longer among those to whom he speaks."

I shuddered.

She saw it, scrutinized my twitch with a chilling, dispassionate gaze. "You are afraid."

"Yes."

"Good. Learn to use that fear as a reminder that there is always an audience, and that you act not only for yourself but within the great theatre that is the universe."

I tried to say something, but lapsed back into a confused silence. In the blink of an eye, she disappeared. One instant she was there, the next she was gone. I couldn't feel her passage, but I knew that she had left, somehow.

That marvelous absence of compulsion stirred me. I got up, and quite casually strolled down the hill, under the freeway, past closed bars and open coffee shops, out onto the beach. I meandered out onto the pier, a favorite place of mine in the days when I still had days, rather than endless night. Out at the far end there are some grotty old benches, where fisherman gather in the daytime. At this hour there wasn't anyone but me; even the make-out artists had gone elsewhere or given up.

I sat down. That was two hours ago.

The surf rolled in beneath me, in a rhythm older than humanity. Older than vampires? I know so little about my kind, since Ranulfson never told me more than I needed to carry out his orders. I understood that I'd learn more after our victory, so that I would be a credit to his coterie when presented to the masters of the Camarilla. Now…well, there are others out there, I suppose. Perhaps they can teach me.

I have no idea what I'll do next.

For the first time since that wretched monster began to displace my blood with his through illusion and trickery, I am under no command. I am under the Haqim's *advice* that I will be watched, but I have no direction. Perhaps…no, somehow, I don't want to destroy myself. I want to understand, first, to know what this has all been about. Then there'll be time to make decisions.

I turn my face to the east and begin to walk back along the pier, toward Los Angeles. I must find out what it is that my life and unlife has been serving, whom my master warred against and whom he served. I will understand, no matter how long it takes, and then when I know I will act.

Angel Mine

Eric Griffin

Sunday, 21 June 1998, 10:00 PM
The Stone Garden
New York City, New York

The moon was the merest sliver as Ernst Lohm hopped the wall of the Stone Garden. The razor-fine crescent lay on its back, supine—a witch's moon. Lohm picked himself up, brushing grass and mud from his hands onto the torn knees of faded and paint-speckled blue jeans. Reorienting himself, he raised one thumb critically at arm's length and sighted along it. Twenty-three degrees, the fickle moon's elevation above the horizon. Perfect.

Immediately he set to work rearranging the carefully ordered tombstones.

His preparations had been painstaking. He worked quickly and expertly. Lohm was a craftsman of the old school, a master of arrangement, balance, composition. He was acutely aware that, should his efforts fall one degree shy of perfection, he might fail utterly to coax forth one of his reluctant dark angels this night. Or worse still, he thought, he might fail to convince it to abandon the multiform wonders of moonlight on marble and return again to the darkling plain from whence it came.

A cruel wind sliced past, drawing a low, shivering groan from his very bones—a bow drawn across cello strings. Lohm glanced distractedly at the shard of moon as if checking his watch. *Yes*, he thought, *time enough*.

Nigel stood at the threshold of the Chantry of the Five Boroughs. Before him, a mere foot length ahead, lay the Grand Foyer. But he could not bring himself to let that foot fall.

He was immaculately, if eclectically, dressed. His costume seemed to cut a bold swath across the ambiguous ground between silk pajamas and a military uniform. Upon closer inspection, the oversized golden buttons were revealed to be coins of ancient minting—of Rome, Carthage, Byzantium. His elaborate, drooping mustaches were more cavalryman than cavalier.

He hesitated on the threshold, caught involuntarily at the crux between the outside world—New York City and its unending progression of night and hunger, mystery and manipulation (all the familiar comforts that the Toreador had learned to call "home")—and this alien inner world, the *sanctum sanctorum*, the lair of the Tremere.

A Tremere chantry. Words a Toreador sire might conjure up to frighten his neonate childer. Nigel knew that few outsiders had ever been granted the double-edged honor of setting foot within this particular domain of the warlocks. Fewer still could be persuaded to recount what they had found lying in wait for them there.

Nigel prided himself on being rather persuasive, but the mysteries that lay beyond the veil that masked the Chantry of Five Boroughs from prying eyes remained impenetrable to him. He pictured the chantry as a dark, undiscovered continent, rife with intrigues and incantations. Nigel had no doubt that a Tremere chantry was a place where all the familiar terrors—of night and hunger, mystery, and manipulation—were distilled down to their purest, most alluring and most lethal forms. The prospect of being invited to partake of this potent liqueur tantalized him at some primal level. This temptation neatly evaded the defenses of judgment and intellect and went directly to work upon gullet, gut and groin.

Or perhaps the allure was something even more primeval. Yes, there was a hierarchy of desire at work here. That was certainly the message implicit in the Tremere's siren song—the never-ending chant of the chantry.

Between the desire and the spasm falls the shadow.

Nigel was discovering that there was some seat of desire that was deeper than the intellectual longing—the cravings to know, to understand, to master, to order, to arrange, to compose. Deeper even than the buried layer of the physical desires—the cravings for food, warmth, sex, blood, youth.

There was, beyond all these, a preeminent desire, an impulse of raw spirit. The revelation broke upon him like a wave. It retreated a brief moment only to crash over him again with redoubled force.

What a strange gift to place before strangers.

The proximity of his own desire lay bare and raw before him. It was an aching to be whole once more. An undeniable urge to return home. An instinctive plunge toward unity, a longing toward belonging. Nigel was overwhelmed by the seduction of the Tremere chantry. Not the expected call to power, but a summons to oneness, an abandonment of self, a simultaneous annihilation and a fulfillment.

Before him, the entry hall soared to dizzying heights. Its spires, galleries and sweeping stairways seemed to be rendered entirely in moonlight through stained glass. The delicate construct seemed wholly ephemeral. Nigel had the distinct and irrational conviction that if he were to blink the entire scene would dissolve and vanish from view.

The paths of the moonbeams streaming in through the colored glass seemed to have more substance than the walls and balustraded galleries of the Grand Foyer itself. Nigel could picture himself ascending the sharply sloping paths of light, climbing the treacherous slope to the very pinnacle of desire.

But some distant part of his mind held him back from abandoning himself to this alien communion of power and desire. As through a dense fog, a voice reached his soaring consciousness. It was the voice of the Gatekeeper, or whatever they called this enigmatic little watchman at the threshold. Talbott.

Talbott waited expectantly to usher Nigel forward to his audience with the Tremere regent. They were expecting him. Talbott's words reached Nigel as if from a great distance: "Your lordship has not previously honored us with a visit?" It was more an explanation than a question.

For a moment Nigel merely stared at him. He had heard each word distinctly, but the syllables found no purchase upon his thoughts. Nigel blinked his eyes experimentally. He clenched and unclenched his fists, manually pumping the vitae to his body's extremities. He felt as one awakening from long sleep or trying to shake off the grip of torpor.

If Talbott noticed Nigel's discomfort, he pointedly ignored it. "She is beautiful, is she not? Captivating."

It was not the words, but something about the tone of Talbott's voice that struck the jarring note—finally breaking in upon Nigel's musings. The words spoke of beauty; but all Nigel heard was danger. With a pang of disappointment and perhaps even betrayal, Nigel realized he was once more on familiar ground. It was a post he had grown accustomed to over the passing of long lifetimes. He was positioned squarely behind his own eyelids, within the comforting walls of his own skull.

Quickly and covertly, he lowered his eyes, glancing sideways and back, scanning for concealed threats in the periphery. He was immediately sorry that he had done so. A wave of vertigo swept over and staggered him. For a moment, he had the distinct impression that the Grand Foyer lay not before him, but behind. He wheeled suddenly back toward his only avenue of escape and found himself, once again, facing the vast moonlit hall.

Talbott smiled back at him from beneath his leonine mane. The smile had all the predatory patience of a great cat. Nigel began to turn again and then thought better of it. He struck what he hoped was a nonchalant stance and forced himself to remain calm. He closed his eyes until little more than a faint impression of light and shadow reached him through the slit of his eyelids.

When he opened his eyes again, Talbott was regarding him curiously. "Are you feeling unwell, sir? There is refreshment within. If you will follow me…"

Again, the hint of danger, and perhaps something else…mockery? A realization was slowly dawning upon Nigel—a realization which grew in proportion to his escalating suspicion of this gatekeeper. Cautiously, with tentative, shuffling steps, he tested his new conviction. It was as he feared. Neither forward nor back, neither advance nor retreat was open to him. It was as if he were caught fast in the complex web of desires that the chantry wove about him.

"You may inform your mistress, that I will await her convenience…here."

It was an admission of defeat. Nigel was aware that, at this moment, he was totally at the mercy of the warlocks. It was not a comforting revelation.

Time stretched uncomfortably. Nigel expected at any moment that his resignation would give way to the cold rush of panic. He was puzzled that, instead, his utter powerlessness brought with it a rather cool clarity of thought.

It is most likely that I am about to die. That was his first thought. Nigel regarded the idea without fear, but with a certain curiosity, almost anticipation. He rolled it around on his tongue, finding it cool, firm, sweet. It *is most likely that I am about to die.*

Again. That was his second thought. It brought with it a rush of unsteadying and poorly suppressed memories. It was not the circumstances of that first death that were most vivid in his mind. If pressed, of course, he could reconstruct every detail of the last view from the cathedral's spire. He could even count the number of stitches in the collar of his sire's intricately embroidered chemise. But the impression that was most real to him, vivid to the point of drowning out all other memories of the event, was the deafening roar of his own heart, spurting, slowing, spurting, slowing…slowing.

That last instant had been infinite. Nigel now found himself outside the ravages of time. Immortal and about to die. Again.

He sized up the Gatekeeper without antipathy. He could pick out the faint telltale flutter of life peeking from Talbott's collar. Desire seized him, mastered him. He reached out one hand to pluck the forbidden fruit, to draw it toward him.

"I am sorry to have kept you waiting."

The voice of lady of the house broke in upon him, and Nigel shook his head to clear it. Sturbridge's presence recalled him to his purpose. He seamlessly shifted obsessions.

"But here is the mistress of the house herself. It would seem that both my liberation and my heart's desire are assured. Aisling, dearest, it is such a delicious cruelty to keep me waiting upon your threshold." Nigel's features composed themselves into a mask of abject contrition. His eyes took on a faraway look as he began to recite:

"She cheats her lover of his due
And still contrives to keep him tied
By first deciding to refuse
And then refusing to decide."

"Hello, Nigel. Ignore him, Talbott. You'll only encourage him. To what do 1 owe this...unexpected pleasure?"

"You will forgive me, my lady. As usual, you seem to have me at something of a disadvantage." The Toreador held out both hands before him, wrists pressed together as if bound.

Sturbridge sighed and made an elaborate sign with her right hand. A peasant superstition. A warding against the evil eye. The tracery of her fingers seemed to linger a few moments too long in the air before her, blazing as if with their own light. Her guest experimentally took one cautious step forward and, finding no obvious harm resulted from it, recovered gracefully, and swept into the room with a flourish of cape. He took her by the arm and began ushering her toward the central fountain.

"You would not believe it," he leaned in confidingly. "The most extraordinary thing has happened. Ernst Lohm is dead."

Sturbridge was keenly aware of the Toreador's trying to remain nonchalant as he watched her shrewdly from the comer of his eye. "The name is familiar," she began guardedly. "He is an artist, is he not? From the Village."

"You know precisely who he is, dear," Nigel countered. "I want to know if you know *where* he is."

"My, you have grown abrupt," Sturbridge deftly extricated her arm from his and continued walking alone. "A severe young German, was he not? I seem to recall seeing some of his scribblings exhibited somewhere or another. He was a pet of yours?"

Instead of rushing to catch up to her, Nigel threw back his head and laughed aloud. He dabbed at his eyes with an immaculately pressed handkerchief which had appeared from a breast pocket. "Oh, that is precious. Ernst? Of mine? Certainly not. You know that, if anything, my failing lies in being far too...possessive. My playthings do not escape so easily."

"Then I do not pretend to understand your obvious interest in the boy. Nor, to be perfectly frank, the purpose for your visit."

"It is a great curse to love a woman with a barbed tongue."

"I seem to recall that they do have a word for those who profess to love dead women, but I do not believe it is cursed. Why have you come, Nigel? And why are you haranguing me with stories about dead artists?"

"Why, my dear, everyone in town knows you have an absolutely morbid fascination with death. Every one who is someone. It's that Irish blood of yours, I suspect. Death comes naturally to you. It's almost a national obsession, a birthright, a legacy. Did you say you had seen Lohm's work?"

Sturbridge shook her head at his persistence. Her gaze flickered deprecatingly down over her own sparse frame. She spread her arms almost apologetically. "The original model had Irish blood. But that was many years ago. The blood that currently worms its way through these old veins hasn't run to the Irish in over a ...but that's not really to the point, is it? Who's Ernst Lohm, and why should I care?"

"Like a mastiff with her teeth in your throat," he muttered just loudly enough to be sure she heard. "Aisling, dearest, surely you recall his work. You always have such a keen mind for details. Lohm's paintings have that delightfully distressing geometry about them. Angles that grate upon your bones. Conic sections that hint at the profane. Intersections of planes that border on the obscene."

"Hmm, yes. I think I recall something of what you mean. Go on."

"Of course you do, dear. Now listen. Someone very close to me, one of my circle of intimates, had set his sights on young Ernst. He decided to bring him home to meet the family, if you understand me."

She rolled her eyes. "Really, Nigel, there is no need to air your clan's dirty laundry for my benefit. This sounds like a skeleton that would be perfectly content to remain in your closet."

"Don't be catty, dear. You know very well that my friend was not the only one who was taken with young Ernst. The word in the back parlor has it that someone else had set his sights on our austere German. Someone who admired his work more for its unorthodox forays into certain disused and forbidden Hermetic *diagramma* than for any inherent aesthetic merit."

Nigel took her arm and pulled her closer, confidingly. "Do you know who that might have been?" he whispered intently.

Sturbridge felt the words instinctively rise up within her in answer to the intensity of his demand, his desire, his need. With an effort of will she choked off the reply before it could pass her lips, but it was already too late. She was flustered. He had learned what he needed to know. He smiled warmly, squeezed her hand, and withdrew a half pace.

She could feel the compelling weight of his attentions lift from her. It rolled back like dark clouds parting. The air between them hung heavy, humid, oppressive. There was the slightest of stillnesses; a calm, pregnant with the first faint crackling of energy. Then lightning flashed in answer to his presumption.

"You will leave now."

A look of perplexity crossed his features. It was quickly replaced with his more familiar stage manner. He was crestfallen. He was desolated. He managed to stammer out, "Forgive me, my lady! I have trespassed upon your hospitality, your kindness. It is unpardonable...."

He soon warmed to the subject, dropping to one knee, the nape of his neck bared as to the axe of judgment. "To allow myself to imagine, for even a moment, that your civility toward a wretch such as myself might be interpreted as...but it is altogether too much to hope for. I am unworthy even to be seen, much less to stand, in your presence."

"Get up, Nigel."

He was jerked to his feet before the words had the opportunity to traverse the intermediary of his ear and volition. He recovered seamlessly by transforming the motion into an impromptu leap. "Oh, my lady, with a word you render me the happiest of men. I..."

"Shut up, Nigel."

He shut up. But his response was more measured this time, more natural. There was no compulsion behind the command. Sturbridge had made her point. He was unlikely to try to get away with anything so clumsy and forthright as that again.

They were silent for a time. He crossed to the fountain and leaned heavily, straight-armed, upon its lip. The aroma of the rich blood was distracting, almost dizzying, as it trickled over the severe Aztec faces. It spilled from upturned mouth to upturned mouth, tumbling down the seven jagged steps of the carved pyramid. The path of its descent was worn smooth by the passing of uncounted lives.

Without turning, he said, "I have to know if he is lost to us, Aisling. If he is here, if he is already among you, I will accept that. But if he is not..."

He was lying, and poorly at that. But he seemed to be authentically at a loss as to the young artist's whereabouts. That would mean that the Toreador had not simply beaten them to the punch. Nigel had not come here to gloat. "But if he is not?" she echoed.

He turned angrily. "Damn it. Is the boy here, or isn't he?"

She smiled coolly and benignly like an icon, knowing she had gained the upper hand. "I can't tell you that, Nigel. Try another tack. You were saying that if he were not here..."

He scowled, considered a pout, and then thought better of it. "All right. If he's not here then he's dead. Just plain dead. And I will know why."

There was fire in his glare, but she stood aloof from it. "I wish you good hunting then, Nigel. You must return to me when you have discovered the truth. I should be disconsolate were I never to know the ending of your peculiar tale."

He took her extended hand and pressed it to his lips. He started toward the door, then turned as if struck with a sudden afterthought. "If the artist is not here…well, it pains me to think that anyone has stolen a march on the both of us."

"What do you mean?"

"It's just that, as embarrassing as it might be to think that this young man had slipped the silken bonds of my associates, how much more of a humiliation for it to be discovered that he was snatched from the iron grip of the Tremere hierarchy…."

"I don't see how that follows, Nigel. The boy is dead. They die all the time, these mortals. It is the single defining act of their existence. Even if one of my brethren had developed an ill-advised interest in this artist of yours—which, I hasten to remind you, has not been established—it does not follow that the designs of this chantry were thwarted in any way."

"As you say," he nodded slowly, deliberately. "No one could possibly take so small an incident for a sign of weakness. Why, simply because someone who had been singled out for the special favor of this august house has disappeared, without any repercussions falling upon the guilty party or parties…well, who could possibly blame you for such shortcomings of justice?"

"Go home, Nigel."

"Then you will look into this matter for me? I shall account it a personal favor. You may rely upon it, my lady: I will not forget your kindness and discretion. It gives my heart cause to hope that I might one day find some small favor in your sight. That I might..."

"Do not come again, Nigel. If I have news for you, I will send my man, Talbott, to you. He is as stubborn as any old half-blind hound of Ulster, and I think you will find him more than a match for even the persuasions of your parlor."

"I will look forward to your gift. Have no fear, I will be thinking only of you while I entice him to reconsider his choice of devotions. Good night, my lady."

―――――――

"You wished to see me, Regentia?" Johanus was obviously uneasy about the sudden summons. The adept wavered uncertainly just inside the threshold of Sturbridge's sanctum, one hand trailing along the doorjamb. This hesitation was not characteristic of her newly appointed Master of Novices—the one his brethren referred to as the Pillar of Fire. He had come by this epithet less for any pyromantic prowess or fiery temper than for the shock of red hair that was usually seen bobbing along just ahead of a column of straggling neophytes. "If this is a bad time..."

"It is, Adeptus. Come in. Close the door."

Johanus scurried forward, barely avoiding being caught in the reinforced steel door as it sang closed of its own accord. It was accompanied by the telltale hissing of hydraulic bolts ramming home.

Sturbridge descended from a throne of precariously balanced books. She strode quickly and purposefully over to him and stood uncomfortably close. He held his ground, but found himself leaning backward slightly.

"Who is Ernst Lohm?"

"Why, he is an artist. In the Village. I think," he added lamely.

"You think?"

Johanus hesitated a moment too long and then the words tumbled from him hurriedly. "Yes, an artist, a painter. I have seen his work. It is extraordinary, really. I can hardly describe it. It all reminds me of abstract equations, spatial formulae, almost a kind of *proto-diagramma*. You would have to see it. You *should see* it, Regentia."

"And you are personally acquainted with the artist?"

Johanus shuffled his feet a bit. "Yes, Regentia. As much as anyone can be said to be on personal terms with Ernst. He is not the type of person who accumulates casual acquaintances."

"Not the right kind of casual acquaintances at any rate," she replied disapprovingly. "Tell me, is collecting artists a regular hobby of yours or is this a special case?"

That shocked him into silence, and he took his time in answering. "It's obvious you're upset about this for some reason, Regentia, but I don't understand why. I haven't done anything wrong here. It's not like I've breached the Masquerade. I have been the very soul of discretion. Ernst is as entirely in the dark about…about the existence of our kind as he was before I first laid eyes on him."

"Are you feeding from him?"

He winced at her blunt question. It was like being asked by his mother if he were sleeping with someone. But to his credit, his answer was unhesitating, without any effort to conceal or deceive. "I have, if you must know. Yes. But not regularly."

"More than once?"

He nodded. "On three occasions. But I really don't see…"

"And the last time would have been?"

"Three nights ago." A look of concern caught up with him. "Why, what has happened?"

"Ernst Lohm is missing, presumed dead. You may be the last one to have seen him alive."

Johanus visibly paled. "But that's impossible. I…" he broke off abruptly. "Three nights? No one has seen him for three nights? It just can't be. Even if he were totally absorbed in a new piece, he could hardly have gone three days and nights without once stirring from his studio. You will excuse me, Regentia. I must go. I have to make certain..."

"You are not going anywhere." There was a note of finality in her voice that preempted all objections. "I need you to think. If Ernst were alive, if he feared for his life, if someone had made him an *uncomfortable* proposition, where would he go?"

"Regentia! Surely you don't believe that I...I did no such thing. You must believe me."

"Must I? I do not recall authorizing any 'recruiting efforts on your part. You are—or you were, your current status may be subject to review after we have resolved the present embarrassment—my Master of Novices. Do you believe that this position somehow entitles you to earmark mortals for your own personal breeding stock?"

"Certainly not." Johanus was fuming, his voice clipped, tight, controlled. "Lohm evidenced a rare and unsettling gift. It bore further observation. He might have, given a decade or two to develop his talent, proven a suitable candidate for admission to the vestibule of House Tremere. Or he might just as easily have descended into the grip of madness or laudanum or spiritualism. Even if I had found him at the point of death," he choked for a moment on words that might prove a bit too close to the truth, "even so, I would not have presumed to act, to free him, without having first sought out your sanction."

"You have already presumed too much. Are you aware that you are not the only one that has been paying court to this young artist? I see you are not. You did not stop to think that our cousins might also take an interest in this shining new talent?"

"You mean the Toreador?" He almost laughed aloud. "Your pardon, Regentia. How could the Toreador ever welcome one such as Ernst into their midst? They hovered around him, certainly, but they were terrified of him, mortified by his work. You should have been there at the exhibition last month. It was glorious. I can see them still, the entire gaggle of hangers-on, involuntarily clutching delicate lace handkerchiefs to their faces in distaste, fanning themselves compulsively. And all the while, as they congregated about the cheese tray, a blasphemous procession of formulae—these improbable guests from beyond the discrete spaces of our world—leered out at them from the keyholes of each and every picture frame. It was sublime."

"You underestimate our cousins at your own peril," Sturbridge replied coldly. "I believe it may have been they who startled your young friend—not the other way around. Assuming, of course, that it was not your own indiscretion that set him to flight. But you have not answered my question. Where would he have gone?"

He managed to ignore the renewed accusation and sat in silence for a time. "The stone garden," he answered at last. "It was a place that he used to come to meet his…that we used to meet. I doubt that the Toreador even know of its existence. I can show you."

"You can tell me. *You* are not going anywhere. You will remain in your quarters until I decide what should be done with you. In the interim, Master Ynnis will see to the novices. That is all."

"But Regentia…"

She only glared at him.

"Yes, Regentia."

He bowed and turned back toward the doorway just as the bolts of the ponderous steel door hissed open. He was halfway through the opening when her voice stopped him.

"Johanus." He half-turned.

"If he is still alive, I will find him."

He seemed about to respond with the obvious question, but the fight had gone out of him. He absently nodded his acknowledgement and withdrew.

———

The small, neat plaque on the gate read, "Wages and Sons." From this distance, Sturbridge at first thought it said, "Wages of Sin," an inscription which she found curious, but not altogether inappropriate.

The gate swung back noiselessly at her touch, despite the carefully polished chrome padlock which was intended to keep the gate from doing precisely that. Nor did the electronic sensor on the strikeplate register the break in the circuit—its usual indication to pass along a warning that the gate had been opened.

Sturbridge noted these things absently, almost after the fact. She did not wave some magic wand or recite any half-forgotten incantation. Doors just opened for her. They always had. Like at the supermarket. It was a basic courtesy which by now she took largely for granted.

Beyond the gate lay a short, curved drive leading up to a carport. She could make out a pair of uncomfortably long black automobiles parked side by side, bedded down for the night. A white pebbled path stretched away across the grounds and wound around to the back of the converted manor house. The building itself was unlit and silent, the funeral parlor closed for the night.

Sturbridge struck out along the path. Her footfalls crunched gratingly against the stillness of the night and the solemnity of the surroundings. The white pebbles gave off a faint, reassuring glow in the diffused moonlight. Sturbridge, however, had eyes only for the single point of shadow marring the path—the one perfect crimson drop that stood out in sharp relief. She bent and extended her forefinger. The droplet latched onto her fingertip and clung tenaciously, surrendering its hold only when touched experimentally to her tongue.

Sturbridge cocked her head quizzically. Not at all what she had expected. She rolled the droplet around on her tongue to make quite certain. Satisfied, she nodded, straightened, and rounded the curve of the path.

On this side of the manor, the wall ran closer to the building, forming a small, enclosed yard—a private cemetery. The path meandered through the smooth marble stones and across the immaculately tailored lawn to the back door of the house. The second trail—the nearly imperceptible thread of dark droplets that Sturbridge followed—stuck closely to the first and vanished among the polished marbles.

But even from here, Sturbridge could tell that something was not right. She was not unaccustomed to the trappings of death, having been there at least once already. But there was something else here. Something that made her uneasy.

The *arrangement of* the stones bothered her, she decided after some thought. They were bunched too close together, as if the dead were simply heaped one on top of the other. And the gleam off the marbles was wrong—too glaring, too uniform, too perfectly reflected. The whole scene felt somehow false, a flawed replica. A trap.

Sturbridge forced herself to move. She had no clear plan of action in mind, but she was all too aware that, in the open space between the house and the little cemetery, she was exposed, an easy target. She advanced cautiously.

Her first realization was that she had certainly found that for which she had been searching. The smell of spilled life here was strong, nearly overwhelming. Something within her stirred in answer to that scent. Something sleek, dark, powerful. It flared its nostrils, snorted, and reared—revealing wicked hooves, each as large as a man's head and shod in glyphs of sizzling neon. She roughly leaned into its neck with all her weight and wrenched its head around and down. This was no time to allow the Beast to take the bit in its teeth.

But there was a clarity in the purely bestial; a single moment free from the cloudy filter of reason. In that instant, all of Sturbridge's senses were alight. She was keenly aware of the body of the young artist lying sprawled, though as yet hidden from sight, in the midst of the carefully arranged tombstones. She also knew without question that his was the only body in this "cemetery." The headstones were immaculate, pristine, unmarred by the rough touch of any chisel. Unburdened by names, dates, epitaphs.

This was no place for the dead. It was a gallery, a showroom. A place where a master stonemason might display his wares to his grieving customers. The only things planted here, Sturbridge realized, were the headstones. *The Stone Garden*. Johanus had called it. *The place where Ernst came to meet his...*

Sturbridge caught the sudden movement out of the corner of her eye. Above her and behind. From the rooftop. The flash of moonlight on metal. She was moving before the impression had time to coalesce into conscious thought. She dived between the headstones, rolled and came abruptly, jarringly, to rest against the corpse of Ernst Lohm.

Three sharp shots rang out. Shards of marble exploded in their wake. Someone's *loaded for bear*, she thought. She closed her eyes tightly in an effort to block out the proximity of the corpse, but it was no good. The scent of life was rich, heady. Her forearms squelched in sweet sticky puddles of it. The Beast tossed its head and stamped the ground, churning earth and spilled life into a thick, rich loam.

Sturbridge cupped her hands, scooping up a double fistful of vitae and the reflected light of pebbles and tombstones. She raised it to her lips.

"*Fiat lux.*"

The nightmare threw back its head and its hooves flashed magnesium bright. A sudden flare erupted from the rooftop. Its searingly bright light reached Sturbridge a fraction of a second ahead of the shriek from the contorted silhouette revealed there.

It was over in an instant, a verdict as swift and unanswerable as a lightning strike. In its wake, the only sound was the heavy thud of a large, inanimate object falling twenty feet to the front lawn. Then solemnity and silence reasserted their claim over the premises.

Sturbridge came to her senses face down in the wreckage of the dead artist's throat. She pushed herself away, angrily wiping at her chin with the back of one mud caked hand. Her left shoulder stung, and a quick investigation revealed a shard of marble still lodged deeply there. It grated against the shoulder blade when she moved. Already she could feel the wound closing, the flesh reknitting. With an effort of will, she stopped the flow of healing blood. She braced herself and ran a cruel fingernail along the length of the wound, reopening it. Better to leave it thus until it could be tended properly back at the chantry.

With her good arm, she unclasped a tiny teardrop-shaped vial from a gold chain at her throat. She stooped again to the body of the young artist and collected what was essential— three perfect beads of spilled blood. The broken remnant of Ernst Lohm she left there among the pristine marbles of his stone garden.

"Aisling, darling, I came as soon as I heard." Nigel seemed disheveled and out of breath. Sturbridge shook her head at his affectations within affectations. He was of course, like all of their kind, quite literally out of breath, and had been so for some time.

"I seem to recall telling you not to come again." That brought him up short, but he recovered immediately.

"Of course you did, dear. But I had to bring back your little watchdog, didn't I? I couldn't bring myself just to turn him out into the street. I'm afraid that, after hearing his news, I found that I would not have the opportunity to play with him as I had so hoped. It is no matter. But you are hurt!" he scolded. "You did not tell me…."

She had winced away as he took her arm. "It's nothing. An ache in the hollow of my shoulder, a souvenir from hanging about cemeteries late at night."

"Let me see that." Nigel made a great fuss of trying to mother her while Sturbridge, just as determinedly, parried his efforts. But there was no hiding the true extent of her injury from him.

"Hanging about cemeteries, indeed! That's a bullet wound. I have not lived so sheltered a life as you seem to believe."

"I assure you, you are mistaken," she countered. "But if you have come here only to offer questionable medical advice, I must conclude our interview. I have no need of a physician, even one with your reputed 'affinity' for the scalpel…."

Nigel tsk-tsked. "Now, play nice. And I was so looking forward to nursing you back to health. I am sorely in need of a diversion. I have been out of sorts since this whole situation with Ernst first arose. Your man, Talbott, he tells me you have found him."

"Yes. He is dead, Nigel, and beyond reach."

A look of irritation flitted across his face. "Dead, do you say? Truly dead? This I must see for myself. Take me to him."

Her voice was calm and level, as if addressing a particularly slow child. "I imagine he is in the morgue by now. They would have found the body this morning."

"You found him and then left his body for the…"

"I did. The boy's body is of no further use, Nigel. He is gone."

Nigel seemed to wrestle with some further accusation but choked it down. "Tell me, how did he die?" His voice was clipped, terse.

Sturbridge studied him for a long moment as if trying to determine how much to reveal. "His throat had been torn out," she replied truthfully, glossing over the strict chronology of events. "There was nothing you could have done for him. Nothing."

Nigel's look had become calculatedly nonchalant once more. "And you have questioned your 'associate' about this matter? About his whereabouts on the evening of the murder?"

If Sturbridge were in the least discomforted by this new line of accusation, she gave no sign of it. "My associate was confined to his quarters, pending the conclusion of my investigation into this matter."

"But how is that possible? When I came here two nights ago..."

"Nigel, Ernst Lohm was killed only last night. I know. I felt the warmth of his blood. It spoke to me. There is very little that the blood conceals from us."

Nigel suppressed an involuntary shudder, his nose wrinkling in distaste. Blood magic. Thaumaturgy. The warlock's dark gift. He had a vision of Sturbridge sitting beside a moonlit corpse, her robes soaked to the elbows in spilled life, distilling truth, sifting entrails, reading omens. But yet the dead man held his peace. His secrets remained his own.

Nigel shook himself to banish the image, suddenly painfully aware of the silence that had fallen between them. He blurted out the first thought that came to mind. "And you found nothing near the body?" It was, perhaps, a miscalculation.

"For instance?"

"I don't know," he snapped back, trying to regain his equilibrium. "Brushes, pigments, canvas..."

"Ah, then you have searched his studio. And recently. Good," she countered. Faced with his puzzled look, she explained further. "You knew that the body was not discovered among his own things."

"Yes, yes," he admitted. "My associate was half-mad with grief. He quite literally tore the studio apart."

"And what did you—excuse me, did *he*—discover?"

"*He*," Nigel replied with emphasis, "could find no sign of...of what Ernst had been working on." *Damn it.* He had not intended to say that much. Sturbridge's insinuations had him ruffled, off balance. Her presumption!

"What was he working on?" Sturbridge pounced on the dangling thread of conversation. Nigel fidgeted, took out an ivory snuffbox and politely offered it to his hostess. Sturbridge waved it aside distractedly. "Nigel, we need to account for about five days' time. If Lohm was working on something—and that something has also disappeared—we need to know what it was. And how far along he was. And who else knew about it."

Sturbridge did not know if it was due to the contents of the snuffbox or the fact that Nigel was himself distracted, but she noted that he neglected to sneeze after taking his pinch of snuff.

"If you must know," he said, dabbing at his nose with an immaculately pressed silk handkerchief. "I am told—by those close to the artist—that it was to be his masterwork. My associate," here he looked hard at Sturbridge as if daring her to contradict him, "says that Ernst would not let anyone near it until it was completed. He kept the studio locked and would not answer to anyone. Not even to his intimates. He says that Ernst called it *The Angel*.

"Thank you, Nigel." Sturbridge stared at him long and calculatingly. At last, she seemed to make up her mind. "I have news for you as well."

He looked as if he might offer some further flowery rhetoric or flattery but thought better of it. He waited for her to continue.

"There was blood found at the scene. Someone else's blood." This was true enough—the droplets of blood on the path. Sturbridge failed to mention that she had also found a significant quantity of this 'other blood' *inside* the body of the victim. Potent blood. Vampiric vitae.

"And you have," again the look of distaste creased Nigel's features, "*examined* this blood?"

"I have."

There was an expectant silence between them. It was Nigel who finally broke it.

"And what did you discover?"

"The blood was that of a Nosferatu. The last being, no doubt, to see Ernst Lohm alive."

Sturbridge had the momentary satisfaction of seeing a look of pure ice and daggers consume her guest's features. He took her hand and pressed it mechanically to his chill lips, forgetting to flush blood and warmth to them as was his customary affectation.

"Thank you, my lady. You have been most helpful. I am in your debt." His cape cracked like a whip as he spun and stalked from the chantry.

———

Sturbridge glanced, for perhaps the hundredth time, at the intricate brass water clock at the north point of the *diagramma hermetica*. The gleaming arcane mechanism gave no indication that more than six hours had passed since Sturbridge had first set it into motion.

Two of the three perfect crimson beads still hung precariously over the beaten-copper basin below. By a potent sympathetic magic, the second droplet would not fall until its owner's blood next spilled upon the ground. It was as if time itself paused and cocked an ear, waiting expectantly for the next droplet to fall.

Sturbridge had not been idle. Even after assembling, adjusting, and attuning the delicate and fickle instrument, she still had to link it to the circle of apportation. Her preparations were patient and precise. She was just refreshing the circle, sating its ravenous thirst with a fresh application of the life's blood of a hawk (hawk for swiftness and surety of flight) when she caught the telltale hint of movement from the brass *mechanica*. She ran her tongue over the blood-tipped feathers of the hawk's breast, sealing the precise incision. Whispering reassuringly, she ran a cold finger down the length of its back and set the magnificent animal back on its perch. At her touch, the bird stirred, blinked, and then shook out its feathers, emerging from its near-petrified state.

Sturbridge had already turned back to the water clock. The second bead of life swelled, drooped, and stretched viscously before surrendering its hold. There was a single chime, deep and low, as it struck the expectant copper basin below. Bracing herself, Sturbridge stepped confidently across the line drawn in blood.

———

There was a whimper and the resounding crack of a whip. A flame sizzled and sputtered to the smell of seared flesh.

"I will ask you again. Where is it?" demanded a voice raised in mounting anger or excitement.

The answering silence was complete, a vacuum. Nature *abhors a vacuum.* Sturbridge thought ruefully, emerging into the dim, rough-hewn chamber. An unsettling feeling of vertigo washed over her, and she stumbled, trying to force her eyes to focus on her new surroundings. She had no doubt that wrath and the crack of the whip would swiftly rush in to fill that vacuum.

"I have been more than patient, wretch. You have stolen something which is precious to me. You will return it now," the voice took on an edge of ice and daggers, "or you will suffer until you do."

There was the slight but unmistakable sound of steel being drawn slowly, patiently across parting flesh. Sturbridge latched onto the glint of metal, a wicked knife. She saw a precious ruby line run the length of the blade and fall neglected to the stone floor. At the exact moment of impact, somewhere behind her, the water clock chimed, low and mournful, for the third and final time.

The room snapped into sharp focus. There were a dozen figures in the dim underground chamber. Thirteen, she corrected herself, counting the unlucky number hung by his wrists from an ancient cast-iron chandelier. Their missing Nosferatu. The last being, save one, to see Ernst Lohm alive.

The unfortunate swung slightly, like a pendulum, bearing mute witness to the subtle stirrings of the earth. It seemed he was already betraying secrets.

The thing which immediately arrested Sturbridge's gaze, however, was not the path he cut through space, but rather the quiet grace with which he did it. If the hanged man were aware of the indignity of coarse ropes, or the kiss of wicked knives, or the sputter of the flaming whip, or even the small lost sound of falling blood—he gave no outward sign.

Rather he seemed transfigured, ennobled. Suspended in midair, the crippling curvature of his spine seemed to fade from view, his silhouette revealing only a gentle, elegant arc of back and neck. The perpetual tension that gnarled his hands into nearly useless bludgeons had fled, abandoning him to solitary peril. The lines of hand that peeked from his bonds seemed graceful, reposed, fluttering gently like delicate white birds. The raw sores that once marred his features had surrendered to the precise ministrations of hot steel. They had sighed, burst, and collapsed into the gentle trickle of blood, washing clean the radiant white marble of cheek and jaw.

He was beautiful. Utterly beautiful. More a piece of sculpture than a creature of flesh and blood. He was a masterwork that might have stepped straight from the Renaissance courts of Florence or the Vatican. A Michelangelo. No, better still, a Donatello. Here was no mythical hero. It was a vibrant figure, a vulnerable figure. A *human* figure.

It was so incredibly lifelike, she half expected the sculpture to move. The whip cracked. The perfect arc of back contorted painfully. The veneer of cool marble crumbled, revealing the writhing form beneath—still clinging tenaciously to the cruel parody of life.

"Enough, Nigel." Her own voice rang out, calm and authoritative. For a moment, she regarded her own words with curiosity, as if they were strangers come upon her unexpectedly in the dark. Resignedly, she stepped forward into the light. There was no turning back now.

The man with the knife spun upon her, wide-eyed, but quickly recovered himself. "You. You have no business here, Aisling. I require no assistance in wringing the information I require from this wretch's blood." The look of polite distaste, so conspicuously absent while he had plied his own bloody trade, reasserted itself.

His circle of intimates edged cautiously forward, drawing a ring around Nigel and Sturbridge. A voice that was nearly a purr accused, "Nigel, dear, you have been holding out on us again. You *must* introduce me to your little playmate. She is simply too…severe."

"This is neither the time, nor the place," he replied coolly, his eyes never leaving Sturbridge.

"Nor the man you are looking for," Sturbridge countered. "This Donatello here did not kill your young artist. You know that."

"I know no such thing. You are the one who led me to him. You and your blood magic. Do you now tell me this is the wrong man?"

She considered. "His blood was certainly at the scene. Although more of it was actually inside your young friend than on his corpse."

"What are you saying? That Ernst was…that he was bound to that thing? That monster?" He gestured angrily at the hanged man with the knife, slinging droplets of blood.

Sturbridge smiled. "I should not be so hard on monsters. But you have it quite backwards. It was our Donatello that found himself indebted to young Ernst. Come now, Nigel. You knew all this. You had been observing our young artist's nocturnal forays for some time now. From the safe vantage point of your 'back parlor'—the funeral parlor which overlooked Ernst's stone garden."

"I did no such…"

"Oh, I'm sure it wasn't you personally. Not all the time. I believe it was one of your associates that I ran into there last night, keeping watch over the bait. Waiting to see if the 'monster' who had defiled your pet artist would be drawn out of hiding."

"That is ridiculous. I did not even know of this creature's existence until you revealed it to me."

"But you did know where Ernst was killed. And you also 'knew' that the injury to my shoulder was from a bullet wound. Now what put you in mind of bullets? I told you it was an ache from hanging about cemeteries late at night—and it was. It was a fragment of a marble headstone that was lodged there. Your associate's shots missed, Nigel."

There was a growl from a familiar silhouette amidst the ring of supporters. Nigel shot him a look that silenced him instantly. "And how do you suggest that I knew that young Ernst had been…misused by that foul wretch?"

"The same way that I did. You fed from him. There would be no concealing the potency of the vitae inside him. Vampiric blood. Nor would a connoisseur like yourself be likely to mistake the taint of the Nosferatu. I tasted it in the blood, of course. The blood conceals nothing from me. But you, what was it that revealed it to you? Was it the boy's supple alabaster skin, gone suddenly coarse and common? Was it the touch of his hand, once satiny, but now inexplicably clammy? Was it..."

"Enough! You will not speak thus to me. I will not justify myself before you. If I released the boy from his bondage to this odious creature, if I took his miserable life, what is that to you? I will not be reproached for doing so. There is no crime in it. He was a mortal, Aisling. Nothing more."

Then she heard her own words parroted slowly, monstrously back to her: "Who's Ernst Lohm and why should I care? The boy is dead. They die all the time, these mortals. It is the single defining act of their existence."

Sturbridge stood in silence for a long while, her head bowed in defeat. At last, she stirred. Without raising her head, she intoned hollowly, "Go, Nigel. Take your friends, take your toys, and go."

"We are not going anywhere until I get some answers from this damnable..."

"Ernst is dead, Nigel. You need to forget him. You need to move on. He struck his own dark bargain." Her voice dropped to a whisper, pitched low so that those gathered around them would not hear. "It may hurt like hell right now. That he would turn his back on you, on all you had to offer him, and choose..." Her voice trailed off and she found herself gazing at the malformed and broken wretch dangling from the ceiling.

His voice was pitched equally low, but it was hard, cruel, threatening. His eyes bore into hers. "If I cannot have the boy, I will have that painting—his final masterwork, his dying breath. I would look upon it. Peer into it and scrutinize him. Interrogate him. There are questions I would put to him, and words." His tone softened as if the fury within him had all but burned itself out. "Words left unspoken between us. That painting is my last link to him, Aisling. My last chance to be near him again. My last chance to say those words. It is my right. You cannot deny me."

She regarded him levelly for a long while, once again finding herself sizing him up, reevaluating. Her voice, when it came, was calm, confident, authoritative. "I will find your painting, Nigel. There is nothing more to be gained here. Go home now. And try to rest. You may come to me again, tomorrow."

He would not meet her gaze, but turned to his circle of intimates, already gathering his stage manner around him like a comforting old cloak. "The witch has given her blood oath. She will extract the necessary information. But come, there is surely more palatable diversion to be found elsewhere. Gentlemen?" He gestured for them to precede him as he bowed low to Sturbridge. "My lady, I leave you to your study of entrails and oracles. Although I must admit it is not you, but rather this unfortunate whom I envy. Tonight, he achieves my fondest hope, for he finds himself in sole possession of your attentions. Until tomorrow then, dearest."

The Nosferatu flinched at the whip-crack of the twirling cape as his inquisitor withdrew. Sturbridge crossed to the hanged man quickly and began searching for some way to lower him to the ground. "Are you all right? I'm going to set you down now. Do you think you can stand?"

He grunted, which she look for an affirmative. The rope ran over the ring of the chandelier and back down to a bracket in the wall. She placed one finger to the knot and it hurriedly unraveled. There was a further grunt as the Nosferatu's feet hit the floor. He staggered, taking up the burden of his own weight once more and bending beneath it.

Sturbridge eased him to the floor and, with a deft twist of fingernail, opened up her wrist. "Here. Drink. I've got no idea where we are, and you'll need your strength before we can go anywhere. I'm Sturbridge," she added, seeing his hesitation. As if that explained everything.

He held up one gnarled and palsied hand before his face, fending off the much-needed nourishment. "Why?" he asked in a husky, broken voice. "Why did you call me *Donatello!*"

Sturbridge drew back at the question, at the intensity of his scrutiny. Returning his stare, she realized the reason for his hesitation. He thought she was mocking him.

"When I saw you hanging there," she began cautiously, as if the sound of her voice alone might be enough to set him to flight. "You reminded me of a sculpture, a statue. A perfect, gleaming figure of white marble standing against the ravages — the indignity — of time. A vibrant, a vulnerable, a *human* figure. A Donatello."

She shrugged, almost apologetically. The blood had run the length of her arm and now fell steadily from her elbow to the floor below. He bowed his head, whether in shame or resignation, she could not tell.

With one mangled hand, he pawed her arm to his lips and drank in great ragged sobbing gulps. After a time, his gasping sobs grew more regular and then ceased entirely. She lowered his head gently to her lap and sealed the now-jagged gash in her wrist.

She looked down at the ruin of his face, now once more in repose. The worst of the knife work had reknit itself, her blood ministering to his wounds from within. Only then did she turn her attentions to the wreckage of his back and what she knew she must find there.

His shirt hung about him in tatters. Carefully, she peeled back the blood-soaked rags. It was a small mercy that the whip had not been barbed. At some point, however, his inquisitors had set fire to its tip—an ancestral enemy which bit far more deeply and lastingly than any steel barb.

The new linen bandages covering most of his back had taken the worst of the scourging, but it remained to see how much lasting damage had been done to the tender flesh beneath. Slowly, with mounting anxiety, Sturbridge peeled back the wrappings.

They came away in one continuous sheet with a wet, sticky sound that spoke of fresh scabs not yet fully formed and old wounds reopened. She gasped.

There, peeking from beneath the bandages, was Ernst Lohm's masterwork, his Angel, worked into the very flesh of the Nosferatu's back. An immortal masterpiece.

Sturbridge peered closer, drinking in every detail. Yes, she was intimately familiar with this dark cowled figure. The wings of purest flame. The mangled right arm dangling limp and useless like a scythe in spring. He was Uriel, the Gatherer—the Angel of Death. Blood stained the hem of his robes. Fresh, raised red weals. The livid crimson stood out boldly, holding its own against the flaming oranges, imperial purples and midnight greens that artist had invoked to breathe life into his harbinger of death.

Sturbridge absently stroked the head that lay in her lap. What a terrible and enigmatic gift to receive at the hand of his devoted and doomed young admirer. For a moment, she was consumed by a simultaneous envy and pity for this dead, crippled husk of a man—this doubly blessed monster who was himself both a timeless work of art and the medium for another's masterpiece.

She cradled the broken shell of his body in her arms. He felt unnaturally light and brittle, as if he might crumble and scatter under the rough caress of a strong draft. A double armful of crisp autumn leaves.

She wondered how he might hope to endure. She could not imagine him facing the physical rigors of the coming nights, much less the far more onerous challenge—the reality of waking each new night knowing only his own deformity and never once being permitted to glimpse the radiant beauty that was ah ways within reach, but ever just beyond his line of sight. Hidden from view. Obfuscated.

Sooner or later, Donatello's patient shadow must catch him up. Sturbridge imagined the Gatherer simply tapping his longtime companion on the shoulder—neutral ground, the no-man's-land midway between them—and leading him home. It was inevitable, as certain as death. But it was not the dying that was difficult, it was finding the strength to remain among the living, to rise each night. To drink life, to endure.

She did not envy him the struggle of waking to this blasphemous parody of the divine gift—of life everlasting—knowing that the Angel of Death himself was ever at his back. Hovering, waiting only for him to stumble, to slip. Just once. Tap.

Sturbridge carefully replaced the linen bandages. Drew up the sheet to cover the face of the dead. Eclipsed, if only for a moment, the immediacy of those terrible, piercing, and hauntingly patient eyes.

Tonight, at least, he would be safe. She curled her arms around him protectively—like raven-dark wings—and he slept soundly, mercifully. The sleep of the dead.

Flesh of My Flesh

Eric Griffin

Friday, 13 August 1999, 11:30 PM
Washington, D.C.

In the wake of the riots, the Mall in Washington, D.C., had assumed the aspect of an armed military encampment. A vast tent city, overflowing with refugees and emergency workers, stretched unbroken between the Capitol and the boarded-up windows of the White House. For the second time in its history, the residence of presidents had been subjected to the indignity of the torch. The First Lady had taken the forced evacuation in stride, recalling the example of her predecessor, Dolley Madison, by making a photo op of rescuing a portrait of George Washington from the conflagration.

The Washington Monument jutted erect and defiant from the press of canvas and unwashed bodies—a finger pointed accusingly at the heavens. Upon closer inspection, however, it was obvious that that the concerted efforts of innumerable vandals were taking their toll. As if sensing the prevailing wind, FEMA workers had at last overcome their awe and reluctance, erecting a makeshift scaffolding in order to paint a bold red cross on each of the obelisk's four sides.

The Smithsonian Institute had shut its doors to the public. The lower level of the Air and Space Museum had been commandeered as the field headquarters of the Maryland State Militia as they tried in vain to restore some semblance of order to the nation's capital. The Natural History Museum had been condemned and cordoned off after the explosion — allegedly set off by would-be diamond thieves — that rocked the building, setting it back down unsteadily on its foundation. Rescue crews were forced to carve their way through the life-sized replica of a blue whale that, once suspended from the ceiling, had precipitated to the floor, sealing off an entire wing of the building.

Of all the buildings on the Mall, however, the one that was most changed was the Castle. Something fundamental about the nostalgic old brick edifice had been altered. The press of teeming life instinctively edged away from its presence. The weeds of rope and canvas would not take root in its shadow.

———

Evening. The tent city was alight with cookfires blazing in metal trashcans and gutted automobiles. The small, crippled figure gave them a wide berth. He knew that if he were unwary enough to straggle too close to one of these tight knots of humanity, he would be rewarded with angry glances and bared steel at best. At worst, he would be robbed, or beaten or…well, many here were starving, he reminded himself. They would hardly scruple at such fare as was abundantly at hand.

He broke from the press of voracious bodies and emerged into a rough circle of open space, the no-man's-land surrounding the Castle. Without glancing around to see if he were observed, he crossed quickly to the front doors. He felt as if the old building were marking his progress through narrowed arrowslit eyes.

Cautiously, he extended one hand to the door. Its surface was rough and knobby, but it seemed to squirm under his touch. Soft and yielding, moist and alive. The portal did not so much open to him as fold around him, engulf him.

He blindly groped, pushed, and battered his way through the viscous membrane, only to find himself spat out into the coolness of the interior. He lost one of his polished brass crutches in the struggle. It skidded across the marble floor and came to rest several feet away with the clatter and reverberating ring of hollow metal.

"William?" came a sharp cry from upstairs. "Is that you, William? You always will make such a racket."

"Yes, Your Eminence, it's me. I am sorry to disturb you. I have…"

"Well come up, then. I am anxious for your news. But do try to be quiet. I should not like for you to further startle the subjects. They are coming along so nicely at present. Do come up."

William shed his traveling clothes and abandoned his remaining crutch in the entryway. He tightened the cinch of the sack around his ribs. What little physical form he had extending below the ribcage—a tangle of vital organs and entrails—was wrapped up in that stained remnant of burlap. Its contents slopped wetly along the floor in his wake as he propelled himself along by means of his grotesquely overdeveloped arms.

William ascended the steps in a tortured series of hops and jerks, his palms slapping resoundingly against the cool marble. Pausing between each step, he waited for the unbalancing rocking motion to subside before assailing the next. After what seemed an eternity, he reached the tower room.

The small circular chamber was stifling. The air was stagnant and musty; the stench of carrion, nearly overpowering. William had the unsettling impression that he had wandered into the nest of some great predatory bird. He could see snatches of sky through the grimed windowpanes of the aerie. The floor of the nest was littered with old bones. Here and there a bright, shiny bauble caught the light—most of them steel, barbed and wickedly edged.

Sascha Vykos perched atop a high stool before a massive antique desk wrought of gopherwood. The piece must have easily weighed three hundred pounds, but the latticework supports gave it a light, almost ephemeral aspect. It put William in mind of the bazaars of Baghdad, of sacks of cinnamon, of swaying girls with navels like perfect almonds.

The stool seemed two sizes too large for the desk. Vykos, her arms folded tightly against her sides like wings, bent nearly double, pecking at the detailed anatomical sketchings before her with one cruel fingernail. Periodically she would cock her head, comparing some nuance of these precise diagrams to the living subjects arrayed around her—splayed open for her scrutiny.

The critical difference here, William thought, was the direction in which the information flowed. He thought of Vesalius and the great anatomists of the Renaissance, forced to ply their trade in secrecy and infamy, hastily scribbling down such *verboten* lore as they gleaned from covert glimpses into the secret depths of the human body.

Here, however, the operation worked in reverse. Vykos was not chronicling her observations of human cadavers. Rather, she was reworking her human subjects according to the blueprint on the desk.

She looked up from her work and, catching sight of William, rose to greet him. "There you are, William. Do come in. I was only just wrapping things up here. Do you have news for me?"

A shuddering moan from the nearest subject testified that Vykos had not yet finished "wrapping things up." William accounted it a sign of weakness in himself that he still took notice of such trifles. The rivers of spilling life; the wet heft of the internal organs; the precise cuts that would separate bone from sinew; all these sights he had mastered and grown numb to. But the moaning, the keening, the gnashing of teeth…

Vykos regarded him coolly, with a look of detached curiosity, as if experimentally rearranging his features in her mind. He swallowed hard and forced himself to focus on the purpose of his visit.

"Yes, Your Eminence. News from the third enclave. All is in readiness. We have breached the outer wardings. I knew you would want to be there yourself, before anything within was disturbed. I have invoked the *noli intrare* and dismissed the excavation crews for the remainder of the evening."

"Excellent. You have done well, William. But tell me, were you not even tempted to enter the enclave yourself? To be the first to wander those disused galleries, abandoned by the enemy in his haste? To gaze upon his lost treasuries, to handle the things that were precious to him? To pry from his musty books and wailing spirits each of his secret hopes?"

Vykos' voice had swelled to a susurrant chorus. William's eyes were fixed in mute horror and fascination upon the severe black tribal tattoos peeking from the archbishop's sleeves. Each seemed to writhe of its own accord and then, with the unmistakable sound of flesh parting, split into a wide, toothless grin. A babble of voices issued forth, each raised in the expectation of some new plunder or vengeance or humiliation near at hand.

William wrenched his gaze away and forced words to his lips. Any words. "Tempted, Your Eminence? Yes, perhaps. But you have been more than generous. The spoils from the first two enclaves—why, without the secrets we uncovered there, I could not hope to have achieved this present level of liberation from the flesh. I am greatly in your debt."

Vykos scowled. "You are a poor liar, William. You did go inside, didn't you? You can tell me. I will understand." She pressed closer.

"No, Your Eminence! I did not...I dared not...I am your faithful servant. You who can dissect all truth from falsehood, you know this is so!"

Vykos looked down impassively at the wretch squirming on the floor before her, inching backward through its own slime trail toward the edge of stairway. A curious insect. She raised one foot to crush it.

"Thank you, my lady!" Enrapt, William curled around the proffered foot, pressing it to his lips.

Vykos hesitated at the crux, savoring the still point between his adoration and annihilation. "Do stop that, William. It is most unseemly." She flipped her toe disdainfully as she withdrew her favor. He flailed wildly, and only narrowly caught himself at the edge of the stair.

"Have the car brought around at once. We will leave immediately."

"Yes, Your Eminence. Thank you, Your Eminence.

The armored personnel carrier rumbled from the subterranean parking deck of the Air and Space Museum. The barricade was hastily reassembled in its wake. The vehicle crossed the street and kept coming, plowing over the curb and into the Mall. Into the no-man's-land surrounding the Castle.

The crowd edged away further, showing its disapproval at this disturbance by means of an intermittent rain of rocks, bottles, and human waste. The APC pulled up tightly to the front doors. It idled for a moment and then pulled away again, a burst of warning shots clearing its path. The crowd shrieked, hurled another volley of abuse, and then shrank back, subsided.

The APC picked its way through the detritus of the city and crossed the last serviceable bridge over the Potomac and into Virginia.

They were deep into the mountains beyond Winchester before the transport came to a halt. The doors slid back and Vykos stepped forth into the cool night air and its pervading scent of pine. She found the vastness of the open space distracting. Perhaps she had been too long among the cramped and dimly lit laboratories, prisons and bunkers which had comprised the entirety of her world of late.

She considered. The last time she could remember being out of doors was the night they had stormed Washington. That had been glorious. No, it was the night of her coronation. She distinctly remembered sitting on the roof of the Castle while the dignitaries of the Sabbat gathered beneath her. But the city had since become a trap for her, a jail.

Vykos had little, if any, interest in the nightly rigors of running a city—especially one of the size and complexity of Washington. The innumerable details and crises that must be dealt with only distracted her from her work, her research. Distracted from it? They preempted it.

But tonight… She drew a great double lungful of wind and starlight and pine. Tonight, she would be free of all such distractions. Here there would be time enough—and space enough—for discoveries. For revelations! Perhaps she would find, within these woods, within this hermitage of her old rival, within his cache of carefully hoarded secrets, some hint to that which had eluded her these long years. Perhaps she would not go back, would never go back.

William cleared his throat uncomfortably, shying away from the unveiled hunger consuming his master's features. It was more terrible than her clinical indifference, her casual dismissal. "The enclave, it is just through here, Your Eminence."

The pass through the wall of briars had been trodden flat. The smell of pine soon gave way to the sickly-sweet reek of magnolia. White-blossoming trees lined both sides of the approach. They leaned together noticeably, their upper reaches meeting high above and forming a bowered colonnade leading up to the decrepit manor house.

Two sentries flanked the semicircular steps which ascended to the front porch. From this distance, they might have been mistaken for a pair of thorny and ill-trimmed hedges. Their impatient rustlings, however, betrayed them. Their stirrings did not coincide with the gusting of the wind.

As the archbishop approached, each of the two thorn bushes disconcertingly dropped to one knee, bending nearly double.

"Good evening, Your Eminence."

"It is a great honor, Your Eminence."

The green men had a wild aspect to them. Their unkempt leafy "hair" stuck out in all directions, barely contained by severe crowns of thorns. The wood of their faces was old, weathered and deeply scored with the passing years. Their features were sharp and angular, a theme carried through to their brittle, twiglike limbs. Wood cracked and snapped at their every motion.

"You," she indicated the guardian at her right hand, "shall accompany us within. We will need a light. William, do hold still a moment." Vykos cupped her hands and blew into them slowly, steadily. A faint, tentative flicker blossomed within the dim recess. As she breathed life into the spark, it grew brilliant, white-hot.

William cried out in alarm, nearly losing his balance atop the brass crutches. His black wool greatcoat slumped to the ground, smoking slightly. Revealed within, the burlap sacking that bound up his entrails blazed with a blinding white light— the network of coarse fibers illuminated like the mesh hood of a propane lamp.

Vykos silenced him with a look. "If you are quite finished, you will be so kind as to lead the way."

The metallic crutches rang along the empty corridors and galleries. It seemed to William that they had been wandering aimlessly for hours. The former occupants of this house had obviously left in a great hurry. The signs of hasty packing could still be read in the scattered personal effects littering the upper chambers. The laboratories had been taken over by noxious vapors and unchecked fungal growths—the descendants of dubious compounds left to their own devices in uncovered beakers and petri dishes.

In the sanctums and workshops, dust had drifted over and obscured the carefully inscribed chalk lines of protective diagrams—the unmistakable sign of rites abandoned midcourse. In the east wing, William could trace a swath of carnage that could only be attributed to a guardian spirit gone renegade. With the pacts that bound it left unfulfilled, the once-faithful servant had rather dramatically and vindictively taken its leave.

"It is the same here as in the other two enclaves that we uncovered," Vykos purred. "I am pleased to see that the loyalty of Goratrix has not gone unrewarded. The pupils have taken a page from their master's book. They have abandoned their post at the first hint of danger."

"They say," William struggled to keep up. "That they were summoned. All of them. Called away. To attend upon their master."

They also say, he reflected, *that Vykos and Goratrix had been the fiercest of rivals, even back in their mortal days—back when both were mere apprentices vying for the attentions of the wizard Tremere. But that was in back in the golden age, when the gods of the night walked among men wearing their true forms—their visages beautiful and terrible to behold. The very sight of them was enough to blast a man's senses for the presumption of gazing upon their betters. But the balefires of the Inquisition ended all that and the affronted Tzimisce turned their radiant and ineffable faces away from even the faithful.*

William had been ever at his master's side as she systematically pillaged each of the hastily abandoned enclaves of House Goratrix. From her occasional unguarded outbursts, William had tried to piece together some hint of what had transpired between the two legendary rivals. His best guess at present was that Goratrix had thought to best his rival by betraying Vykos into the hands of the Radiant Ones. He could not have anticipated, however, that by his actions he would ensure only that their enmity would span a mind-numbing eight centuries. William wisely kept all of these conjectures to himself.

"I know what they say. Do you think we would be here if…" Vykos visibly calmed. "I had heard these rumors, of course, even when I was still in Europe. But I had to see for myself. You understand, don't you, William? But I have heard no news of their master these many months. His silence troubles me. He is very…dear to me."

William was certain that he would not care to be the object of such affections.

"And…and do you think it is possible that he was actually here, Your Eminence? Within these very walls? I must admit, with all that has been whispered about the Betrayer, I begin to doubt that there remains any shred of truth still clinging to the stories about him. All that nonsense about him winning for the Tremere the secret of life eternal. And of his single-handedly rediscovering the lost premises of the Blood Magic. And of his turning upon his master to audaciously declare his own House! Why, if half the things they say about him were true, he would have to have been the greatest warlock ever to…"William broke off abruptly, instantly aware that he had gone too far.

Vykos regarded him levelly. He recognized his master's look. It was that moment of calm into which the blood spills. She held him there squirming with only her gaze. Then with a snort of derision she turned away. "I know a greater."

William hobbled along in silence for a time, reluctant to say anything that might further provoke her. He was content to fall behind. It seemed that they were just traversing the same empty corridors over and over again, but he said nothing. Just ahead Vykos had come to an abrupt halt.

"It has to be here. I distinctly remember being deflected down the length of this corridor at least three times already. William, do you remember searching this storeroom?"

He looked again and saw a small door he had failed to notice during his approach, blocked no doubt by the intimidating figure of Vykos herself. He searched his memory. "Yes, a small pantry. Your Eminence will recall that most of the foodstuffs had collapsed into a sort of red and gray mold."

Their escort had taken note of the discussion and turned back toward the pair. Vykos turned upon the green man as he rejoined them. "Would you be so kind as to make a quick search of that room to confirm William's recollection?"

"Of course, Your Eminence." Opening the door, he peered within, and wrinkled his nose in distaste. He shut it again quickly. "It is exactly as he says. Can't say I blame him. I wouldn't want to spend a lot of time rummaging around down there either." He turned to resume the trek up the corridor.

"*What* is exactly as he says?" Vykos pursued.

The guard looked confused. "The steps. Down to the wine cellar. It looks like the boards are rotted through in places. And from the smell of it, the staircase isn't all that's decomposing down there."

"The wine cellar?" She turned upon William, a look of triumph in her eyes.

"Yes, Your Eminence, the wine cellar. If you feel that is somehow important, 1 imagine we could rig up a harness that I might navigate the broken stairs. I saw some rope in that supply room in the west wing."

"A moment ago, you told me it was a pantry," Vykos persisted.

William seemed flustered. "Maybe I'm disoriented. It feels like we've been wandering in circles for hours." He crossed to the door and, wedging himself between crutch and wall, opened it.

"You are, as usual, quite correct, Your Eminence. It is a pantry, nothing more. I am sorry to have wasted your time. Shall we proceed to search the grounds?"

"No, we will not. We're going through that door. All of us."

"Into the pantry?" William challenged. "I hardly think we would all be able to squeeze in, even if the room were not crammed with rotting foodstuffs. No, I will go, master."

"Imbecile," she muttered. "It is a warding. A lingering trick of old blood magics. It is fogging your perceptions—and apparently your memories as well—of whatever is behind that door." From within the recesses of her sleeve, Vykos conjured a wicked steel blade. William rocked backward in alarm, teetering precariously. She grabbed his shoulder with one hand, steadying him. He felt a surge of heat and panic. Looking down, he saw the knife buried to the hilt in the white-hot mesh that encased his interior organs.

"But, my master! Your Eminence!" he sputtered.

"Do shut up, William." Vykos withdrew the knife. It glowed with stolen fire. She pressed the blade into the wood of the door and, in a single sweeping motion, seared a perfect circle into its surface. She worked quickly, adding runes and arcane glyphs, transforming the circle into a protective diagram. A few more deft strokes and the entire diagram changed again, resolving into the semblance of a great dragon, curled in upon itself, swallowing its own tail.

The knife had grown cold, but the dragon blazed with a radiance of its own. An internal flame. William had slumped back against the wall and slid slowly to the floor. Entrails spilled around him from the tattered remains of the burlap sacking, now extinguished and lifeless. He looked up uncomprehendingly at his master.

"You will wait here, William." She beckoned to the green man to accompany her within. "You may follow us when your wits have cleared."

"Thank you, Your Eminence. You are most generous," William replied.

The room beyond the door opened out into a vast courtyard, open to the sky. There was no trace of a cramped pantry nor of any decaying staircase descending into a dank wine cellar. The once-elaborate gardens were choked with decaying leaves and pools of stagnant water that bred clouds of mosquitoes. Three forking paths—of red, black, and white pebbles, respectively—slithered through the undergrowth.

Vykos stepped into the small circle of cleared space just beyond the door. The floor here was of stone; the weeds and bracken had made little headway against it. To her right was a great jagged boulder draped languidly with broken iron manacles. The chains were stained the dusky red of corrosion and old blood.

The green man bent to examine the inscription carved into the boulder. It read *"Ecce inquit ignis et ligna ubi est victima holocausti"*

"Victims of the Holocaust?" He stared up at the bloody manacles and shook his head. "This is a weird place for a Holocaust memorial."

There was a pained look on Vykos' face as she turned to regard him. "*Victima holocausti* It means 'burnt offering'. Tell me, where exactly did you study...no, never mind. Don't tell me. It will only anger me. The full inscription reads 'Behold the fire and the wood: but where is the lamb for a burnt offering? It's from the Bible," she added hopefully, seeing the blank look on his face. "Perhaps you've heard of it? The story of Abraham and Isaac?"

"'Course I've heard of it." He scuffed angrily at some loose pebbles that had crept into the circle. "Haven't bothered to read it in the Latin."

"When I first learned the story," Vykos' voice was distant, her thoughts already far away, "you couldn't read it in anything *but* the Latin. Or the Hebrew..."

She turned her gaze out over the courtyard, picking out the familiar hint of the Kabbalistic underpinnings that lay beneath the arrangement of the Garden of Forking Paths. Three paths departed from Malkhut, the Earthly Prison, branching, transforming, ascending toward Kether, the Crown. The palace of undiluted divinity. On their journey, the three paths branched, crossed, divided, until they were twenty-two in number—one for each manifestation of the Major Arcana. She could pick out nine other circular clearings besides the one she stood upon, representing the planetary spheres, the waystations upon the journey of inner discovery. Some boasted clogged fountains, others discolored statuary, others still, neglected memorial stones.

As the familiar mystic pattern unfolded before her, however, what Vykos saw was not Jacob's shining ladder ascending step by step from the human to the divine. Rather, she saw a trap. A labyrinth of false turnings, blocked paths, and dead ends. The serpentine routes that should have heralded revelations coiled only inward upon themselves—growing stagnant, brooding, bitter. At the very center of the gardens, the dragon gnawed its tail.

Vykos inhaled deeply, savoring the miasma, the utter refutation of her rival's scheme to grasp immortality. She was sorry Goratrix himself could not be here to witness this, to share in this moment. But perhaps his absence was the most damning refutation of all. Perhaps he had finally succumbed to death's gentle reproof.

"You may follow if you wish," Vykos told the green man. "But be wary. There is death here among the Forking Paths." She strode off boldly down the central path, toward the very heart of the corruption, the dragon's maw. After a while, crunching footfalls told her that her guardian had fallen into step behind her. Foolish. The path of white pebbles was the Axis Mundi, the cosmic pillar; its secret that it knew only departures, never returns.

The path wound toward the central sphere. AF ready she could pick out the stunted apple tree at the heart of the gardens. Many paths converged upon it, forming a crossroads. In her younger days, Vykos remembered, they used to hang people at crossroads. Such a quaint old custom. "It would have been better for you if you had remained at the rock," Vykos called over her shoulder.

Her escort grunted and hurried to catch up. "Gave me the creeps. It felt like there was something hanging over me, circling, waiting. I had to get out from under. That and the smell of the blood. The manacles, they oozed blood! I swear it. I about freaked. And it wasn't like fake blood or special effects either. It was vitae, old and potent. Couldn't figure where it was coming from. Couldn't just ignore it. It was getting all up and inside my head."

"You should have waited outside, with William," Vykos replied sensibly. She brooded in silence for a time as they wended through the undergrowth. "It is well that you did not taste of that blood. It is the blood of the Betrayer. This is his House; those are his chains. They are left there as a reminder, no doubt, for his deluded followers. A sign of the price he paid for their sake."

The path opened out before them into another circle of open ground. A low wall of brick, no more than a foot in height, encircled the clearing. It was clearly the work of a master mason. The bricks fitted together seamlessly, without benefit of mortar or concrete. It was no mean feat to have wrought a perfect circle using solely rectangular bricks. Vykos kicked at the wall, found it solid. This was Yesod, the Foundation.

She drew up short before the weathered statue at the center of the enclosure. "Ah, here you are, my old friend. As ever, your ambition is exceeded only by your modesty."

The statue stood just over eight feet in height, not including its pedestal. The subject was young, dashing, and exultant. His head was thrown back, his upraised fist clenched tightly around some hidden prize.

"This is him? He looks awfully young," her companion said skeptically. Seeing Vykos' disapproving look, he added, "Looks like he just nicked something."

At that Vykos smiled. "He did. He was their Prometheus, their Light-Bringer. But Prometheus stole for man only the secret of fire. Goratrix laid at their feet the secret of the flame eternal, of life everlasting. He struck his Dark Bargain, and he signed it, not only in his own blood, but in the blood of all his brethren. And finally, he paid its price."

"You mean they killed him? Chained him to a rock?"

"Prometheus," Vykos corrected, "was chained to a rock for his presumption. Each day a vulture would tear out and devour his liver, which would regenerate itself for the next day's feast. Goratrix would like us to think that he, like Prometheus, has suffered nobly and unjustly. That his blood is shed nightly for his people. I had hoped that we had seen the last of his blood."

"What's the inscription say?" The green man jerked one thumb in the direction of the pedestal. The writing around its base read: *Quasi tempestas transiens non erit impius iustus autem quasi fundamentum sempiternum.*

Vykos' mood was improving steadily. So much so that she failed to rebuke him as she had William over his lack of classical education. "'As the whirlwind passeth, so is the wicked no more: but the righteous is an everlasting foundation. It's from the…'"

"Oh yeah, the Bible. The wicked is no more, huh? Peculiar epithet for your own memorial. Do you think," he mused aloud as they struck out again from the other side of the clearing, "that he ever actually saw all this? That he might have walked these same paths that we're walking?"

Irritation flickered briefly across her features. This was the second time this evening she had been met with this line of inquiry. But it was not enough to distract her long from the rapture of walking among the ruins of her enemy's house. "I could not say for certain. It is possible. House Goratrix could not have held more than a dozen chantries worldwide. We've discovered and breached three of these enclaves now. Four, if you count the charred ruins of the fatherhouse beneath Mexico City. I'd say it's very likely that he at least put in a single appearance here, perhaps at the dedication of the new community. If only to extract oaths of blood and allegiance."

Before her, the path opened up again. Vykos stepped at last into the central clearing. Her companion cursed as he joined her, pressing his hand over nose and mouth. "Ugh, that stench."

Flies clustered thickly about the pendulous fruit of the blackened tree. This was the focal point of the pattern, the crux where the emanations of the divine met the strivings of the mortal. The place where the dragon's tail and maw met in the humble perfection of the circle. Enrapt, Vykos pressed forward.

There was a marble plaque set against the trunk of the stunted tree. She clawed away the encroaching undergrowth and read aloud, *"Eritis sicut dii scientes bonum et malum..."*

"What's that supposed to mean?"

Vykos did not turn. She squinted up into the tattered canopy of dead branches as if searching for something, some glitter of scale, some flickering of tongue. "And you shall be as gods," she replied, "knowing both good and evil."

Tentatively, she extended one hand to pluck the forbidden fruit. The apple. The Malum. The symbol of House Goratrix and of the temptation with which he had both betrayed and damned the Tremere. *You shall be as gods...*

The cloud of flies parted before her amidst a buzzing of jealous reproaches. In its wake, Vykos saw revealed, not the lustrous red gleam of the Malum, but the deeper red/black tones of a withered human heart.

The tree was festooned with stunted life. With a deft motion, Vykos ruthlessly plucked the pendulous fruit and savored its slimy wet heft. A single bead of blood glistened on the broken aortal stem. Closing her eyes upon the sublime anticipation, she raised the fruit to her lips and bit into the sweet flesh.

There was the unmistakable sound of muscle rending. Crisp, moist, warm. Then the rush of juices. A mouthful of long-forbidden sunlight. Vykos was aware of the warmth spreading throughout her body. Fanning out. Following, not the course of gullet and gut, but rather surging through the atrophied channels of disused veins and arteries.

Vykos felt an answering fire from her own blood. It leapt within her, boiling, raging. She doubled over in ecstatic pain.

There was a shriek from behind her. Vykos forced her eyes open upon a scene of mayhem. The body of the green man had erupted into flames, consumed from within. He raced from the circle, plowing straight through a dense wall of vegetation in his efforts to reach the nearest fountain. Scattered fires caught in his wake, playing among the dried leaves.

The screams and the crashing through the underbrush ceased abruptly. Judging from the location of the wavering column of smoke, he had never reached his destination.

An anxious voice reached Vykos from the direction of Malkhut, the Earthly Prison. The exit. "Are you all right, Your Eminence? I heard..."

William broke off abruptly, catching sight of his mistress. He was propped up unsteadily against the boulder. His entrails dangled freely, twining in and amongst the rusty manacles, blind white serpents testing the air with darting tongues. William was oblivious to the spectacle he presented. He had eyes only for his master.

Vykos was radiant. Transfigured. A brilliant light shone through her. Like a prism, she splintered it into shards of color.

"It's all right, William." The voice was strong, comforting. Not at all the alien musical tones he had come to expect from his master. The prism of light drew closer, moving jerkily. It crunched heavily up the pebbled pathway. It entered the Earthly Prison with the ringing sound of hollow brass striking stone.

With each halting step, its radiance faded, dimming to a calm, reflective luster. William stared in open wonder at the image before him. It was no longer that of his harsh mistress, but rather a reflection of himself. But what a reflection! This was not an image of himself as he was now; it was a reflection of what he might be. The mirror picked out all that was noble, all that was praiseworthy, all that was desirable within him and magnified it. Laid it before him like a gift.

It was disorienting, seeing himself standing there in Vykos' place. He looked upon a William who was a millennium-old predator, a pillar of the Sabbat, the leader of a city feared the world over.

But even as he gazed, the image was already shifting, refining. His double straightened, seeming to hang effortlessly in midair. The clumsy brass crutches fell away, neglected, forgotten. The image twisted, withered, curled in upon itself, a serpent swallowing its own entrails. It shed its skin, its physical form peeling away like layers of cumbersome winter clothing, revealing ever-lighter garments beneath. Wrappings of skin gave way to muscle, and then tissue, and ultimately bone. The trailing clutter of ribs and vertebrae fell to the ground like a gentle rain. The skull followed with the musical sound of hollow bone struck against rock.

He stood before himself as he was in essence: a light, drifting mist of blood. There were tears in his eyes as he reached out one tentative hand.

"Why, whatever is wrong, William?" The voice was little more than a stirring of the mist.

He felt a cool, soothing moisture as the wisps of crimson danced between his fingertips. "Nothing. Absolutely nothing."

He was silent a long while, oblivious to all around him. Then he spoke aloud, to no one in particular, to Vykos (where had she gone?), to himself. "I'm afraid it will end. Fm afraid it will not end."

"William? Come back to me, William."

The cloud resolved into the shape of a face. Vykos' face. She was bent over him in concern. Her features came into sharper focus, resuming their habitual dispassionate scrutiny. A look that wielded a scalpel.

"Your sentry has met with an accident. Some sort of warding, no doubt, to keep the uninitiated from tasting of the fruit of the tree. You really must be more careful in your recruiting efforts. There were some glaring oversights in his formal training. You will keep that in mind when securing a replacement, won't you, William?"

William could not focus on his master's words. His thoughts were still on that simple, dancing wisp of crimson. Physical form distilled to the essential. Already, he knew this was to be his obsession, his calling, his lifework.

It was an ambiguous, double-edged gift that his master had laid before him, here in her rival's Garden of Forking Paths. He pushed himself upright, free of the bloodstained boulder, wondering what price might be exacted of her in return for this indiscretion.

But already, he knew the price.

"Come along, William. You will see to the dismantling of this enclave tomorrow. You may apportion the plunder as you see fit. But make sure that the ruins are burned. And William," she turned back to him, "I will have that statue for my museum.

My *museums*. You will see to it that it is brought to the Castle, won't you?"

"Your will be done, Your Eminence." Ahead of him he saw, not the familiar silhouette of his master, but only a drifting wisp of red. Temptation distilled to its purest, its most essential, its most lethal form. He knew now why he, like all who beheld her, could refuse her nothing.

Sins of the Father

Robert Hatch

Saturday, 9 October 1999, 6:13 PM
Baltimore, Maryland

Derek Joiner was driving south along the connector with ten years of his life in a box.

The box was made of cardboard, and it bore the logo of the Anodyne Corporation, where he'd worked for most of the past decade. They'd given him the box along with his severance package. As he'd packed it, Kincaid had accompanied him from workstation to workstation, to ensure that he didn't steal mouse pads, Post-It notes, or other company property.

If Derek had been thinking about it—which he hadn't, not consciously—he might have reflected that the whole day seemed cursed. The morning had been bad enough, what with angry clients, unreturned emails, and the necessity of signing off on paperwork that his subordinates should have finished months ago. But the real troubles had started in the early afternoon, with the phone call. He'd picked up the phone, expecting an important call from the folks in Marketing Support.

But it had been Melanie, his wife. Melanie, who rarely called him at work except to deliver some kind of bad news. Over the years, Derek had learned to gauge the different types of tension in Melanie's voice as though he were a musician listening for different chords. There was the "l-know-you're-fucking-other-

'women" tension and the "Jeremy's-brought-home-a-bad-progress-report" tension and the "1-just-got-off-the-phone-with-Mother" tension, among countless other notes in the symphony they'd composed together over the years. When he'd picked up the receiver and said "Hello" and she'd said "Derek"—not "Hi, Derek" or "Hey there" or "Hi, sweetie"—he'd recognized the distinctive strains of "Crisis" tension, and his gut had knotted around his Whopper Jr. as he waited for the blow....

"What do you mean, bounced?"

"1 mean that the bank is telling us we don't have *anything* in our checking account and—"

"Did you get the checkbook? A statement? Did you—"

"Derek, please! I went to the bank, talked to the branch manager. She called up the records.... It's not even like somebody got our PIN number and has been stealing from us. It's just—there's no money in there, and the records going back show this decline or something and—"

"But we've got statements from last year, right? Years before that?"

"I... The manager said she'd call the main branch, talk to the folks there, have a meeting with us. She said something about FICA, except that...it's just that it looks like the money was never there, and she gave off this vibe like I was lying or insane for saying it was in the first place!

"And that's not all...then I called the mutual fund service people to check on that, and...all that money's gone, too. I spent more than an hour on the phone with somebody in Customer Service—"

"Fuck Customer Service," Derek growled. "I want the number of the goddamn VP! Look, Melanie, that's impossible! Money doesn't just up and disappear. We had nearly 10K in the checking account, 40K in the mutual fund, now where the fuck is it?"

He'd spent the afternoon trying to pry something reasonable out of Melanie, the bank manager, the mutual-fund people, his voice getting progressively louder and hoarser. Then, while on his fourth phone call with Melanie, Kincaid had come to him. Said Jim Phelan wanted to see him, "just for a minute." No, it couldn't wait. He'd made some excuse, told her he'd take care of it, because this had to be just a glitch or some kind of computer virus or something like that. This kind of thing didn't just happen. Families' money didn't just evaporate like water on hot asphalt.

He went up a flight of stairs and through the Anodyne cubicle farm into Jim's big executive window office, and there was a feeling in the air like he was being called to the principal's. Jim was sitting behind that obnoxious mahogany power desk, and Kincaid, who didn't like Derek and hadn't for years, was standing, tension ever so slightly tautening his skinny frame. They invited Derek to sit down.

Kincaid shut the door behind them. John Phelan did not typically like his office door to be shut.

"Is something wrong?" Derek asked.

As it turned out, yes, there was.

The new position just wasn't working out the way they'd anticipated in Derek's performance review last year. Derek had always been a good production-level person, but success in this position required a more strategic mindset and, frankly, the numbers just weren't what the company had hoped for.

Derek, listening to them, felt as though he were at the center of a thunderclap. He tried to protest. Yes, Derek's division had increased profits by only four percent, but the company as a whole had lost eleven percent over the last fiscal year. Derek had met or exceeded all the goals listed in the job description

Phelan himself had written upon Derek's promotion. How could there possibly be a problem of this magnitude?

And they understood that, surely they did, and no doubt Derek had given his best effort, but the goals that were acceptable for someone coming new into a position just weren't sufficient for someone who'd been on the job for nearly nine months now. Management felt that he wasn't enough of a self-starter, he wasn't aggressive enough, he wasn't displaying enough initiative. And then that electric-chair switch of a phrase: It just wasn't a good fit.

It wasn't a good fit. After a whole fucking decade of "4" and "5" performance reviews, they'd suddenly come to the conclusion that Derek wasn't good at his job anymore. "It wasn't a good fit" meant that that cocksucker Kincaid had finally planted enough poison in Phelan's ear to get Derek canned. Still, he tried; he asked for goals, for measurable performance criteria. In the end, fueled by the thought of the kids, he begged. Phelan was as benign but implacable as a granite statue of a dead president. Of course, having been with the company for so long, he'd receive a generous severance package, as well as whatever letters of recommendation he needed. They were sure he'd land on his feet quickly.

Derek was sure of something, too, concerning their ancestry and morals, and the stress of the day came bubbling out of his mouth like vapor from a tar pit. His voice carried through the door; heads popped over the cubicle walls like those silly clown-heads people whack with a mallet at the carnival. Phelan and Kincaid listened to his tirade impassively—with maybe just a shade of another emotion in Kincaid's case—and said that, while they understood his frustration, it would be better for all concerned if he simply cleared out his desk and left. The implication was plain, and Joiner would be damned if he'd be dragged out of his fucking company by rent-a-cops.

So now Derek Joiner was driving southbound along the connector, from a ruined career to a hysterical wife and a gutted savings portfolio. He handled the Saab as though a cop were behind him. Everything was very clear, very mechanical. It might have interested a casual observer how situations of absolute serenity and absolute chaos sometimes led to the same superficial reactions: autonomic, Zenlike response.

He would go home. He would talk to Melanie and find out what the hell was happening with the finances. He would file a complaint of wrongful dismissal. He would simply go home, and what happened next would just have to happen.

Get off the freeway. Stop at the light. Turn left, then left again. Then right, along the seedy road of Western Unions and adult emporiums that he avoided whenever he had the kids in the car. Then left, and through mazy strings of apartment complexes rented to students whose parents had some money but not so very much. Another right, and it was as though suburbia suddenly flashed up in PowerPoint precision all around him, split-level houses and trimmed, leaf-strewn lawns and Volvos in the driveways. The streetlights made the neighborhood seem ghostly, more a movie set than anything real; a fall breeze rattled the depilated trees as he drove past the familiar vista and into a particular driveway on a particular street. Home.

The sun had set, but the midtown skyscrapers blazed like torches against the night sky, turning the surrounding blackness to an ashy gray. For the most part, the towers remained ablaze for the sake of "civic pride," which is to say ostentation, but a few lights were on for more practical reasons: to accommodate the cleaning crews, or ambitious marketeers hoping to barter long hours for promotions, or the true shareholders and powerbrokers who could not attend the 2 PM meetings, but who issued the most important policies and directives by night.

In one such office, Jan Pieterzoon sat straight, hands folded, and listened to the report of his underling, a spy who had long been in the service of one of Pieterzoon's multitudinous minor foes. Such foes clung like barnacles to all who would swim the seas of Jyhad, and every significant player in the great game had his or her share; still, it was at times necessary to scrape them clean—particularly when the barnacles became overly heavy or cumbersome.

Now, Pieterzoon felt a specific itch, an itch from one especially loathsome parasite who had outlived Jan's indulgence. This week, the parasite had interfered in the operations of the Anodyne Corporation, one of Pieterzoon's holdings, as well as the securities of one to whom Pieterzoon owed a favor. The meddling was nothing major in and of itself, but it was part of a recurring pattern. This *autarkis* this lowly scavenger who skulked from era to era like a tick in the fur of a higher animal, had scratched at the surface of Pieterzoon's power base on previous occasions. There had been the cultivation of the d'Ibervilles, ruined a decade previous to the Terror; there had been the ruination of the Miller & Joiner Trading Company, key to Pieterzoon's drive East, during Victoria's zenith. No mortal blow to a being of Jan's years and cunning—but scrapes, erosions, persistent penetrations of the political and economic armor Pieterzoon had patiently calcified around himself, like a coral polyp, against the ravages of Jyhad.

It reflected poorly on Jan to allow such a creature to trouble him or his allies further. Particularly when, according to his minion's intelligence, the creature would be scuttling into view very soon indeed. Right at the proper time, as it had done for centuries.

No longer.

"So," Pieterzoon replied, after his retainer had ceased to speak, "Gaston moves tonight?"

Derek parked the car at the bottom of the driveway, just like he did on other nights when his life wasn't ruined. The light was on out front, like a false beacon beckoning a ship to crash on reefs. The light was on in the living room. What was he going to say? What was she going to say to him? Incomplete, kaleidoscopic fragments of thought whirled randomly in Derek's head; he began subvocalizing strings of hastily juxtaposed phrases that didn't amount to anything coherent at all.

He came in through the kitchen. No lights were on here; no smell of food greeted him. *Jesus. Melanie, couldn't you have at least picked up some Chinese takeout!* He started to call out to his wife, then decided he'd just find her. He stopped, took a breath, and passed through the kitchen—which was an oddly uncharacteristic mess, papers scattered everywhere, the knife holder tipped over and the knives lying strewn on the floor where Amanda could step on them—and into the familiar beige-and-brown panorama of the living room, with its 36" TV and catalog-purchased accessories.

And there was Melanie, lolling on the sofa, in a blue housedress, hair down, her mouth (one of her most attractive features when it was shut or at least engaged in activities other than talking) red and full and open. And Melanie had another open mouth as well: this one lower, wider, redder, fuller, a jagged clown's mouth of smeared makeup across her throat.

Again, it was like coming into the principal's office. Melanie remained sprawling on the sofa, did not rise to shriek at him about the events of the day, did not acknowledge his entry at all. "Melanie?" he said, his voice suddenly hollow. "Melanie?

What's wrong?" Melanie did not burst into tears, did not speak, did not move. Derek felt as though he was being gripped and shaken by a vast, invisible hand.

It was like taking in a painting. Derek had never really noticed the details of his living room in close to eight years of residency. Now, expanding into his consciousness, came the beige plush carpet, curiously spattered with red stains; the sofa, light brown to complement the carpet, also spattered with stains; the coffee table, topped with glass, purchased from Pier 1 as a Christmas present for Melanie, marbled with crimson smears.

"Melanie?" His voice rose as he advanced. Melanie's blue dress, seen in the light of the Tiffany lamp, was maculated with dark mottlings. Melanie's eyes were wide open, staring like those of trout pulled from a lake. Her throat was a mass of ragged meat.

"Omigod!" Derek breathed. He knelt before his mangled wife, gripping her shoulders, frantically and inexpertly flailing at her to rouse signs of life. Derek had been in the same room with death before, on banal occasions like funerals of relatives whom he'd known mainly from the checks they sent him at birthdays and Christmas. He had never felt death so close, so palpable in the air around him.

And then, like a scalpel, an all-consuming thought sliced through the webs tightening about his consciousness. *The children!*

Jeremy... He remembered a fragment of conversation Melanie had tossed to him with his cereal, something about Jeremy staying the night with his friend Brian.... *Jeremy out of house. Amanda...*

"Amanda!" Amanda was their two-year-old. Was she in the house?

He shot to his feet, spinning toward the corridor to the upstairs area and Amanda's room.

"Amanda!" he shrieked, but the cry caught in his throat as he saw what was standing in the living-room door.

A man, tall and clad in shapeless dark garments, leaned insouciantly against the frame. Derek registered long brown hair, three-days growth of beard, skin of shocking pallor in the glow from the Tiffany lamp, a black coat. Most of all he registered the fact that the man held the white-bundled form of his daughter.

"Let my daughter…what do you want—"

"Sit down," the stranger snarled. And instantly, with shocking suddenness, Derek crumpled onto the sofa next to the corpse of his wife, as though he'd just had the wind knocked out of him. His muscles, which a moment ago had been humming with adrenaline, now felt as though they were balloons that had had the air let out of them.

"Let her go," Derek repeated as, despite his sudden weakness, he rose again.

"I said sit down. And *stop* talking," the stranger hissed.

Once more, Derek collapsed onto the sofa. As if to reinforce his point, the stranger delicately raised the cradled form of Amanda, who mercifully seemed to be asleep.

That gesture took the fight out of Derek. The entire room, the scene, reeled before him—but he had to act correctly now, more than when he was fighting for his job, had to react in the right way to save his daughter. "Who are you?" Derek breathed. "What do you want?"

"Well," the stranger drawled, "I'm the person—well, not *person* exactly, but first things first—who's just ruined your life. Your paltry little hoard of savings? Gone, courtesy of me. Your yoke of a career? Plucked from you like the wing of a fly, courtesy of me. Your toothsome wife? Even colder and more bloodless than in life… again, compliments of yours truly." The stranger made a mocking bow, dipping Amanda in front of him as he did so.

This was, of course, impossible: that this lunatic, whom he'd never seen before, could crash into his life like a tidal wave to wash away most of the foundation of his existence. This was all some sort of...prank, gag?

Melanie would stand up and wash away the greasepaint blood from her neck, and Phelan would call, and everybody would laugh about the whole tasteless and morbid but forgivable joke. He could forgive this; he'd go to sleep and delete the whole thing from his world as though it were an annoying spreadsheet entry at work.

Instead, he blurted, "Why are you doing this?" Watching the stranger holding Amanda...watching Melanie staring at him in death more accusingly than ever she had in life... More than anger or grief or anything (except fear for his Amanda), he wanted to comprehend, to understand this...thing enough to react to it before his daughter was hurt.

"Well, Mr. Joiner, that's a very sensible question," came the stranger's reply. "And to answer it, we have to turn our mind's eye across the Atlantic, to a little province in the Midi, in the south of the land you now call France, and we have to stretch our memory back, oh, about six hundred years...."

"Just answer the fucking question! What do you want?" The words rasped out of Derek's mouth, nearly cracking as they did so.

In response, the stranger simply picked up Amanda, and then he opened his mouth.

In the lamp's glow, long, impossibly sharp teeth gleamed, in menacing juxtaposition to Amanda's smooth skin.

"Stop Jesus, stop! Just stop! Okay...okay...okay...don't hurt her...okay..." The words were tumbling out of his mouth like tokens from a slot machine, and about as randomly.

The stranger pouted, as though offended, and slowly lowered Amanda, holding her before him in a gesture of obvious significance. "Ahem. Well, then. Let us cast our mind's eye back to the lands of the Sieur d'Joinville, hereditary ruler of a small fiefdom in the area during the late Middle Ages. Not so very important—kind of middle-management, I suppose, much like you were until today—though, like many petty rulers, full of an overweening pride. But, as mentioned, this description could apply to so many persons of the age, and this weary age as well…and the Sieur d'Joinville was, for me, a very special tyrant. Tell me, Mr. Joiner…do you know who the Sieur d'Joinville was?"

Derek simply stared blankly at the babbler. He was focusing on the words the way a driver in dangerous congestion absently listens to the traffic report, the better part of his brain seeking any conceivable way to get his daughter from this madman. The stranger, seemingly nonplussed by the lack of response, nonetheless continued.

"You are as ill-mannered as the rest of your line, and as hopelessly unskilled at repartee. Hmph. Well, he—the sieur— was a very wicked man, a brute even by the standards of the age, and his serfs and hirelings loathed him even more than you do your Mr. Kincaid." The stranger paused, looked crookedly at Derek. "Of more relevance to you, of course, is the fact that the Sieur d'Joinville was your ancestor." The stranger paused again for effect, got no response. "Your great-great-great-et cetera grandfather, twenty-three generations removed. Exactly twenty-three generations. I know; I have counted them most meticulously." At that, the stranger chuckled, a grating, guttural noise.

Derek had to focus—for his daughter's sake, had to respond to this craziness rationally. "I don't know anything about my family history. Look, you don't want to be doing this; we need to get my wife to a hospital and—"

"Don't tell me what I want and don't want!" the stranger screamed. As if in answer, Amanda woke with a cry, began to kick, and shriek. The stranger held up his wriggling burden, looked into the toddler's face, and whispered, "Sleep. *Sleep.*" The child quieted as though she'd been given a tranquilizer.

"Now look what's happened, Mr. Joiner. You made me upset the child! The situation before you, Mr. Joiner, is this: I have a story to tell you, and if you wish to escape this…incident with anything of you and yours left intact, you are going to listen to me. Otherwise…" The stranger lifted Amanda to his lips, began to kiss her cheek.

"Okay! Okay!" Derek raised his hands in a pleading gesture. "Tell me your story, tell me what you want, just don't hurt her…."

"Excellent. Now, we were speaking of the Sieur d'Joinville. As I said, your departed ancestor was a tyrant of no mean reputation in an age of monsters. Of birth as lowly as one could be and still be adjudged *noble*, the sieur sought to assuage his multitudinous insecurities by administering his turnip patch of a fiefdom like a bloody-handed Saracen. Hard was the lot of the serfs who need must labor in the sieur's fields; the soil was as stony as the sieur's heart, and the taxes nearly double those of the more prosperous surrounding fiefdoms. Indeed, the sole grace standing between the people and abject starvation was the sieur's propensity to hang men on the slightest pretext, which served to reduce the fief's population of hungry mouths.

"Such troubles continued for many a weary year—but not forever. For of course, even in that fatalistic age, conduct as monstrous as the sieur's bred resentment, desperation…ultimately, rebellion. It came to pass that grumbling arose among the stony fields, in the hovels after sunset, in the filthy church where filthy serfs prayed for deliverance; and certain of the bolder or more desperate among the young village men swore that they would bring down the sieur, or die trying.

"I remember when it began—late autumn it was, as I and the other young men defied the sieur's curfew, meeting in my crude dwelling to hammer out such crude plots as farmers fashion. We had no skill at arms, but we had numbers, and hate, and the sieur's forces were little more than brigands and poorly paid to boot.

"I suppose the others looked to me because I had once been an involuntary conscript when the sieur had been forced to send troops to fulfill an obligation to the neighboring count. I had spent over a month bran-dishing a pole-lashed knife that was supposed to pass for a spear, and staying as far from the fray of battle as possible; the fact that I'd survived the struggle at all, I suppose, made me the veriest hero in my village." The stranger coughed.

"I approached a particular lieutenant among the guards, a villainous ruffian and habitual drunkard who was no friend of either the sieur or his own captain. To him I proposed a bargain: If he could persuade a few men to lower the sieur's drawbridge to our invading band while simultaneously causing chaos among the ranks of the guards, we would allow the lieutenant and his men to loot the manse, taking what they could carry. The mutiny of a few guards would be overlooked in the general rebellion, and we would subsequently swear that the rapine was the work of the bandits that roamed like wolves between the provinces.

"The deal was struck and the night set. All through the next month we labored in the evening, lashing and beating farm implements into crude weapons of war. Finally, the night came, and our band stole to the manse—only to scatter as arrows buzzed among us like angry wasps. Someone—almost certainly the lieutenant—had betrayed the plot to the sieur, and his men-at-arms lay in wait for our band. We were farmers, not soldiers, and our resolve melted like ice in spring. Fools that we were, to trust any among the jackals who would serve the sieur!

"Many among us were captured; seeing my chance early, I escaped into the forest on the outskirts of the sieur's lands. I had grown up among those groves, and I knew enough of woodcraft to evade the initial pursuit of the guards, though once the sieur's huntsmen were deployed, things looked ill for me. Even so, little did I reck the vengeance of the sieur! A captive disclosed the genesis of the conspiracy, doubtless under the sieur's irons. From my vantage point, close at hand yet concealed as only a fearful peasant could hide, I saw a plume of smoke rising from a flaming shell where my hovel had been. I saw the antlike figures of my wife and children as they were dragged to the sieur.

"I crept closer, sick to my soul, yet afraid and helpless to act. The sieur's men dragged my wife and children in front of the castle walls. A public assembly had been called, over which the sieur himself presided from the battlements. The sieur ordered my family stripped naked and flogged with bridle straps until the bones lay bare. My daughters and youngest son did not survive such punishment. My wife and eldest son, alas, did.

"He next had their hands and feet amputated and the wounds cauterized so they would not immediately die. He then ordered them blinded with heated pokers. Then he forced them to crawl from the castle to the village square, where waited, at last, the mercy of the gallows. The sieur had them hang in the square for days, where his guards flung urine and offal on them as an object lesson. Finally, when the stench threatened to invite plague, he had their bodies cut down and tossed in the rubbish heap, to be fought over by the dogs." The stranger said this last in a monotone, as though it was a litany that he'd rehearsed and repeated again and again.

"And God had decreed that I watch all this from hiding, yet my heart prove too cowardly to make an attempt at rescue! Sick to my soul, I turned from my home. I was alone and bereaved in the darksome forest. If the sieur's huntsmen did not find me—a near inevitability—surely I would be prey for brigands, the filthy rabble that swarmed between fiefdoms like aphids in those nights. Or perhaps—perhaps, Mr. Joiner, I would be prey for something worse. You know, folk were superstitious in those nights, and all manner of the Devil's children were reputed to haunt the depths of the forests.

"I cared not. I stumbled uncaring through the dark, little heeding whether my path would take me to the sieur's vengeance or to safety or to Hell itself. I think, in retrospect, my destination was indeed the lattermost of my choices. You see, that night, a…thing found me, Mr. Joiner.

"Oh, the sieur was a foul and wicked beast, and by day he was the fat tick that battened on the people's lifeblood. By night, though, other monsters rose from hidden places, and they also sought to rob the people of their lifeblood in far more…literal…fashion than the sieur. And so, as I heedlessly stumbled through the undergrowth, something came for me from the dark deep woods, something that sought to lay open my veins and suck the blood from my body until I was empty and cold.

"But it did not immediately drag me into death, despite its ravening hunger. My action—or lack thereof—had piqued its curiosity. For you see, this thing was most frightful in appearance and disposition, and most of its victims tried to run, to struggle, at least to cry and plead for their lives. But I…1 cared little, even for a tryst with a night-thing on a lonely forest road. When it came for me, I simply waited passively, for no fiend could do more to me than the sieur had already done. And so, this being a most unusual behavior, as it gripped me and pulled me to it, it queried me as to why I would so uncaringly give myself to its embrace.

"Inspired, perhaps, by a sense of irony, I told my story to the fiend as though it were a priest at confessional. And the monster listened with interest, and something—sport or mockery or perhaps even pity—stayed its fangs. As it told me later, even among its kind there were estates, and lords and chattel, oppressors and oppressed, tyrants and those who would be free. The monster I had encountered was called *autarkis*. Anarch, a renegade from its own parliament of monsters. Evidently, something of my story...moved it.

"The grinning monster made a devil's bargain with me that night. In exchange for becoming its vassal, I was to die, my blood sucked from my veins. But as I passed from this world, I would take its blood into my body, and I would become reborn as a monster like itself. For eternity I would be a damned, night-stalking thing like it, forever shunning the sun and any sustenance save the blood of mortals. But in return I would gain life eternal—life of a sort, anyway—and, more importantly, sufficient strength to revenge myself on the sieur. Severed from my ties to life and to God, I would gain the strength of five mortal men, and neither flesh nor steel could do me any abiding harm.

"I made the bargain, and for weeks thereafter I learned how to hunt, and feed, and how to call upon the Devil for unholy power. Then, my apprenticeship completed, I went back to the sieur's miserable castle. Gaining entry was as naught for a wielder of Hell's power. I had not learned the ways of subtlety, nor sought to use them. As the sieur cowered in his bedchamber, I rent his treacherous guards limb from limb. Ever calking the sieur's name, I dragged his lady and children into the sieur's own dining hall, slaying them outright or binding them for later as the mood took me. Then I smashed down the oaken door behind which the sieur cowered. He swung at me with his ancestral blade; the impact was as meaningless as the bite of a marsh-fly. I dragged the wretch howling through gore-stained corridors and down into his own dungeons, where I bound him with iron chains. Would that I had time to enact a proper revenge...ah, but word of the attack would spread, so I had but a night. One night!

"Oh, but for the sieur, every second of that night felt like a thousand years in Hell. I was no expert torturer, but hate more than compensated for lack of skill. On him I employed the blade, the bastinado, the lash, the hot iron; and I also practiced certain gifts that had been given to me with my rebirth. I made him watch as I slew his wife and children, and when the sieur's death threatened to interrupt my vengeance, I made him whole again with a miraculous draught of my devil's blood, only to break him anew!

"Finally, certain pains and fatigue peculiar to my…new form heralded the coming morning, and the hateful sun that I could not endure. Alas! I would have to depart. I could hardly repose at the estate; even in that benighted age, word of the sieur's downfall would swiftly spread. After all he had done to me, I would be forced to grant the sieur his mercy blow.

"I turned to him, prepared to orchestrate his or deal to one final agonizing crescendo—and do you know what happened then? The sieur no longer had a tongue with which to plead or curse, but what was left of his face bore an expression, not of hate or fear or desperation, but of *resignation*. Resignation! Can you believe the temerity of the man? 'Just get it over with, his expression seemed to say, superciliously mocking me the entire time!

"I could not send him to Hell then, for in so doing I had not yet made him suffer as I had. But what more could I do to him? I had ruined his; estate, violated his body in innumerable ways, destroyed his family….

"And then the thought came to me! His family… You see, in those days, naught mattered so much to the nobility as the continuation of their family line. I was now immortal, forever suspended outside Time's clutches, unlike the sieur and his sons and his sons thereafter, who would be born and age and die. And then I realized the bitterness of the weapon, the dagger that I could drive into the sieur's soul!

"So, Mr. Joiner, do you know what I told the sieur?"

"What?" Derek's voice seemed to well up from a vast, weary distance. "What did you tell him?"

"I told him that I had destroyed him and his estate and such kin as I could immediately reach. But I told him that I would let one scion—little Henri—live until the age of maturity. You see, Henri was not present at the castle. He was currently a page in a neighboring noble's court, and so would know only that his lands and family had been the victims of a 'rebellion' or 'bandit uprising. Yes, little Henri would grow up, and marry and start a family of his own, and in this was the seed of the sieur's final calm. But—I told the sieur—once Henri himself had offspring, I would come for him, and I would destroy Henri in the same manner that 1 had destroyed the sieur, allowing but a sole family member to escape the ruin. And every generation hence—every two at most—I would reenact my vengeance, taking revenge on child after child after child after puking bastard child for the sins of the sieur! And as that curse descended like a hammer-blow on the countenance of the now-pleading wretch, I sent the sieur to Hell.

"Aye, for centuries a great curse descended on the House of Joinville! Their name became blighted by tragedy and misfortune. They became pariahs among the aristocracy, and by the time of the Terror their fortune and name had long since withered. Only I remembered! I, who am a truer relative than many who have borne your accursed name.

"If you had the time before you, I would invite you to go back into the Joiner familial records. Even a cursory study of your line reveals a litany of tragic deaths, reversals of fortune, and similar incidents. Was not your paternal grandfather the sole survivor of a mysterious accident in the early part of the twentieth century? Alas, I have had much…nocturnal business to attend to this century, and so too many of your immediate forbears have escaped for the nonce. But your death should give your father and grandfather great anguish, and so my revenge will continue on and on and on!"

Derek stared blankly at the gloating creature before him. The man was obviously insane, some kind of psycho from an asylum. And yet, there were those eyes, that sapped him of strength…and those fangs with which he threatened his little girl…. "And so now it's my turn?" Derek asked.

"Of course. You see, Mr. Joiner, for over six centuries I have cultivated your line as a gardener nurtures a shrub, ever ready with his pruning shears. Sometimes my wrath is great, or a particular descendant very much reminds me of the sieur, and I strike twice within a few decades of each other. Sometimes I have other business to attend to, and so your family gains respite for two, perhaps three generations. But always — always! I return to batten on the filthy spawn of the sieur.

"And so — if it's any comfort to you, which it won't be — sweet Jeremy will survive this night. You, of course, will join your wife in Hell very shortly. But Jeremy I shall let live and grow, after a fashion, as a fowl grows in a wire cage to be slaughtered at a time of its owner's choosing."

"Amanda?" said Derek. "Look…if your goal was to ruin my life, you've…you've done a hell of a job. If what you say is…I mean, you've trashed my career, you've…my wife," he choked. He couldn't bring himself to say the word, or to look at the husk sprawled next to him on the sofa. "But for God's sake," he pleaded, nearly gagging on every word, "if you've got to kill me, if that's the only thing that'll make you happy, can't you leave my daughter out of this? Sweet Jesus, she's only two! She's innocent—"

"As were my children," the stranger hissed.

"Then you know what it feels like! You know what it feels like to see a little child hurt!" Derek leaned forward, every muscle taut, even as another part of his numbed brain gauged the chances of somehow, even with Amanda held hostage, making one desperate lunge. The stranger didn't appear to be carrying a gun. If he knocked the stranger back... the carpet was plush; Amanda could take a fall; if it was the only way.... "Whatever it is...whatever happened to you...it shouldn't involve a little girl! Please, show some pity!" This was going to be it, Derek knew; he had to at least try to get his daughter out of the killer's hands.

"Well..." The stranger looked down at the bundled toddler, and his face momentarily seemed to—soften? "She is a sweet child, for a Joinville. Would you bar gain your life for hers?"

Derek leaned forward, hands formed into claws. "Look, do what you want to me. Kill me...kill me slowly if that's what makes you feel good. We'll go to a neighbor's house, I won't say a word, we can drop off Amanda, you can take me back here and...do your worst." Incongruously, a laugh forced itself from Derek's throat. "I won't fight it. I won't fight it."

"Very well. Perhaps I shall let her live as well...." Derek released a sharp exhalation, still terrorized but grateful beyond words. As he reached tremblingly towards his child, the stranger's smile widened cruelly. "Hope is such a pathetic thing, is it not, Mr. Joiner? No, I think I'll rip your little bitch daughter's head off and drink from her neck right in front of you."

With those words, the lethargy that had gripped Derek was lifted as though it were a veil. Roaring, Derek launched himself at the stranger's torso. He heard his daughter shriek into wakefulness as he tackled the stranger, flailing at any part of him he could hit, driving him into the wood-paneled wall with a thud.

The stranger's flesh was as chill as an ice sculpture. Though Derek had played rugby in college and stood an even six feet, his assault seemed as futile as though his target were made of wood. The stranger never even lost his grip on the girl. With a hiss of disgust, the stranger swung his left forearm like a club;

Derek's head reeled, and knees buckled as the blow drove him to the ground. Dimly, his tongue registered shredded lips, the salty taste of his own blood filling his mouth. The thought of Amanda pistoned him up to clutch at the stranger's knees; this time, a kick propelled him into the sofa, his back snapping into the wood with a sharp crack. The impact dislodged the corpse of Melanie; the body slumped prone, and Melanie's dead hand flopped onto Derek's face and shoulder, like a spider descending on a line.

Stunned into immobility, with a former athlete's certain knowledge of his opponent's physical superiority, Derek nonetheless sought to muster what feeble reserves he had left; Amanda's screaming demanded that he try. The stranger observed Derek's writhing as though evaluating a future project, clutching the toddler above his head with one arm.

"You are as stubborn and strong-willed as all your line," the stranger muttered. "Know this: The pain you feel now is but the merest inkling of what I will do to you once I drag you and your daughter to your basement. You've been a good little yuppie, Mr. Joiner: electrical tape and cordage and power tools, all hanging neat and orderly on the wall. I am old, but I can imagine the caress of your power sander on little Amanda's dainty skin, and—"

"Gaston." The interrupting voice came from the kitchen entrance. Another man stood there, having evidently let himself in through the garage. Derek registered a man of middle height and youngish middle years, blond, paler perhaps than the stranger himself, dressed in a charcoal Armani suit and with an expression of calm resolve.

At the sight of the newcomer, the stranger hissed like a feral cat, his expression twisting into a rictus of rage. "Pieterzoon!" the stranger snarled. "What are you doing here? My business here is of no concern to you, nor our rivalry—"

"'Rivalry[1] is perhaps too...generous a term, Gaston," the newcomer retorted. "I reserve the term *rival for* those opponents of mine who are sufficiently clever not to creep into the living word every few decades, like a slug from under a rock, to befoul the environs with their peculiar slime. I believe the word...*annoyance* might suit you better. Nonetheless, I find your recent financial chicanery against the resources of Anodyne Corporation, a company in which I have holdings...intolerable. Moreover, your ridiculous vendetta — absurdly irresponsible even in times before the police had their fingerprints and computers and DNA tests — is unacceptable in these nights.

"It is over, Gaston. Your dalliance in the lives of these kine ends tonight."

The newcomer advanced; the stranger tried to stand his ground, but took an indecisive step back. Derek, trying to shut out the pain and rise, heard the newcomer's monologue as though his ears were packed with cotton; all that stood out to him were Amanda's struggles and heart-wrenching shrieks. The newcomer continued. "I have spoken to the prince, and the blood hunt your sloppy obsession has brought down on you in two continents is in force in this domain as well. I will not deign to remind you of the shocking breach of the Masquerade which...this..." Pieterzoon gestured contemptuously at the entire scene, "constitutes. Nonetheless, I give you the option to surrender yourself, *autarkis.* You may come before the prince and the other officials who have assembled to judge you, and perhaps they will show mercy.

"First, though," the newcomer ordered, "give me the girl, Gaston." The newcomer's stare transfixed the stranger. Mechanically, Gaston delivered the whimpering child into Pieterzoon's hands. Keeping his gazed firmly affixed on his foe's eyes, Pieterzoon handed Amanda into Derek's trembling, nerveless grip. In his eagerness, Derek nearly dropped the child. For the briefest of instants, Pieterzoon had had to turn away. Gaston leaped forward at that moment, arms splayed to grapple, and fangs exposed in a fearful snarl. Pivoting with seemingly effortless grace, Pieterzoon sidestepped the monster's rush, then, with seeming effortlessness, gripped Gaston in a practiced hold. Freeing one arm, Pieterzoon torqued back Gaston's head, exposing his neck. Pieterzoon's lips darted to that neck, and a deep-rooted instinct told Derek it would be best to look away. Derek buried Amanda's sobbing face in his shoulder, then shut his eyes, pressed on two sides by the limp weights of his living daughter and dead wife.

For a time, perhaps several seconds, the world was a black symphony of sobs, heartbeats, and wet sucking noises. Derek cradled Amanda to him as though the world were about to end.

The noise ceased. Derek opened his eyes. The newcomer, Pieterzoon, stood above him. His pristine suit was stained with what appeared to be dirt or soot of some sort. At his feet was a pile of filthy, soot-covered rags. Of the stranger, Gaston, there was no sign. Derek gripped his daughter and clenched his fists to hurl himself at the stranger if need be.

Pieterzoon sighed contemptuously at the pile of ash on the floor, then turned his attention to the kine and his daughter. The tiny pale thing was clinging to her father's shoulder, sobbing. He was clutching her to him. The man's eyes were as glazed as those of a salmon; there was little left behind them. Moreover, the kine was clearly in pain, and nigh delirious. "Sleep," Pieterzoon whispered. He picked up father and child and laid them on the sofa, then, from his pocket, pulled a small knife. It would not do to have the kine sent to a hospital, so Pieterzoon would be forced to use other means to heal his injuries. He jabbed the blade into his own wrist, then set to work repairing the mess Gaston had made....

Pieterzoon's gaze enveloped Derek, his eyes widening to orbs the size of the moon, and the room and Melanie and even

Amanda seemed to float away like a distant dream. As though from a great distance above him, these words reverberated down: "You will forget the events of this day. You will have memories of a tragedy, of your wife dying at the hands of an intruder. You will take a suitable sabbatical to grieve, following which you will apply for a position at the San Francisco branch of the Anodyne Company. For now, you will leave your home and take your family to the Downtown Hyatt Regency, where suite 1814 has been prepared for you. You may return to your home in a week's time."

As Derek's car pulled away from the ruined home, Pieterzoon reflected on the wasteful scene around him. Jan was far from sentimental, but the senselessness of this incident made him feel...hollow, somehow. The idea—of carrying the pettiest of vengeances down through an immortal's centuries, until one's own doom was ensured thereby.

Then again, Pieterzoon reflected, was Gaston so very different from the rest of us who played the game? Or simply less skilled, and more honest?

The thought stayed with him as he finished his tasks, shut out the lights, and left the silent house to the night and the dead.

Queen of the Night

Bruce Baugh

Sunday, 5 November 1999, 9:42 PM
Flag Pavilion, Seattle Center
Seattle, Washington

She spoke to him on a whim.

"Excuse me," she said as she raised a gloved hand to point at his guitar case. Just below the case's top latch, a bumper sticker displayed a sunlit cathedral at the summit of a steep hill and the word "Zaragosa." She shook a raindrop off her glove, then ran one finger along the word. "Have you been to Zaragosa?"

He pivoted on one boot, turning away from the Space Needle to look her up and down for a moment. Her face was unlined, but her eyes were cold, and her jaw was set in a very determined way that reminded him of boxers he'd known. Her clothes looked custom-fitted, and while they were all in shades of gray, they all had elaborate designs in the weave—heraldry in the umbrella, geometric designs in the coat and boots. Everything was immaculately groomed, with just a few splashes of mud around her boot heels to mar the perfect image. She didn't look like another society matron out to pick up an artistic boy-toy. He didn't know what she was, and that might be interesting.

"Yeah," he answered. "I spent a couple of years there. Worked in the studios for a couple of old students of Fernandez and Ferrer." She looked surprised, and he liked that. He figured that she'd pegged him as a typical music-making slacker. Her problem, if she didn't think a really good luthier could feel comfortable in baggy jeans and army jacket. "I did an apprenticeship with the Manitos—" he was surprised back, as she nodded in an understanding way "—and they arranged it for me and another guy in my class."

She'd looked up to watch him talk, then looked down again at the sticker. He couldn't read her expression at all, and with this one he hated to guess. She spoke with a faint hint of an old-fashioned accent. "You make guitars, then." It was a statement.

"Yeah."

"Are you good?"

He was quiet again, thinking about his answer. It was a rude enough question, he wouldn't feel bad if he gave her some smartass answer. But he didn't feel like brushing her off, for some reason he couldn't quite identify. "Yeah, I am. Not as good as I could be, I think. Getting better, and when people pay me good money, I'm not ripping them off."

She looked over his shoulder, down the twin rows of world flags toward the Space Needle. Its white columns gleamed even in the light evening rain showers, and the spotlight on top cast a glittering wake overhead. The Seattle Center monorail station loomed up from behind intervening buildings, but she found it vulgar with its multi-colored lights and recorded music.

The Space Needle's towering whiteness, however, caught her fancy as a work in pristine isolation. The elevator rising between the tower's three legs was wrapped in dark-tinted glass to repel daytime glare, and its incandescent lamps illuminated only shadowy forms. The tower stood apart even when humanity wrapped itself around and tried to climb. It would not mourn the passing of its architect, nor fear the loss of trusted counselors, nor dread that some older building might

wake one day and seek to feast on it. It… She realized she'd
grown maudlin, and scowled briefly.

He saw the frown and misunderstood it. "Look, you seem
like you know what you're talking about. You're probably all
busy and stuff, but let me get you one of my cards." He patted
half a dozen coat pockets before finding the one he wanted. She
stared blankly at his extended card folder, caught herself, and
took the topmost card.

"Just a moment." She made a show of checking her watch.
"Let's step inside." Gently, she tapped the sticker. "Do you have
a specimen of your work I could see?" For the first time that
evening, she showed a brief flash of pleasure. "I grew up in
Aragon, you see, right in Zaragosa itself part of the time. Fine
work reminds me of home."

As a come-on line, it wasn't bad, he thought. He was a little
disappointed. She was apparently just an unusually
knowledgeable society matron. Still, money was where you
found it. He shrugged. "Sure. In fact, I was taking this over to
the opera house for the assistant concertmaster to take a look at.
C'mon and you can have a look there."

The wind picked up suddenly, and crevasses opened
through the rain clouds. One last downpour washed away, its
passage marked by a little wave rolling down the cobblestones
and concrete paths. An arc of moonlight fell on the gigantic
fountain where she'd been standing as he walked by. Its central
dome, eight feet across, was brushed aluminum, and with its
fresh coating of rainwater made a fine mirror. He set down the
case and drew out a comb to primp a moment for her.

Then he realized that she cast no reflection.

"Um…" the syllable froze partway out of his mouth.

"Forget," she told him.

If she'd had breath to draw, she would have given a brief
sigh. She chose not to waste the effort just at the moment, and
simply walked into the nearest shadow. She folded the

umbrella and propped it neatly near a doorway, hoping that someone who needed it might find it. Her coat, boots, and skin all faded into dusky intangibility, and she was gone.

He stood motionless until the clouds closed, the moonlight drifted away, and the showers resumed. He looked down at the dropped card and shrugged. As the rain fell more heavily, he stuffed the case partway under his jacket and sprinted from one awning to the next, toward the opera house. By the time he'd maneuvered around two courtyards, a construction site, and two parking lots, any trace from her gloves had washed off the sticker, leaving it as blank as she'd made his thoughts.

Wednesday, 15 June 1791, 10:59 PM
Theater auf de Wieden
Vienna, Austria

Wolfgang paused in the courtyard of the Theater auf de Wieden and listened for the lobby clock to strike. He nodded in time with its eleven strokes. His opera was still a little long, but today's changes had certainly helped the second act. Schikaneder was perfectly happy with a libretto which portrayed the enemies of enlightenment in completely stereotypical terms, and didn't understand why Wolfgang kept casting around for something more interesting to do with the Queen of the Night in the first act. Wolfgang had long since given up explaining about such things to the librettist. As a Masonic brother, as a comrade in the endless struggle to enlighten the world, as a guide to the fine things in Viennese life, Schikaneder had no faults. Never mind, then, that any deep notion of dramatic tension slipped off him like melting snow.

It was a fine summer night, the stars crisp overhead. He knew from long practice that it was fifteen- or twenty-minutes direct walk to his apartment in the *Rauhensteingasse*, within the city itself. Tonight, though, he felt like ambling a little. The tenements around the Theater—from which, indeed, the Theater itself was constructed—filled him with a great sorrow and compassion. In his thirty-five years on the earth so far, Wolfgang had known his share of poverty and disgrace as well as success. But he knew the difference between a downturn in fortune and a life doomed to misery itself. In his mind, the music he'd written for Sarastro, high priest of Wisdom, Reason, and Nature, echoed to his footsteps. Wolfgang dreamed of a time when the sleeping masses around him would rest in peace rather than exhaustion and hunger, when the world would seem their ally and servant rather than enemy and master.

He paused on a low rise, his eye caught by some movement along the rooftops farther from the city center. At first, he thought it a cloud scudding along, but he quickly realized that the wind was blowing at right angles to its movement. Then he saw it gather about a human figure, and decided it must be a great cloak. The figure leapt in pursuit of some blurry target Wolfgang couldn't properly make out. As the pursuer was briefly silhouetted against a still-lit inn window, he realized that the cloaked person was a woman. Truly, he thought, here was a Queen of the Night, no doubt on some errand of brigandage.

Then his breath froze in his throat. Unmistakably, long tendrils of pure darkness extended from the woman's hands and her face, lashing out with amazing speed to whip around the blur. As they pinioned it, Wolfgang could see it resolve into the figure of a struggling man with a long beard that whirled about as he twisted in frantic struggles for freedom. The woman walked along a rooftop and jumped casually to a dormer to stand beside her prey. Absolute darkness spread about them both. Wolfgang would never know for sure whether he heard a cry or merely imagined it. In a few heartbeats, the darkness lifted. Neither figure could be seen anywhere. He waited many minutes in an agony of fear and wonder, but saw nothing more out of the ordinary.

Wolfgang thought about his feeble efforts to capture a lady of darkness in song. This figure he'd seen, this was the true Queen of the Night. Could he evoke the majesty of her confidence, her terrible command over darkness? What music could match that effortlessly super-human leap? The Masons among whom Wolfgang moved spoke of the emancipation of women, but he suspected that none of them had dreamed of woman as graceful killer any more than he had.

Only a fool could live a life at court and gain no hint of a secret world in the shadows. Wolfgang was not a fool. He knew that behind the appearances shown to the public, there were strange things of many breeds. He had himself *seen* only a few of these, and nothing compared to the dread majesty of this night's vision. The awe he felt unleashed a torrent of counter-balancing emotion: rage, above all, that a human being, given the divine gift of reason, should feel fear at a creature in human guise. He understood Sarastro's deep anger better. A fresh melody for the Queen of the Night came to Wolfgang then, a hymn to the dark arts of deceit and terror, and to human limitations.

As he resumed his walk home, he thought about orchestrations. He would need to foreshadow the main motif in the opening scene. The joys of his craft gradually soothed his still-trembling body. When he arrived home, he would take up his pen and write two new arias and a new chorus. *The Magic Flute* would yet shine as he wanted it to.

———

Sunday, 5 November 1999, 10:01 PM
Seattle Opera House

Seattle, Washington

Lucita did not smile as she stepped under the awnings proclaiming, "Seattle Opera House Renovation: Newer, Better, For You." Nonetheless, she was just as glad to be out from under the rain—she'd experienced far worse, but she didn't *like* getting wet needlessly. She shook her coat (and regretted leaving her umbrella behind), closed her eyes, and listened to the spaces around her.

The encounter with the guitar maker had reinforced her melancholy. Seattle struck her as a beautiful city, though in a very modem sort of way. It had none of the grace that comes from a real historical legacy, but it had vigor, and many of its homes and offices were built in pleasing styles. She admired the rich greenery everywhere, remembering the dryness of her home and how gardens had been a sign of power and wealth. Here even commoners, the people who now thought of themselves as "labor" and "middle class," filled their properties with plants of all sorts. She admired, as well, the energy of its inhabitants. For all the talk of "slackers" and the like, she saw tremendous industry at work, albeit in generally unproductive pursuits. There was much potential here.

But she had no one with whom to share her thoughts.

She thought of her lost sire and her lost companion of the ages. What would Moncada have thought? Something scheming, no doubt. He'd have identified half a dozen social weak points already and used his encounters with passersby to set some complex intrigue in motion, which would culminate a decade later with all the city's major institutions in his hands. In the process he'd have blighted the city, driving wedges between communities, encouraging violence and dissolution as cover for his soldier's schemes, draining the vitality of the city to make it one more set of predictable pawns.

And Anatole? She never knew in advance what the seer might say, and couldn't predict him in his absence. He would have seen signs, she knew, that she missed: warnings in the folds of coats and the patterns of birds pointing toward the evils that might stir nearby. Heaven and earth told him of impending calamities. She imagined the city in flames, while overhead deathly creations carried their unliving masters to survey their handiwork. Or perhaps the carnage might come in some form mortals wouldn't recognize: volcano, or earthquake, or flood, or war. Were Seattle's people even now marching ahead minute by minute toward another act in the tragical farce that was Gehenna? She didn't know, and couldn't ask.

Lucita had been to Seattle before, when this country had been at war with European and Asian powers. She could probably find some of her old contacts from that time. Many, perhaps most, of the vampires who dwelled in the city then still did, despite the chaos that sometimes spilled north out of the Anarch cesspit. No doubt some of the young soldiers and their would-be sweethearts were still here too, albeit aging. But would any of them care to see her? She thought not. She'd been here on business, and in her experience very few clients wished to be reminded that, yes, they had in fact hired an assassin to settle their affairs. She recalled how the servants in her father's castle had tried to fade into the walls as the royal family passed. That was what her clients wanted of her, not friendly conversation.

The tide of her thoughts disturbed her; she opened her eyes and relaxed her concentration. For the moment, she surveyed the scene only with the senses in her own body. Her own eyes peered up the tree-lined street at the proliferating garages. (So many cars. What did the people *do* with them all?) Her own ears heard erratic winds rattle in the leafy branches overhead and the rain patter on the plastic tarpaulins spread over the tom-open opera-house roof Her own nose smelled the cooling tar laid down during the day, while she'd slept in the cargo hold of a chartered jet parked at one end of Sea-Tac Airport. Her own fingers felt through her gloves, tracing the light coating of sandblasted grit over the opera house's brown brick sidings. She was aware of more than any mortal observer would have been, her body tuned as none that still lived could be, but she was in one place only and using senses that differed in degree rather than fundamental kind.

The exercise helped her calm. She worried about the distracting reminiscences, which came more and more frequently. Her mortal days were such a tiny fraction of her existence, but they loomed large in her thoughts and reactions. She knew too well that this was often a sign of impending self-destruction: She'd exploited that unwillingness to continue as a vampire in many of her targets over the centuries. If some young would-be rival were stalking her now, he'd find it disturbingly easy to sneak up on her when she was lost in this sort of reverie. She'd tell herself to save it for her haven, if there were any place that truly seemed like home to her.

Freshly aware of herself here and now, she closed her eyes again and reached out through shadow. She could feel the dull flickers of mortal minds. Tourists, many gathering for late dinners at the Space Needle or nearby restaurants. Janitors and custodians, toiling after hours to preserve the daytime illusion that properties maintained themselves and that there was no underclass to embarrass the latter-day merchants and financiers and clerks who occupied these offices. In the opera house itself, the performers and mechanics she'd expected, busily performing not for a real audience but for recording machinery.

There were faint traces that other vampires had passed nearby not long ago. At least two of the custodians released the faint but distinctive musk of vitae, and she wondered if they'd become ghouls willingly or otherwise. One of the mechanics (she caught the term "second camera operator" in the woman's thoughts) had also drunk of vitae, and more of it. This one was fully blood bound to one of Lucita's kind. And there, at the far side of the hall, was the stronger pulse of willpower that marked a vampire. She shifted her senses along paths of shadow inside the opera house to study it more closely.

She looked out from eight vantage points spread across the main concert hall, mostly in high comers and behind the gantries the mechanics called light bridges. Two of her chosen shadows proved to offer no useful view, thanks to intervening glare, and she drifted down to peer out from behind mid-row seats instead. She could look up at the back of the auditorium and see five places where the ceiling had been pierced to let mechanics work on the building's plumbing or some other hidden system, but subdued tapestries made of thick synthetic fabrics covered them all. Apart from that, there was no sign within the main hall of the work so visible from outside.

The stage itself was arrayed for a production of *The Magic Flute*. Lucita remembered when she had first heard about the opera and its villainous "Queen of the Night," sometime in the early nineteenth century. It must have been before 1848, since the young Lasombra who'd told her about it perished accidentally during the uprising in Paris that year. Lucita had been startled; she remembered the brood of aging Anarchs she'd hunted down in Vienna in 1791, and wondered if she'd inspired the character. Most of a month later, she was finally satisfied that she hadn't, having established that the libretto was done well before she'd entered the city. She'd dismissed the coincidence as one more of the many twists of fate that confound the damned.

This production was, she gathered from conversations throughout the building, a "postmodern" production, whatever that might mean. The set consisted entirely of geometric shapes, each in a single flat color, except for highly detailed and supremely realistic Greek temple colonnades. The intended effect was lost on Lucita, but then she'd never quite grasped the Renaissance notions of theater, nor their successors. There was no regular audience, however, just a bouquet of cameras and microphones. Her target sat to one side in the front row, and occasionally spoke into a little microphone attached to his lapel, giving comments to the "director" who apparently oversaw the operation as with cinema. The crew was recording the performance; she caught a mention of "DVD" and "Webcast," and realized that this *was* cinema, cinema apparently intended to provide the audience the experience of a command performance. *An aristocratic pleasure for so loudly egalitarian an age*, she thought.

She gathered her consciousness behind the drawn-back curtain closest to her target, and whispered to him, "Havel Fedlos, I must speak with you."

Friday, 20 August 1915, 7:27 PM
Vinohrady
Prague, Austro-Hungarian Empire

Havel Fedlos realized quite suddenly one day that he wished to separate himself from his sire and all the other members of his clan. He woke up with the realization in the forefront of his thoughts, and hoped that no early-rising eavesdropper had overheard his intentions. It was with some trepidation that he rose from his bier and dressed for the night, speaking calmly (he hoped) to the servants and sensing nothing out of the ordinary. He engaged in a respectable minimum of polite conversation with the others at the evening meal, helped his younger brother in the blood dispose of the corpses, and set out for a stroll around the Prague palace.

Original thoughts had come only rarely to Havel in life, and even more rarely after his Embrace into the ranks of the undead. He pondered his motive now, and eventually decided that it was in large measure the fault of the story he'd read the night before. It was by the young living writer, Kafka, whom Havel sometimes heard perform impromptu readings at coffee houses they both frequented, but this particular piece was new to Havel. It was about a young man who transformed into a giant insect, and ended with his death as the fitting end to a pointless existence. It made Havel uncomfortable. His own existence was altogether too reminiscent of the fictional torments Gregor suffered after metamorphosis, and seemed no more likely to end happily.

However, Havel could act as Gregor could not. He needed no help to slip out into the surrounding world, nor would he always stand out as a freak, not if he were careful. As long as he avoided alerting his sire or the rest of the Vinohrady brood, he could (he hoped) simply fade into the night and build a new existence for himself. With care, perhaps he might become a patron of the arts, even though the curse had undermined whatever creativity his mortal mind had once housed.

It could be a better existence than the bug's, at least.

Sunday, 5 November 1999, 11:30 PM
Seattle Opera House, Seattle Center
Seattle, Washington

For twenty years he'd been Harold Grushkin, immigrant from some vaguely identified Eastern European nation, cautious investor, and lover of fine arts. In the early '80s he attracted some attention in the classical music scene for his sponsorship of videotaped concerts, far more carefully edited and mixed than most of his rivals. By the mid-'90s, the Grushkin Productions logo guaranteed a small but tremendously reliable volume of sales to connoisseurs. He established a cheap line aimed primarily at schools and libraries, and an elite imprint for customers to whom money was no object. For the last half decade, he'd scarcely needed to touch his original investments at all, and let his lawyers handle them while he managed the studio.

It was a fine existence, much better than his earlier experiments. Nobody was likely to connect a Viennese Anarch of most of a century ago with the genteel American video enthusiast. This time he didn't just have papers and a well-placed administrative cover, but plausible ancestry for two generations. That had cost him in favors, but now they were all paid off, thanks to desperate refugees from the East Coast struggle needing help at any cost. Those who might have embarrassed Havel were all fled, and in any event they had more pressing concerns. In time he might have some of them assassinated, but while removing loose ends was good, being beholden to assassins wasn't.

Havel's real passion was blood magic. Chance encounters in the 1930s had introduced him to the little communities of blood magicians outside the Tremere pyramid, and to his surprise he found himself an apt pupil. While Harold Grushkin maintained a scrupulously conservative routine, Havel was never more than a few contacts away from all the decadents and mortal occultists he could want, so that he never lacked for apprentices and fodder. Grushkin charitable donations gave him more access to local universities, where he could arrange for long-term experiments to unfold without interruption. Grushkin trips to sponsors, subscribers, and potential recording sites let Havel search for some of the countless lost troves all thaumaturgists hoped to find. Occasionally the effort succeeded, and his lore grew quietly.

He thought sometimes about creating a childe, but he had yet to find anyone he really wanted to spend indefinite years with, and it would complicate his existence. He had a fine crop of ghouls among his current crew, and they served his needs well. Some night, perhaps…

The shadows spoke to him. "Havel Fedlos, I must speak with you."

He thought about fleeing, but decided against it. He'd heard tales of vampires who could move through shadows and had no wish to find out how many of the stories were true. If the Sabbat had come for him, he could at least pass with dignity. "It's been some time since I used that name, sir or madam. May I help you?"

The curtain twitched briefly and revealed an elegantly dressed woman. She might have been Hispanic or Mediterranean in origin, though Havel knew that features could and usually did deceive among vampires. "I would like to speak with you privately, if I may."

This was not the usual sort of Sabbat attack, though her powers marked her as the offspring of Antediluvian-destroyers. "Certainly. One moment." Havel turned on his microphone. "Jerri, please continue taping. I have to attend to a matter in my office, but should be back in…" He paused, and saw the woman raise her gloved fingers. "Ten minutes, no more." The label microphone came off with one tug, and he laid it on his theater seat. "Now, madam, I am at your disposal. This way." Trying not to tremble, he walked past the intruder, up the side stairs, around a comer, and up a second half-flight of stairs to his office. She followed with measured steps.

His companion shut the door after them and made a small gesture. Havel watched shadows flow out over the windows which looked down onto the orchestra pit and backstage. From outside, he supposed, it must look like drawn curtains, or simply the absence of light. To his continuing surprise, she did not attack him. She merely looked at him curiously.

Finally, he couldn't bear to remain silent. "Are you here to destroy me?"

"Perhaps."

"An indecisive Sabbat? That must be one of the unspoken signs of Gehenna."

She smiled. "I am not of the Sabbat."

"But clearly you…"

"My clan would not speak well of me, any more than I do of them."

"Ah." Havel felt his palms become damp, and looked down to see blood sweat rising. "Then what would bring you to destroy me?"

"I often destroy others of our kind. For this I have been well paid."

The blood sweat thickened in Havel's palms, despite his efforts to nonchalantly wipe it away. "If it's a question of money…"

"Not money only. Rather, I have questions."

"An interrogation?"

"Of a sort." She paused, then sat in the chair closest to the office door. He sat in his desk chair. "Mr. Fedlos…"

"Grushkin, if you please. This is not just a mask I wear. It is the existence I have made for myself."

"Grushkin, then. Tell me about what sent you out of Vienna."

He looked surprised. If she could read auras, he thought, she must surely sense the depth of his confusion. "Why do you want to know about that?"

"My purposes need not concern you. Tell me."

He gathered his thoughts. As best he could, he described the stagnation of his brood, of old imperial ways preserved even as modernity swirled around them. He recalled the ache of his lost life, tedious as it had been, and his yearning for art. Gradually his narrative spiraled back and forth from planning to execution, converging on that story of the giant bug. She sat motionless and took it all in.

"Thank you," she said at last. "You need fear no follow-up." She disappeared in what would have been a mortal's blink. Even with his acute perception, Havel could barely see her flatten out and merge with the shadows she'd laid over the windows. A blink later, they disappeared as well.

Monday, 6 November 1999, 6:51 AM
Sheraton Hotel
Seattle, Washington

"No, Herr Wiscz, I haven't yet found him. Mr. Grushkin wasn't your lost childe any more than the previous three candidates were. You would perhaps save yourself and me some effort if you were to give me the rest of the list rather than doling out names one at a time." Lucita returned the hotel phone to its cradle and watched the first early-morning tugs crawl out into the harbor.

She wasn't quite sure why she'd lied to the arrogant ancilla that way. He was far from the most arrogant client she'd ever had, after all. It was something about Grushkin....

This is not just a mask I wear. That was it.

Lucita was aware that in her time she'd worn many masks. In recent years alone she'd gone from callous modem woman in her dealings with Fatima and that last encounter with her sire to this current guise, lady of Aragon out of time. None of them were her, she supposed, but was there anything at all underneath the mask?

Fedlos had found someone to be. He was doing what he wanted to. The quiet stench of blood magic filled his office and might someday get him into trouble, but then it wasn't likely that many other vampires would ever be there. He wasn't part of the "night society," adhered to no sect. If he survived, he'd make a fine addition to the Inconnu, a rumor of music and magic for sires to threaten their childer with. If not, well, at least he'd had satisfactions on the way.

Lucita didn't know who she wanted to be. It wasn't enough to be the anti-Moncada anymore (if it had ever been, but she wasn't ready for *that* thought yet). While being the lady of Aragon was comfortable, in truth it was an act. As a living woman, she'd yearned for some other role, and it was a slap at her own earlier self to pretend now that she was comfortable as a regal mistress.

She thought of the masks she'd seen actors in Greece wear while performing one of the ancient tragedies. At the time they hadn't mattered much to her, just part of the background for her second hunt of 1955. Now they crowded in from all sides of her mind's eye. Even these illusions had more complexity than her real soul, insofar as she could identify one. The masks showed the marks of years in scars and wrinkles—imagined years for made-up characters, but were her unlined face and empty heart so much better? She yearned for a mask into which she might grow, as Fedlos had grown into Grushkin.

The sky across Puget Sound was still dark, and no hint of dawn yet glimmered above the distant mountains. But she felt the sun's approach in her bones. She suddenly imagined herself refusing to move, facing the sun, feeling the pure light, burning, crumbling....

No. Not yet, at least. Not until she knew who it was who'd perish in that final blaze. Not today. She drew the curtains, hung a blanket as additional protection, and stretched out on the bed to await another day's sleep.

Meet in Her Aspect and Her Eyes

Eric Griffin

Tuesday, 7 December 1999, 10:45 PM
New York City, New York

With a screech of steel, the subway car lurched heavily to one side. Someone behind Ramona screamed as the lights flickered out. The oppressive darkness of the tunnel clamped down.

"This is not funny," she yelled at no one in particular. The human noises around her went suddenly silent. Ramona pushed her way toward the doors and felt for the crack between them. There. Claws parted the rotted weather gasket. With a heave, she wrenched them apart and was rewarded with a face full of foul, stagnant air.

There was a crackling noise from the car speaker, "...will not be nezezzary, Miz Zalvadore."

The sound of her name brought her up short. She turned, her already-keen senses going to full battle readiness. Pinpointing the source of the sound, she edged cautiously toward it. She was surprised that she did not have to fight against a press of bodies stampeding toward the exit. There was no other human sound in the darkness.

"Pleaze ztep away from the doorz." The doors resealed behind her. There was the familiar rumble of a train starting up and pulling away. A flicker of receding lights shone through the grimed windows. The car Ramona was standing in did not budge.

Ramona carefully crossed to the intercom, half expecting, hoping, to trip over a few bodies lying on the floor. Nada. Angrily, she mashed the button. "I said, this isn't funny. Now you knock this crap off right now and help me get these people out of here or I'll…"

The dim emergency lighting hummed and shuddered to life. The car was empty.

Ramona pressed her face right up against the speaker and yelled directly into it, "All right, what the hell did you do to them?!"

"They are fine, Miss Salvadore," the voice came, not from the tinny speaker, but from a shadowy form standing at the far end of the train car. "For them, the train lost power for a moment only and then continued on its way."

Ramona whirled upon the newcomer.

The hunched form stepped forward, leaning heavily against the seatbacks as he came. Ramona kept straining to pick out the sound of broken gasps that must accompany such labored progress, but the air did not stir.

"You had requested an audience, my dear. A *private* audience. I have gone to some pains to secure a place where we might be alone. Privacy is such an indulgence here. All too often, I find myself unable to justify the expense of importing it. And there is always someone else jealous of such decadence. But you have not come to hear of my distractions. Sit here, next to me, and tell me why you have come."

He lowered himself torturously into a double seat facing the aisle.

"I didn't ask to be hijacked." Ramona grumpily took the seat opposite him. "I know you've got offices for receiving visitors. Couldn't we just have met in one of those bunkers of yours carved out underneath…oh." Ramona followed the thought through to its logical conclusion and found she had answered her own question. Those places she had met with Calebros before, where they had openly discussed the secrets of the Eye with Hesha—those places had not been 'private'. Their conversations had been overheard, documented, replayed, analyzed, annotated, collated, and distributed.

"How long do we have?" she asked shrewdly.

"A better question. At least twenty minutes or so, before I'm missed, and someone starts asking questions."

"Boy, you're not kidding about that lack-of-privacy thing."

"Somewhere this week, I seem to have lost my sense of humor. This 'provisional council' idea looked a lot better on paper."

Ramona shook her head. "How'd you get roped into that, anyway? Holding the city together while the rest of polite society is out there butchering each other in the streets—and all for a shot at a seat on some fledgling primogen council. It's just stupid. It would serve them right if the Sabbat just marched back in and spanked the lot of them. No offense."

"I believe that I was what they call a 'compromise candidate.'" Calebros smiled self-deprecatingly.

"They *told* you that? I'd leave them to run their own damn city."

"You are not alone in that opinion. I believe that many of your relations have felt that way throughout this struggle. No, I'm afraid that, as a Gangrel, you will find that the doors to the backroom intrigues of the Camarilla will no longer open to you—even if you were inclined to knock."

"If I were interested, I wouldn't bother knocking."

Calebros chuckled low, a sound like an engine turning. "No, I don't imagine you would. I will miss your straightforward style, Ramona. I find it refreshing. But already you know that there is no longer any place for you here. In the midst of battle—against the Sabbat and later, against Leopold and the Eye—we could afford certain marriages of convenience. But these partnerships will not survive the challenges of peacetime. Your associates, Mr. Ruhadze and Mr. Ravana, they found themselves in much the same position. Each has already left New York."

"What?! You let Hesha go? With the Eye? Are you *nuts?*" Ramona was out of her seat. "That's why I came to you tonight. I thought you were on the level. That maybe you would help. That maybe there was a place for me here, somewhere. What the hell was I thinking?"

"Please calm yourself, my dear. Mr. Ruhadze did not seek out my permission in this matter. But I was certainly in no position to deny him what had already been pledged by the justicars. It was a *fait accompli.* Nothing worth getting worked up over. You don't think him so foolish as to attempt to use the Eye? Not after…"

"Damn it, he snowed you too." Ramona's fist cracked the plastic seat next to her. "And you knew better. What the hell do you think he's going to do with the Eye? Put it on his mantelpiece and forget about it? Is it just me? I can't be the only one in this whole damn city to have ever seen a B-movie. Here, let me set the scene for you. Fade in a temple interior. A Priest of Set, robed and masked, gloats over the ancient gem he has stolen. It is shaped like a giant, malevolent eye. He holds it up to the adulation of a throng of thuggee fanatics. A mammoth golden idol of a serpent presides over the debacle. One of its eye-sockets gapes emptily…"

"This isn't Hollywood, Ramona. Sometimes, the dark, mysterious stranger keeps his word."

"Yeah, and sometimes the heroes hunt people down and murder them and drink their blood. Sometimes they do it just to stay 'alive.' Sometimes they do it just for kicks. And sometimes they do it just to hurt somebody else—someone close to the victim. Shit, this ain't Hollywood, it's daytime TV."

Calebros was silent for a time, letting her wind down. "I'm sorry I couldn't help you with the Eye, Ramona. And I'm sorry you will have to leave us. Believe me, I would like nothing better than to find a place for you here. I will have sore need of people who can be relied upon in the nights ahead. But you know what you would be up against if you remained here — the posturing, the none-too-subtle snubbing, the outright backstabbing. You are a rarity among our kind, Ramona. But because you are different, you will be hated and eventually destroyed if you stay among the society of the damned. Know that I will remember our time together fondly. If I can be of any assistance to you in relocating…"

"No, I understand. It's 'thanks for your help; here's your bus ticket.' Well, I don't need any of your favors.

I don't like the strings attached to them. And I resent the fact that you think I'm so stupid that I'll let you screw me over and then thank you for it."

"Ramona…"

"No, you won. I killed that bastard Leopold for you. *Killed* him. Your honorable Mr. Ruhadze never said anything about it killing him. He said it would cut the connection with Eye. Well, it certainly did that. Lying bastard."

"I thought you wanted Leopold dead," Calebros replied guardedly. "He butchered your people. He twisted them into that blasphemous…"

"You think I don't know what he did?! I was there, all right? He deserved to die. But you didn't see him, at the end. When the nerve unraveled and the influence of the Eye lifted from him… Forget it, you wouldn't understand."

"Ramona, you can't go around blaming yourself for Leopold's death — nor is it going to do any good to blame Hesha, or me. He was lost to us as soon as he took up the Eye. A victim, nothing more. A walking corpse."

"Yeah, whatever. Look, it's been real nice reminiscing over old times with you. Now are you going to let me out of here, or do I need to find my own way out?"

"I suspect you will not be happy until you find your own way out. Goodbye, Ramona. If you need…"

"I don't need anything from you." The subway car lurched forward, pitching her over sideways. She caught herself and, straightening up, found that the figure across from her was gone.

"You're welcome," she shouted after him.

———

Ramona turned her back on the city and began walking north. She had no particular destination in mind, she just needed to put as much distance as possible between herself and New York. There were too many memories for her there—and every one of them a death or a betrayal or a reproach. Her thoughts kept returning to the first time she had seen the city, rising out of the swampy miasma of the Jersey Turnpike. It had filled the entire horizon, the sharp buildings piercing the soft underbelly of the sky like a fistful of knives.

Damn, she had been naive. All of them had, Jen, Darnell… If they could just get to New York! The promise of it had kept them going through that entire hellish trip across the country. And what had they found when they got here?

Ramona brushed the thought aside brusquely. It just didn't matter anymore. Jen and Darnell were dead, killed by that monster Leopold. And Zhavon…

She *had* found Zhavon, and that counted for something. It had to count for something. Ramona clung to that. But there was pain there too. Ramona used the anger to keep it down, to keep the hurt at bay. But she could not deny the fact that she had failed Zhavon. She couldn't help her, she couldn't 'rescue' her, and she sure as hell hadn't been able to prevent her death.

Ramona knew that there was nothing here for her anymore, in New York. She had gradually come to despise the city and all it represented. A low, roiling anger churned in the pit of her stomach. She had been duped and manipulated ever since she set foot back in the city. By Hesha, by Kahlil, by the damned Camarilla. The meeting with Calebros had been only the final indignity. She had gone to him for help, and he had dismissed her out of hand—banished her. Where the hell did he get off bossing her around? She certainly didn't remember voting him in as king.

She just needed to get away for a while. Not because they told her to. But because she needed to prove to herself that they didn't really matter—that all their insular little slights and intrigues and posturings didn't amount to much out here, beyond the outskirts of the city. That all their strivings and betrayals were just a sad sort of pantomime. Children fighting over sandbox real estate.

New York was a trap. She knew that now. A very pretty trap, decked out in bright neon and raw altitude, dressed in the decadence of power and wealth, and wrapped in a brightly colored shawl of ethnic diversity. But every skyscraper cast an even longer shadow in which dark things festered. And every immaculately tailored suit carried the subtle but unmistakable reek of the sweatshop. And each different cultural group huddled apart, brooding upon its own hatreds and sheltering behind its own fears.

Ramona was still running when the sunrise caught her and pressed her gently back down into the earth's arms.

———

Ramona stretched, her fingers scrabbling through the loosely packed soil. Instinctively they sought out the only significant direction in this subterranean world—up. Her hands broke the surface, planted themselves firmly and pushed—dragging the rest of her body from the earth.

She brushed away the worst of the dirt from her clothes, casting about, trying to get her bearings. This was the third night since she had escaped the city. She was already deep within the Alleghenies and, she realized with growing apprehension, her surroundings were beginning to look familiar. She had not intended to return here, but she could not fail to recognize the path her feet were taking. Back toward Zhavon's grave. Back toward Table Rock. Back toward the cave where Leopold had massacred her people.

No. She was not yet ready to face that again. But where would she go? The question had not really occurred to her before. Not back to New York, that was for sure. For a moment, she thought of returning home, to L.A., but there was nothing waiting for her there either. Nor did the thought of attempting the perilous cross-country journey alone appeal to her.

It seemed she didn't belong anywhere anymore. She couldn't blame her feet for carrying her back here. Back to her dead.

She almost laughed aloud at the thought. She knew better. She didn't even have a place among the dead anymore. Of course, she would never find any place among the living that would accept her. She was not of the living. She did not belong among them any more than she belonged among the dead.

Well, that didn't leave her a lot of options. She could seek out others of her kind, but she had no reason to expect any better reception from that quarter. She knew all too well what she would receive at the hands of the Camarilla—their polite scorn, their casual betrayals. Ramona was not about to lower herself to their level—to spend decades learning the polite nuances of their little games. She wasn't even convinced that, if she did so, she would be accepted among them, much less treated as an equal. She simply did not rate in their world. They would always look down at her as an outsider, a wanna-be. No thanks.

That left the Sabbat. Frankly, Ramona had seen enough of that debacle back in New York to last her a lifetime or two. The Sabbat seemed to thrive on frenzy. They reveled in the Beast. Ramona had already received two very personal and unambiguous warnings as to what awaited those of her kind who abandoned themselves to that path. She absently stroked the coarse fur behind one sharp lupine ear—a transformation she had discovered upon emerging from a particularly murderous rage. One that had gotten the better of her. Her feet also bore the mark of the beast. Now, that was a sight! The very bones had twisted into gnarled animal paws. She could not even wear normal shoes anymore.

She looked down at the clumsy, oversized boots. At night, at a distance, they might pass for human footwear. But they were uncomfortable as hell, and she couldn't tie them tight enough to keep them from spinning around and pointing the wrong way after a few hours of walking. When Calebros first gave them to her he had said...

Calebros. Ramona sat down on a nearby rock and patiently unlaced the boots. She left them there, arranged neatly like a pair of slippers peeking out from beneath the edge of a bed. She didn't need his damned help.

She was close now. She could feel the proximity of her dead all around her. They flickered at the periphery of her vision, trying desperately to get her attention, tugging at her.

"Damn it, leave me alone!"

Even the dead wanted something from her. And she was getting just a little bit tired of not living up to everybody's expectations. "I don't owe you anything. You're not my real relatives. You weren't there for me. When Jen got killed, and Darnell and Zhavon, where were you then, huh? When were you ever there for me? I'll tell you when—never. Where the hell do you get off thinking I need to drop whatever I'm doing and do something for you? You are nothing to me, you get it? Nothing."

Her words seemed to have the exact opposite of the desired effect. The shades pressed closer, drinking in her anger, and growing more substantial. They hung about her like a tattered cloak.

"Just get the hell off of me!" She batted at them, trying unsuccessfully to dislodge their ravenous maws. "I didn't ask for this. Any of this. Do you think I wanted to end up this way, stuck here, in between? With you? You think I wanted to be like you? You think I asked that bastard Tanner to do this to me? To leave me like this? Fuck you. All of you. I don't need you. 1 don't need some stupid 'clan'—especially one full of nothing but a bunch of dead, pushy losers."

She broke away from the press of the dead and stumbled out into a clearing. At its center a huge, horizontal slab of granite lay atop a jumble of boulders. Its surface was rough, pitted, and not quite level. It sloped down to the east at a perceptible tilt. Table Rock.

Ramona felt the heat of shame and anger welling up behind her eyes. It was here that that damned mystic, Blackfeather, had forced the second indignity upon her. She remembered her awe at the seer's occult mutterings, his preposterous ritual. He had forged a sacred hoop of chalk and firelight atop Table Rock. He had drawn her into its intimate circle. He had pressed the ashes into her eyes. And from that time forward she could not shut out the visions. The ghost sight.

She thought of it as her "ghost sight," but that didn't really capture it. It wasn't so much that she saw spooks—what she saw was the interconnectedness of things. Like seeing Xavier standing atop Table Rock as the very personification of the hunt. Like perceiving the link between herself and the wolf that precipitated the first time she stepped outside her human skin.

And like seeing the connection between Leopold and the Eye as a pulsing optic nerve binding him inextricably to…well, to whatever the hell that thing was that had risen up and consumed him. Hazimel, she guessed. Whoever he was.

Here, at Table Rock, she always saw her dead. They slipped in and out of the clearing, calling to one another in greeting or in challenge. Reciting their lineages and their deeds. Tussling for dominance. The old habits were so ingrained, her people could not abandon them, even in death.

No, that wasn't fair, Ramona thought. She knew that these were not really the spirits of the dead, denied their final rest and doomed to linger here for all eternity. The truth was nothing so romantic. These were only dim afterimages, reminiscences. As quaint and beside the point as silent movies.

It had something to do with integrity. People who lived authentically left an impression on a place by their very presence. A lasting impression. Table Rock was a receptive place, a place of power. If she gazed at the stone with her ghost sight, to Ramona the slab looked like a picture of the Rosetta Stone she had seen once in a magazine—its polished surface crowded with carved letters and pictograms of many different tongues. Proclaiming the legacy of her people across the flimsy barriers of language and time.

She shut her eyes tightly to block out the vision. She had no desire to read the condemnation that was graven in that stone. The tale of the massacre of her people; the story of her own failure.

Was it always going to be like this? Seeing reproaches in every outcropping of rock? Damn these eyes of hers, and damn Blackfeather. She hadn't asked for this.

Against her will, she found herself thinking of Leopold. She had been thinking of little else of late. Of his face at the very end. When he was finally free of the Eye.

He had turned to her. He must have known that she had just killed him — that the stroke that severed him from the Eye was a mortal blow. But there was no fear in his face. No hatred, no reproach, not even surprise.

The look he gave her was one of recognition and of sadness. In those final moments when he was finally himself once more, he'd smiled at her, damn him. With the last vestiges of *his* unnatural sight, he had *seen* her. In that instant, he knew her for what she was — cursed, spent, and discarded. Just like him. Alone.

He had called her by name and spoken words of compassion she would not soon forget or forgive him. Where the hell did he get off pitying her? That monstrosity. That sick, murdering bastard.

Even as the accusations formed, however, Ramona knew them for what they were: shallow. Empty. It was not Leopold that had massacred her people and desecrated their remains. It was whatever he had become under the influence of that blasphemous Eye.

He was lost to us as soon as he took up the Eye. A victim, nothing more. A walking corpse. Calebros's words came back to her, but they brought no comfort. Instead, they only fueled her outrage.

"We're all walking corpses, you self-righteous bastard." The words she could not give voice to three nights ago would no longer stay down. "That makes it okay? Okay for him to kill my people and then leave them like *that*[7]. Because the Eye made him do it? Bullshit. If the Eye was making him do all that sick shit, if the Eye was consuming his identity and turning him into something he despised, why didn't he just reach up and pluck..."

A realization dawned upon Ramona, and not a pleasant one. The anger drained away from her as under the shock of cold water. She thought of Theo Bell, the Brujah Archon, going toe to toe with Leopold. Bell would have killed him as a matter of course. Dispassionately, perhaps even with a hint of annoyance, like someone might feel at having to take out the trash. But Bell couldn't kill him.

Hesha would have stolen the Eye. He would have manipulated, cheated, and yes, even killed without the slightest hint of remorse, to secure the priceless artifact. But he could not take the Eye. He could not perceive the bond that joined it to Leopold—much less sever the connection.

But Ramona could. With her "gift," her sight, she had stolen the eye for Hesha. With her sight, she had murdered Leopold for Theo and his damned Camarilla. She was no better than Leopold. Her ghost sight had made her a less scrupulous thief than the infamous Hesha Ruhadze, and a more callous murderer than the Camarilla's avenging angel, Theo Bell.

She felt dirty, polluted, like she wanted to throw up. It was as if she were responsible, not only for Leopold's death, but for the deaths of countless others—of all her people. She was complicit in all of Leopold's crimes. She had compounded his offense by heaping another victim upon his already considerable pile of skulls. And it was no good blaming it all on this damned ghost sight. That did not absolve her of a single drop of the blood she had spilled.

Damn it, she was no thief, and she was no killer. Leopold hadn't had the balls to break free of the power of the Eye and reclaim his own identity. "But you'd better believe I do, you bastards," Ramona's voice was low and rumbling, like a storm breaking. She was unaware she had spoken aloud.

She planted her elbows firmly on Table Rock, as if to steady her resolve, clenching and unclenching her fists. The soft pads covering her fingertips slid back, revealing vicious claws which extended with aching patience until they brushed gently against fluttering eyelids.

She thought of Tanner's caress as he'd pressed closed those eyelids, drawing her into an Embrace from which she would never emerge. She thought of the pressure of the heel of Blackfeather's palm as he ground ashes and vision into her tightly shut orbs. She felt the white-hot fire of the third and final indignity—the gouging claws, groping for and severing tenacious optic nerves. Ramona threw back her head and howled in agony and release, scattering droplets of precious vitae on all sides.

———

The Dreamstalkers found her there, pitched forward across Table Rock. She was lying heavily upon one arm, her claws still deeply lodged in the furrows they had gouged into the slab's surface. The newcomers spared hardly a glance for these ambiguous runes, Ramona's epithet. In defiance, or perhaps despair, she had carved her mark upon the ongoing story of the people. It was not for them to interpret that mark, to give it meaning.

They gathered the little one up in their arms and, lifting her gently over the threshold of the night wind, carried her home to her people.

A Friendly Neighborhood Place to Drink

Richard Dansky

Tuesday, 14 December 1999, 6:47 PM
Fort Lee, New Jersey

"Motherfucking Jersey."

That pretty much summed up everything Theo Bell was feeling at the moment, so he just shook his head and watched the traffic pour slowly by. Down the street, a neon sign shone redly against the night, promising passersby a cool Budweiser and not much else. City sounds floated through the air, indelicately, and the breeze smelled like car exhaust and spilled beer.

There was no pedestrian traffic, no one on the sidewalk besides Theo, and he liked it that way just fine. He'd had entirely too much of other folks lately, living and dead, and he would be much happier if he didn't have to speak to anyone for the next ten or fifteen years, easy.

Mind you, the chances of that were about the same as Theo's chances of going for an afternoon stroll, so he just spat once on the sidewalk and decided to enjoy what time he had. Picking a direction at random, he set off at a slow pace. Moving too fast was still painful: The shotgun bolstered across his back rubbed neatly against where some Sabbat shithead had inserted a length of copper pipe into his liver. He'd killed the man, of course, and God alone knew how many others, but even for a Kindred of Theo's strength, that sort of thing took a little while to heal.

One of the pockets of Theo's vest bulged with ammo, but that and the shotgun was all he carried. Clothes, money, luxuries—Theo had learned that those could be found easily, regardless of circumstance. A fistful of dragonsbreath rounds and a way to put them right down the fanged asshole that passed for a Sabbat flunky's throat—those were traveling essentials.

Up ahead, a traffic light made up its mind to go red. Brakes squealed, someone cursed, and otherwise life went on without paying Theo any mind. He liked that. He liked that no one was trying to kill him, that no one was telling him to go places where people would try to kill him, and that he didn't have to kill anyone else at the moment. The fact that the battle for New York had ended up more or less victorious was all well and good—if nothing else, it meant that a few of the justicars would be too busy handing out attaboys and fighting over territory to get in his hair for a while. What he really wanted, though, was to find some godforsaken town that was such a shithole that neither the Camarilla nor Sabbat wanted it, and he could kick back and watch everyone else tear the crap out of one another for a change.

Unfortunately, Fort Lee, New Jersey, did not meet any of those requirements. It did, however, have a bar conveniently stationed across the street from where Theo now stood, a shabby little place with a half-lit sign promising "A friendly place to drink and socialize" in faded red letters. The door was red, too—some sort of fake leather with grimy brass studs holding it to the wood—and in the dark window cool red light still offered that ice-cold Bud.

"There's a lot of goddamn red light in this town," Theo muttered to himself, then crossed the street toward the bar. He'd never actually had a beer—he'd been turned before the opportunity had presented itself—but he understood very clearly what the place was really selling.

Sanctuary.

Theo had been in a thousand joints like that, and they were all the same. *Come inside and forget the world,* they whispered. *Your wife can't find you here. The bills can't find you here. The boss can't find you here.*

"That's a fucking joke," growled Theo. "Fucker can find me anywhere on the planet just by waving his dick around." But he went into the bar anyway.

As grim as the outside of the bar was, the inside was grimmer. The lighting had been designed to be low, but time and the frailties of tungsten filaments made it even lower. Tables and ice-cream-parlor-style chairs were scattered across the floor haphazardly; most were upright, and few were occupied. Booths with tom red Naugahyde seating lined the walls, and a dim sign marked the location of the restroom, singular, in the back. The bar was against the wall to the right-hand side, the patrons maintaining stony silence and a distance of at least one empty seat from each to each. The barkeep was a middle-aged white man in an ugly shirt. He had a pot belly and a bad haircut, and Theo knew without a doubt that he had an over under tucked under the beer cooler in case of trouble.

Every other bartender in every other place like this he'd visited did, after all.

The other patrons—mostly men—noted Theo's presence by pointedly ignoring him. That was just fine by Theo, as he had no desire to talk to anyone here. He'd spent nights in the salons of Paris's Toreador elders, listening to centuries-worth of distilled wit and philosophy; he had no interest in speaking with anyone here. For one thing, sooner or later the conversation would inevitably turn to sports, which Theo mostly despised, and for another, conversation was contrary to the point of the place. You came here to be alone with your troubles, not mix them with someone else's.

After a half-second's deliberation, Theo picked a booth and slid into it. From where he sat, he could see both front door and rest room, and get a more or less decent view through the window. The table was bolted to the floor, but not well, and he could easily overturn it for cover if the situation demanded. And while Theo somehow doubted that he was going to be dealing with any problems of that nature here tonight, old habits of survival die hard. You had to be vigilant at his age, or you just plain stopped being.

It took a few minutes, but eventually the bartender wandered over to where Theo sat. "What'll you have?" he more or less said, though he couldn't appear less interested in the answer.

"Gimme a beer," Theo found himself saying, and suddenly he grinned. Why the hell not? He'd trained himself to be able to keep food down, at least for a little while, so a beer shouldn't be too much of a problem.

"What kind?"

"What you got?"

"Bud, Bud Lite, Icehouse, MGD, Miller Lite, Coors, Coors Lite, Genny Cream Ale and Keystone. Read the sign," the bartender said, and gestured toward the barely legible blackboard that hung next to the bar.

Theo turned. If he squinted, he could lie to himself and claim he saw those words scrawled in chalk. As things stood, he just took the bartender's word for it. "Screw it. What sucks the least?"

"Genny it is," the fat man mumbled, and turned back to the bar. He returned a few minutes later, saying something that sounded like "Tree-fiftee" and bearing a mug that was half filled with foam. Theo threw a five at him, took the beer, and then stared pointedly until the man shuffled away. "Asshole," the bartender muttered under his breath, and then vanished back behind the counter.

Theo just stared after him while the beer quietly sat on the table. After a minute, he shrugged and lifted it—the damn thing almost seemed to be staring him—and immediately wished he hadn't. "Tastes like drinking piss from a three-day-dead horse," he said under his breath, and put the mug down. No one heard him, or if they did, none of the other patrons cared. Each just huddled over his own drink and shut out the rest of the world. Taking advantage of that, Theo discreetly spit his beer back into the glass. While he was reasonably sure that keeping that stuff in his system wouldn't do him any permanent harm, he wasn't dead certain, and these days he took no chances.

So intent was he in getting the beer back into the glass that he didn't notice the man who slid into the booth across from him, at least not until the stranger addressed him. "Bell, I presume?" The man spoke with a noticeable English accent, and he was smiling as he said it.

Theo sat up like a shot. "Who the fuck are you?" he asked, even as his foot found the base of the table in preparation for shoving it at the stranger, hard. "And how the fuck did you sneak up on me?"

The stranger shrugged and spread his arms in a r rueful gesture. "I was able to sneak up on you because you let me, Theo." His grin left no doubt that he felt that he just might have been able to accomplish the feat on his own. "And my name is Talley."

"Son of a bitch…" Theo's voice trailed off as he stared at the other man. Talley was tall, thin, and pale in a way that would have attracted notice even if he weren't dead. He wore a black suit in a very conservative cut, and his hair was close-cropped to his skull. Leather driving gloves were on his hands, and a no doubt expensive pair of sunglasses peeked out of a breast pocket.

The shirt underneath the suit was, of course, black.

Theo growled. "War's over, dog. Your side lost. Did you need a reminder of that?" He leaned forward and the table groaned under the pressure of his hands. "What are you doing here?"

Talley hastily turned his hands palm-forward. "Please. I'm just here to talk. Just talk."

"And what if I don't feel like talking?" Theo was halfway across the table now, and Talley still hadn't budged.

"Then I let a shadow rip off the bartender's head, and while you're trying to tape the Masquerade back together, I stroll out the front door safe as houses. It's your choice."

Theo stopped and just stared. "I'm fast enough to take you before you do that, you know."

Talley eased back in the booth and shrugged. "Perhaps. Perhaps not. I'm reasonably quick myself, you know. As I said, the choice is yours."

For a long second, Theo's eyes held Talley's. There was a smile there, and a challenge, and something else, something Theo didn't recognize. He sat back in his seat and crossed his arms. "Fine. So talk. I'm all motherfucking ears." A sudden thought struck him. "The beer's yours, if you want it."

With a sickly grin, Talley put his arms down. "No, thank you. The bartender spat in it before you did, you know. Just in case you were wondering."

"Huh. Probably improved the taste. But if you came all this way to talk to me about beer, you're shit out of luck. Besides, I thought you were flying the friendly skies back to sunny Spain. What happened—Moncada get a new poodle?"

"Cut the shite, Bell. The cardinal's dead and you know it, and you probably knew about it ten minutes after it happened. Don't play games, or by God I will turn this hole into an abattoir and smear your fingerprints all over it for Pascek to find. Do you understand me? Good. I'm glad we understand each other."

Theo smiled, thinly. "I knew the fat man was dead. Didn't know if you knew that I did, and didn't know where you fit in. I think I do, now. So tell me, why are you here? If you want to start something, I'll finish it. You're not taking New York back by yourself, Talley."

"You're welcome to it, Bell, stinking cesspool that it is. I told you, I came here to talk, and I came here to talk to you. Why do you think I made this dive so appealing to you? It's public enough that we can't afford to tangle. If I wanted to fight, we'd be fighting and you'd be wondering who turned out the lights. I just want words. No one knows I'm here, not even Moncada'ssuccessor."

"Is that what you're here for? Asylum? You want to defect, and think I can arrange protection? Or are you just here to sell info? Which is it? Let's make a deal here."

"Would you believe none of the above?" Talley's voice was clipped and quiet, full of menace. "I decided to get out of Spain while the getting was good until the situation resolved itself and my role was known. I have no interest in joining your little club, Bell, now or ever. I am here. To. Talk." With each word, he slammed his fist down on the table. At the bar, patrons turned to look, then began whispering to one another, lazily.

"Whatever. But I don't know what we've got to talk about, in that case. How 'bout them Mets?"

"Look, Bell, I'm serious here. You and I have more in common with one another than we do with the idiots we work for. Tell me what you think of Pascek. Tell me what you honestly think of him. Come on. Say something *nice* about that arrogant bastard. I dare you."

"I can't." Theo shook his head. "But that's not the point. You know that."

"No, I don't. You get old enough—give yourself a few centuries—and you start asking questions. I've got six centuries on you, Bell, and after all that time, I find myself finally starting to ask why. And so I ask you: Why do you put up with it? Why do you deal with the shame of being subordinate to a man who's clearly your lesser, who clearly despises you and who clearly would gladly be rid of you? Seize the moment, Bell— make your own path. Or at least tell me why you stick to theirs."

Theo eased himself out of the booth. "I could ask you the same question. Why do you put up with the shit?" He took two steps toward the door. "Your job's the same as mine, Talley. You look at the bigger picture and figure it's worth shoveling shit to make the whole damn garden grow. I don't do this for Pascek. I don't do it for those bastards on the Seven. I don't do it for anyone but me, because I decided it was worth doing. And you know what? You made the same decision yourself a long time ago when you turned yourself into Moncada's dog. Just deal, Talley. We made ourselves what we are. Get used to it. Now you can either go back home, or you can decided to do something new—but we both know which way you're going to jump. Don't we?" He paused for a second and stared at Talley, who eventually looked away. "Hah. Thought so." He walked toward the door. "Call me if you really have something you want to talk about. Otherwise, don't bother. And keep the beer."

Behind him, Talley stood. "You really believe in it, don't you? You actually believe it's worth it?" His tone was incredulous.

Theo turned. "Until something better comes along, yeah. I believe. You happy now?"

"Disappointed, actually." Talley shook his head, and spread his arms wide. "All the power of the centuries in front of you, Bell, and this is the best you can do? It's your damn job? You're no better than they are." One by one, the bar's patrons turned to stare. "Oh yes, my good people, didn't your new friend warn you? He's a vampire." Talley's voice took on a mock-conspiratorial tone. "But don't worry. He's a nice vampire. He doesn't want to cause any trouble."

"Talley…" Theo's voice was a low warning. Talley ignored him.

"Oh, hush, Theo. They don't believe me. Your precious little Masquerade isn't going to fall down from that. It might, however, from this!" Even as Theo leaped for him, he brought his arms up in a gesture that might have been stolen from a circus ringmaster.

Pillars of shadow exploded from every comer. Two passed through and shredded the hapless bartender. Others battered patrons. One smashed the mirror behind the counter, filling the air with shattered glass and screams. Though it all, Talley just smiled, even as Bell smashed into him with fangs bared. The two tumbled to the floor with a crash, Bell on top. Around them, the shadow tentacles continued their rampage.

"Why the fuck did you do that?" he snarled. "I'm going to kill you for that."

Unexpectedly, Talley laughed. "Do that. Take the time to kill me. And in the meantime, the survivors of this little fiasco will be taking to the streets. Running away. Spreading their stories. What's that going to do to the Masquerade, Bell? Or is it worth putting the job aside for a minute just to try to kill me?" A shuddering crash distracted both of them for a second, as one of the tentacles punched through the front door and withdrew. A patron, seeing his chance, burst for the exit. "What's it going to be?"

With a muttered curse, Bell threw himself off of his opponent and chased after the fleeing patron. "Nobody move a fucking muscle," he bellowed as he went through the doorway. "I'll be right back."

Talley dusted himself off, stood up, and snapped his fingers. The shadow tentacles faded. For a second, the only noise was the quiet sobbing of one of the wounded patrons, and the gentle gurgle of beer leaking from broken bottles. "He will, you know. More's the pity." With that, he, too, strode out the door into the night—and then vanished. Behind him, the remaining mortals sat, or stood, and just waited. After all, Theo had ordered them to.

A block down, Theo sprinted with inhuman speed after the fleeing patron. He was *pretty* sure this was the only one who'd gotten away, but the uncertainty kept him glancing from side to side, and had prevented him from quite reaching his target yet. "Come back!" he yelled fruitlessly over the traffic. "I'm not going to hurt you!" But *if this takes much longer, I'm gonna motherfucking kill you*, he muttered under his breath. Ahead of him, the man ran heedlessly on.

Talley was right, unfortunately. He had to stomp this one, nip it in the bud. If there was a Masquerade breach with him at the center, and with Talley sitting across the table, Pascek would have his balls in an egg cup for breakfast. He'd just have to trust that he hadn't missed anyone, and go get this guy now. With that decision, Theo put his head down, concentrated for a second and put on additional burst of speed. This had to end.

Ahead of him, the runaway turned a comer and slammed into an abandoned newsstand. He went down, hard. Theo was on him in an instant, grabbing the front of his shirt and hauling him to his feet. "Listen to me, you saw nothing back there, do you hear me? Nothing!" He'd done this a million times before— convince some kine that he hadn't just seen a lame-ass vampire pull something stupid. But this time, he hesitated, hearing

Talley's words in the back of his head. Why was he doing this? To protect the Masquerade? Habit? Or just to cover his own ass? Did it even matter? He shook his head and tried to concentrate again, but it was too late.

With a tearing sound, the guy's shirt ripped, leaving Theo holding a double handful of fabric. The mortal staggered out into the street, eyes wide with panic, then turned and caught a city bus full in the face. It dragged him for half a city block, then screeched to a halt. A babble of voices broke out, but by then, Theo was gone. Only a double handful of cloth, drifting to the sidewalk, showed that he'd ever been there.

It was a bare fifteen minutes later when Theo left the wreckage of the bar once more. All of the patrons had been spoken to and had their memories readjusted; each had been given a story sure to contradict the others so that the cops would tie themselves in knots trying to figure out the truth. Ambulances had been called, as had the police, and it was time to get a move on. In the distance, flashing red lights indicated that an ambulance had arrived to deal with the accident victim. Sirens howled in the night air, getting closer. There was no reason to stay any longer.

Theo crossed the street and cut through an alley, pausing to stamp his feet in some standing water to get the mirror shards off his boots. The pants were a loss, but he'd replace them as soon as possible. A good pair of boots was like an old friend, though. You didn't give those up unless you had to. Soundlessly he padded off again, putting as much distance as he could between him and what had happened earlier in the night. There'd be hell to pay over that, but he wouldn't be the one to pay it.

A soft sound from above caught his attention. Alert, he slid into a shadow and looked around for the source. He didn't have to look long.

Up above, on a fire escape, stood Talley. The moon was behind him, and he was looking down at Theo, smiling. The sound came from Talley's hands. He was applauding, slowly. Then, he bowed.

"I was wrong," he mouthed. "You win." And then, as a cloud passed over the moon, he vanished.

Theo shook his head. "Motherfucking Jersey" was all he said, and continued on.

Self-Portrait

Gherbod Fleming

Friday, 17 December 1999, 8:15 PM
Broadway Avenue
New York City, New York

The outside lane was already full with taxis disgorging theatre-goers, so Benjamin Neil's cabby did what to him, a cabdriver in midtown Manhattan, seemed perfectly reasonable. He triple-parked. The northbound lanes of Broadway, now completely blocked, rapidly degenerated into a snarled, angry mass of immobilized, horn-blowing vehicles.

"Six eighty," the cabby said with a thick Indian accent.

Benjamin handed him eight dollars and slipped from the cab. He could feel the curses of the other drivers, already lined up a block and a half deep, but the insults and enmity slid off his shoulders as easily as did the cold, pelting rain that caused the pearled and tuxedoed theatre-goers to cower beneath black umbrellas and hurry toward the relative shelter of the marquee. The show was a revival of "Annie Get Your Gun," with Bernadette Peters and some cast-off television actor. Benjamin was not attending the show; he did not stoop to such mawkish fare. Benjamin attended the opera on occasion.

Tonight, however, was a working night. He navigated through the sea of cabs and past the theatre to the front door of his gallery. It wasn't, technically speaking, *his* gallery. He merely managed the establishment for Mr. Stephenson—*the*

Mr. Stephenson of the Stephenson Gallery. Although for all practical intents and purposes, Benjamin *was* the Stephenson Gallery. He oversaw day-to-day operations. It was he who maintained relations with the artistic community as well as the influential museums. He made all of the financial and exhibit decisions. Except for tonight.

Benjamin thrust his key into the front door's temperamental lock and twisted it like the knife he wished it were in Mr. Stephenson's back. Previously, the owner had always treated Benjamin well. So confident was Stephenson that the gallery was in competent hands, in fact, that he had not visited the premises in just over three years, leaving everything to Benjamin. Why, then, Benjamin wondered as he stepped inside and pushed closed the heavy door with a bit more force than was required, had Stephenson forced tonight's client upon him without explanation, or even twenty-four hours' warning?

Benjamin had been compelled to close the previous exhibit early and delay the opening of the next, a new collection of oils by Jacopo Finini. The artist would be outraged, and with good reason. There were also -financial repercussions, of course. Benjamin had already decided that, should Stephenson hold him responsible for the owner's own erratic and unreasonable demands, he would resign. Just quit and walk away from the gallery that he had transformed from a nothing to a shining star of the Manhattan museum scene. Benjamin simply would not allow anyone, not even Mr. Stephenson, who had been so good to him, to ruin Benjamin's good name in the art community. Credibility was as fragile as the most delicate orchid, requiring perfect conditions to flourish, but so easily destroyed by carelessness or neglect.

Mark had urged Benjamin to quit tonight, to stand up the intrusive client and tell Mr. Stephenson what he could do with his gallery. But then again, Mark tended to overreact. Benjamin wasn't one for burning bridges. Not yet.

His steps echoed from the sparkling black tile of the walls and stairwell as he hurried up from street level to the double glass doors of the gallery proper. Benjamin glanced at his watch and then punched in the combination for the door's electronic lock. He had plenty of time. The client wasn't scheduled to arrive for another two hours—an inconvenient late-night appointment for Benjamin, but not out of the ordinary for a client operating on European or maybe West Coast time. Benjamin wasn't sure from whence or where this mystery client hailed. Another irritant, that.

Benjamin shrugged off his overcoat and had started to toss it on the receptionist's desk in the lobby when he saw the elegant fur already draped across the desk. His hand stopped in mid-throwing motion, but the overcoat was already out of his grasp and struck the front of the desk, then slid off onto the floor.

He stood staring at the fur for a long moment. Who the hell had left that on the receptionist's desk? It was not the receptionist, that was certain. Benjamin compensated Lilia handsomely, but the sleek sable cape on the desk would have cost her nearly a year's salary, and Benjamin knew for a fact that at least half of every pay check went straight up her nose. Who then?

Slowly, he bent down and retrieved his coat. He wiped absently with his fingers at the water that had dripped from his wrap onto the hardwood floor. Standing just as slowly, Benjamin stepped carefully around the desk, watching the for as if it might move, and laid his coat over the receptionist's chair.

Strange. The client, even if she'd arrived early, would have been locked out, and burglars, even art burglars, Benjamin imagined, didn't generally wear fur to a heist. Maybe some senile dowager had left the fur and arranged with Lilia to pick it up in the morning. That seemed the most reasonable explanation.

As Benjamin made his way through the empty rooms of the gallery, his footsteps seemed to thunder resoundingly, the sound of each step blending with those before and after to create a rolling military tattoo. Perhaps the exaggerated sound was merely his imagination, or it could have been because the gallery was so completely empty. Literally empty. Of patrons and of art. Except for one painting.

Benjamin had seen hundreds of exhibits come and go. He had chosen what pieces would go where, in which room, on which wall. Never before, even when every piece had been taken down and packed away, had the gallery felt so empty to him. Never had the walls seemed so stark white, sanitary, void of life. Never had the hardwood floors felt so cold and sterile.

He strode through the main gallery, poking his head into the four smaller chambers that flanked the central room. All silent as the grave. He moved toward the three rear galleries, thinking about the one painting, the only work on display, that hung in the rearmost room. He'd supervised Raul's hanging the rather largish piece this afternoon. Benjamin had had specific instructions from Mr. Stephenson concerning exactly where the portrait should be displayed. The alleged portrait. Mr. Stephenson's letter had mentioned that it was a portrait, but the letter had also been quite emphatic that the silk tapestry attached to the frame and covering the painting itself not be removed. So Benjamin had not yet seen the painting. That, he assumed, would wait until the client arrived later tonight.

Perhaps Mr. Stephenson was arranging a sale to this self-important person. That seemed the likeliest scenario, though Benjamin, grinding his teeth as he thought about it, would have appreciated the courtesy of an explanation. He felt that, considering his loyalty and proven ability, he deserved that much at the very least.

Benjamin continued on through the first two of the rear galleries. He almost expected the staccato percussion of his footsteps to shatter the empty display cases. Absorbed by thoughts of the many things he would like to tell Mr. Stephenson, he turned the corner into the last gallery and started violently, his shoes squeaking on the heavily polished floor. Despite the fur, he hadn't been expecting to find anyone, least of all a goddess.

She wore an ivory, sleeveless gown with a fitted bodice and long, flowing skirt. Her hands, in matching formal gloves, were propped gracefully on her hips. The lines of her cheeks were rounded, narrowing considerably toward the chin, the effect unusual, interesting, perfect, entrancing. The soft tone of her gown and the milky white of her skin, far from causing her to appear bland or washed out, served to set off the auburn curls of her hair, the similar dark red of her lips, and her vibrant emerald eyes.

"Mr. Neil," she said, and the syllables eased from her tongue like a guilty pleasure.

He stared at her. "Ms. Ash," he managed at last. He began toward her, surprised to find his knees weak. He ran a hand through his prematurely thinning hair, felt the raindrops still resting there, and noticed in contrast how dry his mouth suddenly was.

"I hope you don't mind my arriving early," she said, unconcerned. "Emil sent me a key and the combination, and I just couldn't help myself."

Emil. Benjamin's mind was blank for a moment, then he realized. Emil Stephenson. Mr. Stephenson. Mention of Benjamin's employer rekindled his ire somewhat. Mr. Stephenson had given her a key? And without so much as consulting Benjamin? He was more than a little irked at his boss and, by extension, at this woman, the mysterious client. But her voice was a warm, sensual shower, and there was something about her eyes….

"You do understand, don't you?"

Benjamin blinked repeatedly. She had said something, asked him a questions. "I…understand? Beg your pardon?"

"I said, Benny, that I just couldn't wait any longer to drop by." Her eyes shone brilliantly. Her smile was very slight, and perhaps a bit cruel, like that of a child pulling legs off a spider.

"Benjamin, please," he said, recovering his earlier irritation. No one called him Benny except Mark. Benjamin dealt daily with beautiful men and women, and with wealthy, affected eccentrics. They often needed a reminder that theirs was a business relationship, not the dealings of master and slave. They needed, in short, someone to put them in their place, and Benjamin was pleased to accommodate. "Your visit *per se* is not a problem, but quite frankly the suddenness of your exhibit—"

"*Watch your tongue, you petulant child*, she hissed, then very sweetly added, "or I'll tear it out."

Benjamin's knees again nearly failed him. He stood dumbfounded, mouth agape. His stomach churned. The intimate gallery was suddenly cavernous, and he, exposed, vulnerable, standing alone in the center of it. He wanted to flee from the room, but his feet, rooted to the spot, were not his to command. He couldn't have just heard what he thought he had. For an instant, he thought his client's eyes burned bright red…but no, they were the same enticing emerald, and he couldn't explain the visceral fear that had just swept over him and receded in the space of two heartbeats.

His collar was too tight. Benjamin tugged at his black shirt, buttoned to the top. A bead of sweat trickled down his side.

"Are you quite all right, Mr. Neil?" Her eyes were watching him, encompassing him with her gaze, delving into him.

"I… Would you excuse me? I need a Perrier."

"Certainly."

"May I get you something?"

"No, thank you. Not at present."

Benjamin turned on his heels and beat a hasty retreat from the room. Away from her he began breathing regularly again, realized that he'd been holding his breath. His heart was pounding. He glanced over his shoulder, sure that he was still in the line of sight of those bright green eyes, but he was alone. Had she just threatened to pull out his tongue? Impossible. His analyst was going to have a field day with this one. Did the woman remind him of his bitch mother? Had she tapped into some repressed childhood memory? Benjamin stretched his mouth and eyes open wide, then squeezed them shut. He flicked beads of sweat from his forehead.

Before he remembered it was locked, Benjamin tried to turn the knob and walked face first into his office door. He stood stunned for several seconds. Finally, he laughed, a bit nervously. There was no one to witness his embarrassment. He was alone.

He unlocked his office and took a bottle of Perrier from the refrigerator. On second thought, he put the bottle back, poured himself two fingers of Scotch from the bar instead, and gulped down the sweet liquid fire. Thus fortified, he returned to the rear gallery. His heart raced to keep time with the rataplan of his shoes across the hardwood.

"And she wouldn't show you the picture?" Mark asked incredulously.

"No. It was covered the entire time. A beautiful silk tapestry, by the way," Benjamin said. He poked at his unfinished dinner.

"What a *bitch*" It wasn't the herbal tea Mark was sipping that left the sour look on his face.

Benjamin gazed out the window of the bistro at the throng of people passing along the sidewalks and across the streets of Times Square. He was practiced at guessing which passersby were the tourists and which were native New Yorkers. It was all in the bearing, the attitude. The city had a spirit that infused its inhabitants and spurred them on to flamboyance and greatness. The punks were more rebellious here, green spikes of hair, giant stud piercings. The young professionals were sexier, short skirts and spiked heels that showed off sculpted calves and thighs; tight blouses and crisp suits, accentuating gravity-defying breasts and stone-hard pecs. The intelligentsia here were more brilliant, the artists more gifted.

Yet compared to Victoria Ash, they were all but pale, faded ghosts devoid of substance.

"You don't listen to me anymore," Mark said.

"What?" Benjamin was drawn back within the bistro and confronted by Mark's expression of habitual irritation, slightly pursed lips, brow furrowed. "Of course I do. You were…complaining about something." That was a safe enough guess.

Mark snorted derisively. He was wearing a snug T-shirt, the short sleeves cuffed. He never wore a jacket, even though it was cold out; he liked to show off his work at the gym. "You should've told her to go fuck herself."

"Oh, that's good for business. Not to mention job security. My employer sends me an obviously rich-as-sin client, so I insult her and turn away her business. Mr. Stephenson would love that."

"Oh, fuck Mr. Stephenson," said Mark, rolling his eyes. "That gallery would be *nothing* without you. He might as well shoot himself in the head as fire you."

"Flattery will get you everywhere," Benjamin said, anxious to change the subject. He squeezed Mark's knee under the table.

"It already has, dearie." Mark grinned conspiratorially, but then became serious again. "But none of that means you should take any guff from this woman. What's her name?"

"Victoria Ash." There was a long pause before Benjamin registered his companion's displeasure. "What?"

"I don't like the way you say her name."

"What? What are you talking about? That's her name. Victoria Ash. I didn't make it up."

Mark crossed his muscled arms. "It's not her name that bothers me. Although…Victoria…it's rather pretentious, don't you think? No, it's how *you* say it that bothers me. *Victoria Ash.* All dreamy and gaga. Did you fuck her?"

"No! Of course not. And I didn't say her name gaga. You are so paranoid. This is a client."

"That never stopped you before."

"Oh, here we go. You are *so* juvenile. I am *not* going to have this conversation. I refuse."

"You did fuck her."

"I did not," Benjamin said. "Listen to me." He grabbed Mark's hand but Mark resisted and looked away. "Fine," Benjamin said through clenched teeth. "I'm not the one who banged a fucking cocktail waitress. And how about the buff young usher? At least I had some class. But *nothing* happened with this woman."

They sat for several minutes without speaking, an eddy of high-strung silence amidst the swirling bodies, neon, and flashing digital projections of Times Square. Benjamin was less concerned by Mark's surliness than by his own inability to remember exactly what *had* happened last night.

Finally, he stood. "I have to go." He leaned over and kissed, unrequited, Mark's pursed lips.

————

She was waiting for him at the gallery. He knew she would be. Benjamin was trying to convince himself that Ms. Ash must be paying an obscene amount for Mr. Stephenson to have agreed to all this. That had to be the explanation. The gallery remained bare, all white walls and vacant pedestals, except for the alleged portrait. All thought of the financial side of the affair fled Benjamin's mind, however, when he stepped into her presence.

She wore a simple white, starched blouse tonight, and a calf-length, form-fitting black skirt with black heels. A string of pearls graced her chest beneath her open collar; two more pearls dangled gently from her delicate earlobes. She was black and white against the bare expanse of gallery, again her hair, lips, and eyes the only dashes of color.

"Would you like to see?" she asked as Benjamin approached.

Only then did he realized that the tapestry was removed from the frame of the painting. The silk lay on the floor beneath.

"I…" Never in his life had Benjamin found himself so tongue-tied. Of course he wanted to see the mysterious painting. He was unable to feign disinterest, unable even to try.

He came within a few steps of Victoria. She stood in virtually the same spot as last night, directly aligned with the painting several feet away. Only when she gestured toward the piece did Benjamin manage to look away from her and at it.

The portrait was tall, life-sized, and before Benjamin stood the mirror image of the goddess at his side. He looked back and forth between the visions of beauty, two but one. Impossible. Judging by the slight darkening of the oil pigmentation, Benjamin would have guessed that the painting was a hundred-fifty, maybe two hundred years old. Yet the likeness was too uncanny to be coincidental. On the canvas, Victoria's auburn tresses flowed over her shoulders and down her back. The artist had *almost* captured the vibrant eyes; the color was right, but how could he have hoped to reproduce the gaze that drove

Benjamin to distraction? The lips were full, rounded perfectly, enticing. Benjamin only vaguely noted the background: trees, Grecian columns, broken, one overturned. Victoria, too, wore classical trappings, a white robe draped over a shoulder, clinging to her hips, her right breast bare.

Impossible, Benjamin told himself again. The age alone... But his mind could not completely discount what his eyes told him: The portrait was of Victoria.

Of it all, Benjamin's mind fastened upon the lips. There was the faintest hint of a smile—the same amused, cruel smile that he had seen last night.

"The likeness is very good, don't you think?" Victoria asked. She was very near him. Had she stepped closer? Her alluring scent filled his awareness. "Would you like to touch it?"

Benjamin watched his hand rising toward the canvas. He wanted very much to touch it, to touch Victoria. His fingers brushed her lips, traced the line of her strong cheekbone, but returned to the lips, lingered there.

"The artist mixed a few drops of my blood with the red to get just the right shade for the lips," she whispered to him. "The nipple as well. I think the effect is... pleasing."

But this picture is over a hundred years old. Benjamin wanted to say. Instead, he leaned close to the wall. The texture of the layered paint was strangely electric. His fingertips tingled. *Literally* tingled. A distant, nagging thought tried to break in on his reverie. Had she said *blood?*

But then he found himself with his lips against Victoria's, tasting her, his tongue padding back and forth against the canvas. Mixed with the acrid taste and smell of the oils was something arousing, stimulating. He pressed his body against the canvas....

"Mr. Neil?"

Benjamin froze. It was as if a fuse popped in his brain. He was suddenly and painfully aware that he was standing in front of the most influential client he'd ever met, perhaps the most important client his employer had. And he was kissing, *licking*, practically humping, a portrait. *Of her.*

"Emil said you were a lover of fine art," Ms. Ash said.

Benjamin jumped back from the wall as if the current he'd felt had spiked, shocking him. He was mortified to discover that, beneath his sleek black slacks, he was, quite obviously, erect.

"Oh my God," he sputtered. He had spent years dealing with arrogant, narcissistic patrons, and had constructed his own wall of disdainful egotism as a defense, as an *offense*, but nothing he'd ever encountered had prepared him for this demon.

"I'd hate to know what you do to portraits you don't like," Victoria said.

Benjamin cursed her in that instant, as she mocked his confusion. If he could have, he would have taken her by her perfect neck and throttled her, squeezed until her eyes bulged and no breath entered her body. But he could not. He could only look into those green eyes and watch as she laughed at him. Gone was the pretense that anything going on here was normal, and with it Benjamin's embarrassment. So what if he'd tried to hump the fucking picture? Inconsequential. What was the point of modesty in the face of something so unnatural, so deviant? Benjamin desperately wanted to choke her with his bare hands, he desperately wanted to hurt her, he desperately *wanted her.*

He reached for her, determined to rip the blouse from her shoulders, determined to grasp the perfect breast exposed on canvas behind him, determined to bruise and bloody her nipple between his teeth. *Then* he would throttle her, *then* he would—

Her fingers were around his wrist. He hadn't seen her move, but she stopped his hand, twisted it backward. Benjamin cried out and fell to his knees. The angel of death swooped down upon him.

————

Benjamin left the gallery shortly before daybreak. In the back of his mind, he thought he would walk home. He needed the fresh air. At some point during the first hour, he realized that he'd forgotten his overcoat. A biting wind whipped through the mazelike streets of Manhattan. The streets themselves, the buildings, the landmarks, were unfamiliar to Benjamin. On several occasions, he stared at one street sign or another, reading the name but uncomprehending. Walking, home should have been roughly half an hour away, but after something like three hours, he still couldn't orient himself, couldn't place his surroundings or decipher the sights and sounds that he'd experienced every day for years.

The business day began. The streets grew crowded. Benjamin wandered among the people, not really noticing them except when he bumped shoulders with someone walking the other way. Eventually he reached a river; it was the Hudson or the East, but which one? The sun, largely obscured by gray clouds, climbed higher in the sky, but the day did not warm. At some point after noon, Benjamin gave up. He slumped onto a park bench and remained there, shivering and crying.

People continued to pass, hurried past him, in fact. None of them was Mark; none of them was Victoria.

Victoria. Benjamin shuddered, doubled over in pain, retched. "Oh, God," he muttered as he nearly choked on warm, steaming bile. He was afraid to look at the splattered sidewalk, afraid he would see blood. *Blood.* She had slit her own wrist and fed him *blood.* And he had drunk…and wanted more! No, he was wrong, must be wrong, delusional. He staggered to his feet, forced himself to walk, to keep moving. If he col lapsed on the bench, a policeman might find him. Would a cop think he was a drunk and haul him away, or try to help, ask him if he was all right? What would Benjamin say? How could he explain what he did not himself understand?

Keep walking. Things would come into focus, get better. They had to. They couldn't get worse. And gradually his mind did begin to clear. And things were worse. As the sun began its descent, Benjamin was finally able to concentrate, to hold a coherent thought, a recognizable image, in his mind. But that image was Victoria. Hundred-year-old canvas or perfect flesh. The distinction was unclear. He had tasted her blood from both. His tongue and throat burned at the memory. Emerald eyes, rose-red blood. It was true. They were all that were there, in the empty white expanse of his gallery. The place where he'd spent most of his waking hours over the past three years was now changed, foreign, repulsive.

Benjamin stumbled through the landscape of his mind. He felt the sickening nothingness as his foot tried for a step that was not there. Glaring lights. Blaring horn. He caught his balance. Looked up at the lights, looked down at the curb he'd stumbled from. Music, as a window rolled down.

"Hey, mon, you get in?"

A taxi. A city of taxis waiting to take him where he could not go by himself. Hand sliding along the hood. Fumbling at the handle. Exhaustion pulled him into the seat. Sickly sweet air freshener didn't really cover the scent of *ganja.* Dreadlocks helicoptered in slow motion as the driver turned. The music wasn't reggae. Zydeco. Benjamin laughed. Said the address. Closed his eyes.

"Mon, that's only three blocks. You sure?" And in the next instant, "Here you go, mon."

Benjamin gave him a bill, left the door open, struggled with the door to his own building. So close now. His feet and hands and head were heavy, pulling him down. The key turned. Through the foyer, another locked door, stairs, home.

He shed clothes from the door to the bed. Shoes, socks, shirt, belt, slacks, silk boxers. Finally, between the satin sheets. They were warm after the cold outside. His fingers and toes were numb, but he was home. Peace.

"You were with her, weren't you?"

Benjamin buried his face in the forgiving pillow, pulled the sheet tightly around himself. Peace. Sleep.

"You were, weren't you?" Mark said. "Fuck you."

Benjamin didn't respond. He was so cold, chilled to the bone by the long day outside without his overcoat. But the body beside him provided little warmth, and no comfort. Benjamin felt the tears on his face; they washed over the grime of the city as he wept silently. His nose was running on the pillow. "I don't feel…well, Mark."

"You are such a fucking bastard."

Benjamin closed his eyes tightly but could not stop the tears that flowed more fiercely now. His sobs shook the bed. The room spun, and as his world turned upside down, he could no longer deny what he had long suspected, what he had long struggled to hide from himself. There was no love in the man beside him, only possession and envy. And there was no love between them, only dependence, desperation, tired routine. "How could I have ever loved you?" Benjamin whispered. "It must have been my fault. Must have been." When had it died? When had the joy drained away from their lives?

Mark lashed out. He flung an elbow at Benjamin, cracked him on the back of the head. "Fuck you."

Benjamin shot up in bed and smacked Mark in the face…then realized what he'd done. It was the first time he'd ever hit Mark. And it felt good. The slap enraged Mark. His face contorted horribly, and he smashed a fist across Benjamin's jaw. Suddenly the world was streaks of light and dark, dancing colors—then just as suddenly Benjamin's face was in his pillow, and he could taste blood.

"Oh, God, Benny...I'm sorry, so sorry.... You shouldn't have hit me."

Benjamin waited for the hesitant, gentle touch on his shoulder. So many of their fights went this way. Mark lost control and then felt guilty; they kissed, made up, made love. It was so clear now—how Mark abused him, emotionally as much as physically. Mark was a monster, a user. Had been from the start. Benjamin had always let him be, had played his part in the game. It was as much his own fault; he'd never complained, never threatened to leave.

And there, the gentle touch on his shoulder...

Benjamin whirled and smashed his head into Mark's nose, felt the crunch, smelled the blood gushing through Mark's fingers as he screamed his shock and outrage. Benjamin couldn't believe what he'd done, couldn't believe what he was doing, because he didn't stop. Something about the blood fueled his fever. He slammed his head into Mark's face again. Bones, not just cartilage, crunched this time. Mark fell back, stunned. Benjamin threw himself on top of Mark and latched his fingers around the throat of his lover, his tormentor. The urge to throttle came back easily; it felt right, natural, overdue.

Benjamin's hands were stronger than he'd ever imagined. He savored the strength, the control. But suddenly it was Victoria's delicate neck his hands were around. He redoubled his efforts. If only it could be...

From beneath, Mark's hands thrashed wildly at his face, but Benjamin didn't ease the pressure. Mark's fingers clawed at his eyes, his mouth. Benjamin bit down hard and felt a digit come free between his teeth. More blood. He relived all the abuse, all the cruel words, all the violent sex that had left him, *always him*, bruised and bleeding.

Never again. Never again.

———————

Benjamin was a dead man walking to the street door of the gallery. He was showered, his hair still wet, his skin brutally scrubbed, pink and raw, but he still felt the filth of the city clinging to him. He felt the blood on his hands, on his face, in his mouth. He was completely certain that every person who passed him on the street knew exactly what heinous crime he'd just committed. It was much like the feeling he'd experienced as a young man having come to realize he was queer—the surety that eyes were following him, that others had access to his deepest secrets. He looked into the glass of a storefront and saw the heavy, dark circles under his eyes; he hadn't slept at all tonight, or last night.

He fumbled with his key as he took it from his pocket. The lock, temperamental at the best of times, thwarted his repeated attempts. Giving in to fatigue and tension, he cursed and kicked wildly at the door for a moment. His frantic burst of energy and rage quickly spent, he noticed the patrol car driving slowly past, New York's finest observing his erratic behavior. He felt the word "murderer" was tattooed across his forehead. Perhaps, he thought, he should reach for his wallet and hope the police gunned him down. The punishment would fit the crime. It was one thing to have discovered that, somewhere through the years, his love had died; it was quite another to have strangled his lover until Mark's eyes and tongue had bulged. But this was the classy part of town, and Benjamin well-dressed and neatly groomed, so the police continued on their way.

Benjamin attempted the door again, but still his murderer's fingers could not make the key work. Something was not right, something was different. Then the door opened, and Lilia was staring out at him. "I thought I heard somebody."

"My key wouldn't work," he said numbly.

"Yeah. Ms. Ash had the locks changed." Lilia was too cheerful; she must have scored some high-quality powder. "She is a beautiful woman, isn't she?" she said. "I mean, really *beautiful*."

"She changed the locks?"

"Yeah. Come on up. I've got a key for you."

His footsteps rang hollow as he followed her up the black tile stairs. The corridor was dark and bleak and barren. And then at the top of the stairs—"She had me change this combination too."—the gallery shone with bright white light, but, like Benjamin, it was cold and dead. "She's in the back with somebody. I didn't see who."

Benjamin threw his coat onto Lilia's desk. "Hang it up with her fur," he said sharply, and left her. Back in the sterile, empty gallery, Benjamin managed to recoup a portion of his spirit, his will. It was all going to stop, all the strangeness. Blood-drinking, indeed. He'd obviously been suffering some sort of episode, some severe dementia. He'd best act while his mind was relatively clear, and then seek professional help. *He* had been the victim here; he'd been Mark's victim, and Ms. Ash's victim. She was at the root of this somehow. Benjamin had had enough of this farce, he decided as he strode toward the rearmost gallery. What did he have to lose by kicking out his employer's rich and beautiful client? He'd already killed his lover. *She is a beautiful woman, isn't she?* He could have smacked Lilia. Of course, Ms. Ash was beautiful. But she was a beast, a cruel, inhuman monster. This was all her doing. Benjamin would throw her out, bodily if she forced him to that. He would deal with the police later. He'd confess everything about Mark; he could plead self-defense maybe. But first he must rid himself of this woman. He wasn't sure exactly how she had taken advantage of his lapse into mental illness, or how she had caused it, but he was certain she had.

He gained strength and determination with each step. The stark, white walls were his evidence against her. For the gallery to sit empty at her whim was a crime. She wasn't the one who had made this place what it was. By the time he reached the final room, he'd built up a full head of steam.

And it promptly dissipated, every ounce of his fury stolen by shock and dismay.

Victoria, stunning in a green velvet gown, stood admiring the portrait with the most hideous creature Benjamin had ever seen. He wasn't sure at first that it was a man, that it was *human*. It wore clothes, a long coat, and it held a fedora in its twisted fingers—but any number of freakish creatures could be dressed up and put on display. Was this what Victoria—herself the subject of an impossibly old portrait—would do with the gallery? Turn it into a freak show? Benjamin was speechless.

Victoria, unsurprisingly, was not. "Benny, do come meet our guest, Mr. Pug."

Benjamin was unable to step forward until the pressure of their expectant gazes overcame his shock. He moved closer—to Victoria, to the repulsive Mr. Pug.

This room had become a gallery of the impossible, the bizarre—Victoria threatening to have out his tongue; the painting; Benjamin attempting to fornicate with that painting, then attacking a client, and, in the end, *drinking her blood*. But the impossible had latched onto Benjamin, had followed him beyond the gallery, had infected him. He'd killed his lover, strangled Mark with bare, impossibly strong hands. Why not a freakish monster of a Mr. Pug? Why not? The creature was short, just over five feet tall, and thick in the middle. Its face was sprinkled with boils and smashed flat as if by violence, the nose easily wider than the squared chin. The eyes bulged out—like Mark's dead eyes—and the grinning mouth was full of jagged fangs. It offered a hand, each nub-like finger decorated with protruding bone knobs at the joints, to shake. Benjamin hesitated. He could feel Victoria's glare. He touched the proffered hand, shook it.

"The pleasure is mine," said Mr. Pug.

Benjamin laughed nervously, his earlier determination having drained away under the onslaught of giddy, ineffable delirium. His stomach was tied in knots, his ears ringing. The *pleasure…* He bit his lip lest he slide into hysterics. Perhaps madness would be a blessing.

Victoria's voice interrupted, if not diminished, the tension. "In looking through your files, I decided that far too many people have access to the gallery. As you've no doubt discovered, the locks and combination are changed. I've given Mr. Pug a key to the rear door, so he may come and go as he pleases." Her voice was hard and cold. It was ice down Benjamin's spine, but still barely managed to penetrate the thick fog of his mind, the onrushing madness. She was giving him instructions, *orders*, as if she were master of the gallery. Benjamin blanched. What had she done to Mr. Stephenson? *Emil. So* familiar, so intimate. Had she fed him blood from her perfect body? Had she destroyed his life?

"This room is to be walled off," she said. "Lilia is making arrangements with contractors I have used before. The portrait is to remain, and no one other than Mr. Pug is to enter the room. When the new construction is completed, then you may prepare the next exhibit."

Construction…walled off. She would defile his gallery, create a shrine to her own likeness? And the inhuman Mr. Pug would be her first supplicant? Not her first, Benjamin realized.

"And I've spoken to Jacopo," Victoria added. "He understands the delay and sends his regards."

Jacopo. Jacopo Finini, important painter, and pompous ass who would *never* in one thousand years consent to such a slight, much less send his regards. "My God," Benjamin muttered under his breath. She'd gotten to Finini too. Twisted him with her blood. How many others? And over how many years?

"Is that clear?" she asked, as one might address the lowliest of servants.

Benjamin realized he was still staring at Mr. Pug, turned his eyes from the grotesque and looked upon the sublime, though truly Victoria was but the grotesque in a different guise. This was the woman who had destroyed his life with but a few sips of her blood. Benjamin didn't understand what had happened, *could* not understand. None of this could be *real*. Mr. Stephenson was still master of the gallery; Mark was waiting at home, in bed, *alive;* neither of these people was standing here. Benjamin remembered his resolve to evict her from the premises, to carry her out the door and fling her down the steps, and then he opened his mouth. "I killed Mark."

Victoria and Mr. Pug regarded him curiously for a moment. "Did you now?" Victoria asked. "And what did you do with him?"

Benjamin felt he was going to be sick. His legs were going to give way. He'd said it, made it real by his acknowledgement. How had it happened? How? But more mystifying than what he had said, than what he had done, was the matter-of-fact reaction from these two...*creatures*. "I...I didn't know what to do. I left him."

"Not a good idea, leaving bodies lying around," said Mr. Pug, shaking his head.

"Pug, could you be a dear and take care of that little problem for us?" Victoria asked with an unconcerned smile.

"Where is it you left him?"

"Was it your home, Benny? Give him your address, Benny. Pug will see to it."

Pug promptly left them. Benjamin had said the words, given his address, followed instructions. With mounting trepidation, he watched the oddity go. Even the company of the hideous Mr. Pug seemed preferable to being alone with Victoria. Benjamin couldn't trust himself with her. He wanted to be with her too much. He couldn't be sure of what he would say or do. At least Mr. Pug's monstrousness was readily visible.

"Poor, poor Mark," Victoria said. "You've been very evil, Benny."

Finally, his legs did give way, and he sank to the floor at her feet. He despised her. He hated the fact that he would kiss the hem of her garment if she so commanded. And so, he tried not to look at her, as he sat there in her shadow.

"Up now, Benny," she said. "Look at me."

She read his thoughts. She ordered him to do that which he would not. And he did. He climbed to his knees. He looked at the cold, green, monstrous eyes. It wasn't even a real struggle. He had sacrificed his world to her, and he would give his life if she asked it. He watched as one of her long, white fingernails gouged a red line along her forearm.

"You look so tired, Benny. You must keep your strength up." She lowered her bleeding arm to him. Benjamin drank in her poison—poison that had freed him only to enslave him to a world far darker than he'd ever believed could exist. He drank, and he hated her, and he thanked her.

The Cellar

Gherbod Fleming

Thursday, 23 December 1999, 7:45 PM
Brooklyn
New York City, New York

The falling snow muffled the rhythmic clanging of the bell and speckled white the faded red Santa suit. Pristine flakes drifted gently, lazily, to earth, where the city claimed them as its own, and countless feet and tires churned them to gray sludge. Heavy clouds lay low, obscuring the tops of buildings; the horizon was close, never more than a block or two away. Amidst the muted winter wonderland, nocturnal hands lifted aside from underneath the wide, steel storm grate that stretched across the sidewalk. The gently falling snow muffled the sounds of the brief struggle, and in the end, there was only a silent bell and a faded red Santa cap lying in the churned snow of the sidewalk.

The door slammed open and Colin stormed in cursing. In the past three hours he'd made the rounds of his whores and his dealers and taken out some of his frustration on each of them in turn. He felt warm and flushed with blood now, but was soothed not at all.

"You break the door and you gotta fix it," Gordon said from his perch in the comer atop a sprawling pile of sofa cushions. The dilapidated couch frame, rotted wood and a bent metal sleeper frame, was in another comer. Little remained in the way of intact furniture in the squalid apartment.

"I'm not gonna break your stupid door," Colin snapped, kicking it shut.

"He's still there, huh?"

"It's a disgrace! That's what it is, a damn disgrace, I tell you," Colin raged as he stalked about the room looking for something to break. He settled on the couch frame and gave it a few good whacks. "I do what I'm supposed to. I never gave Michaela no problems. I got my little neighborhood—"

"Our," Gordon interrupted.

"Huh?"

"Our little neighborhood."

"Right. Our little neighborhood. But that's not the point." Colin resumed his pacing. "I've always done what I'm supposed to. Okay, maybe not always, but pretty damned close. As close as anybody. I keep things quiet in our neighborhood. I don't cause no waves. Sabbat thugs roll through—I lay low instead of causing a fuss that's gonna attract a lot of attention. You know, the Masquerade, First Tradition, all that stuff. And I help out with trouble. We got all these new high-and-mighty types rolling into town, kicking the Sabbat out. I was at Throgs Neck. I did my part. Man, I was standing right behind that Nosferatu guy, the archon, when Polonia split his freaking skull in two. Anyway, I come back home, and what do I find? Some dirtbag loser has holed up in my territory. *Our* territory."

"So, I guess he's still there," Gordon said. He was scratching and biting at a patch of hair on his shoulder that itched constantly, tearing it out with his teeth, never mind that it would be back tomorrow night.

"Yes, he's still there. Haven't you been listening to anything I've said?"

"You didn't say he was still there."

"Well, he is. And you know what I'm gonna do? I'm gonna kill him. I know, I know. We're all dead already. Don't give me that. I'm gonna kill him *dead-dead*. Permanent-like. I'm gonna cut off his head and drink his stupid-squatter blood. Ho, ho, ho, and Merry Christmas, and screw him." Colin had continued stalking around the room throughout his rant, but now he stopped. He looked warily into the comers, at the ceiling, at the door. An important fact had just popped into his mind: The new prince was a Nosferatu. People said he had spies everywhere. They could hear what you were talking about, and you'd never have a clue that they were there. Colin walked to the other doorway and peeked into the closet-like kitchenette. "Figuratively, I mean."

"What?" Gordon paused from his grooming. "You're gonna kill him and drink his blood figuratively?"

"Right. It was a…you know…a metaphor."

"Like one of those things spelled the same way frontwards and backwards?"

"'Cause killing him," Colin continued as he walked deliberately to the center of the room and scanned the ceiling, "killing him would be against the…uh…against one of the traditions."

"Why are you talking to the light fixture?"

"No, I'm not killing anybody. I'm gonna take this to the prince, 'cause I'm in the right here. That building and that cellar are my—our territory. I done my part, and Prince Calebros has always been good to me."

"You always told me you hated those stinking Nossie bastards."

"*Shut up.* You don't know what you're talking about. You don't even know if you're *part* of the Camarilla anymore," Colin said in an attempt to change the subject.

"Yeah, tell me about it. Nobody tells me nothing," Gordon said. "But I don't really care what Xaviar does, or what anybody says he does. I'm staying right here in Brooklyn. The city's been good to me."

"So, you'll go with me to the prince?" Colin asked.

"You're really not gonna kill this squatter guy?"

"*What* did I say?" Colin looked around again. "I-don't-kill-nobody." And he'd seen this squatter guy in action—not the kind of guy Colin wanted to mess with. Otherwise, he would have killed him already.

"I brought you something."

The prince of New York peered over the stacks of papers that ringed his massive, battered desk like battlements. Emmett handed him yet another piece of paper, which Calebros set aside without perusing. Emmett was one of the few Kindred welcome in Calebros's "office." Aside from the desk, the countless papers, and the trusty Smith Corona practically buried beneath them, the subterranean grotto was crammed with shelves and boxes, themselves crammed full of more papers, reports, bundles of photographs and newspaper clippings.

"You probably want to read that," Emmett suggested.

"Oh, do I? I suppose you know better than I what I want."

"I suppose I do."

Calebros scowled at Emmett but elicited no response from his broodmate's familiar features—familiar because Calebros had known him for so many years, and because the face and body very nearly matched Calebros's own. Bald, rough head and jagged ears; wide, deep-set eyes; flat nose; long, unevenly spaced fangs; gnarled, bony fingers that ended in sharp talons. Calebros retrieved the sheet of paper Emmett had given him and read it by the light of the candelabra situated near—but not too near—his desk. His former desk lamp had met an unfortunate end; its base currently protruded from his rubbish can. Calebros read the paper.

"So? Another petition to the prince," he noted dryly. "This is the kind of thing the council should take care of." The *provisional* council of primogen, just as Calebros was the *provisional* prince of the city. This council was the successor to the Council of Twelve, which had selected him prince. That council had been the brainchild of justicars Jaroslav Pascek of Clan Brujah and Lucinde of Clan Ventrue. They had arranged for the selection of a new prince—but Calebros was not who they had planned to have chosen.

After the destruction of Prince Michaela at the hands of Cardinal Polonia of the Sabbat during the Battle of Throgs Neck, the Camarilla powers-that-be had determined that Victoria Ash should assume the mantle of prince of New York, and they had arranged the Council of Twelve to see to that end. The justicars must have felt confident that they could bully and cajole her to do their bidding. The backroom deals had been made, and all was ready—except Victoria had inexplicably refused the position. She had walked out of the council meeting, leaving all present stunned. Cock Robin, justicar of Clan Nosferatu, had then swooped in like a vulture upon carrion to see his candidate enthroned as prince.

Calebros, Prince of the Sewers, some called him, which was fine with Calebros. He was less kindly disposed toward those who referred to him as the Shit King, or the Fecal Regal. He made no attempt to curb the epithets, but neither did he forget those who were heard to utter them. The Nosferatu did not forget.

At any rate, the Council of Twelve, it turned out, did not hold ultimate authority in the matter of selecting a suitable prince—or so read a statement issued shortly thereafter by Justicar Pascek, who had not been present himself at the meeting. Any decision made by appointees of the Inner Circle, he claimed, must subsequently be ratified by the Kindred inhabiting the territory in question. As there was no mechanism to confirm the decision, and since neither Pascek nor Lucinde had seen fit call a conclave to address the matter, and Cock Robin had left the city for parts unknown, both prince and his newly formed council of primogen were to be considered of a provisional nature. Provisional. Temporary. Illegitimate.

The designation was a slap in the face, a procedural and petty lashing out by Pascek, who was himself petty and vain. His candidate having proved a mistake, he was not willing to remove his fingers from the affairs and governance of the city. The stigma attached to the word *provisional* was not crippling— Calebros was accustomed to stigma—but it made his job of restoring order and security to the city that much more difficult. Why should Kindred flock to his banner when the implication was that he might not be around all that long? None opposed him openly; none save a few of the stupid, inconsequential, or more radical and foolhardy among the Anarch element. Calebros even took some amusement from the fact that many of those who conspired against him in private often went to incredible lengths to ensure the secrecy of their plotting—with mixed results. One of those individuals in particular—the *almost* prince—interested Calebros a great deal.

"Have you spoken with Pug?" he asked.

"The petition…"

"Later, later," Calebros waved off his broodmate's complaint. "Have you spoken with Pug?"

"I thought it'd be better if 1 didn't question him directly. Wouldn't want to raise any suspicions. Tundlight is keeping tabs on him for me."

"And what does Mike have to say?"

"He's been to meet her all right. At that gallery. He's been back several times—he has a key to the back entrance—but Victoria hasn't been there many of the times."

Calebros pondered that. Victoria had not appeared pleased when she'd rejected the council's offer, yet she had elaborated to no one her reasons for doing so. "Has Pug mentioned his visits to anyone, any of our people?" Calebros asked, and frowned when Emmett shook his head. "He's not the secretive type."

"Not usually," Emmett said. "Should we be worried, you think?"

"Concerned." Anyone dealing with Victoria Ash on a regular basis was a concern. She had a habit of bending the weak to her own needs and wants, and while Pug was a productive member of the warren, he was not the craftiest or most astute.

"I could question him," Emmett suggested.

"No. I'm sure you could get to the bottom of it, but I think I'd rather… have Mike continue to watch him and report back. Pug isn't normally included in sensitive discussions—"

"But you want that to change."

"Exactly. Very gradually, though. I don't want him to notice. Just a few more responsibilities, a bit more trust given him," Calebros said.

"Limited range of topics?"

"Yes. Toss him a few tidbits that Victoria will be interested in if she is getting anything from him. Perhaps some dirt on Robert Gainesmil. She'd like that. Just enough to convince her that she has an open channel to sources close to the prince."

"You think she's…pumping him for information?"

"Oh, please," Calebros rolled his large eyes. "You're beginning to sound like Colchester. By the way—"

"No, no sign of him. Others are still missing too. Since before most of the fighting with the Sabbat and after. Jeremiah for one. Hilda for another. How's that for a scary couple? Hilda and Colchester."

"I don't want to think about it."

"Then think about that petition instead."

Calebros snatched the paper back up with a snort of disgust. "Territory dispute. Let the council handle it."

Emmett folded his arms. "Would I bring that to you if I didn't have a good reason? Look again."

Calebros's scowl deepened. He read the paper again, more carefully this time. "The Shaft. This location is near it." Emmett nodded, a smug expression taking shape on his face. "Yes, I asked you to keep an eye on that area," Calebros acknowledged. "So go check it out."

"Did," said Emmett, quite pleased with himself now. "And, I found, among other things…this? He tossed a filthy canvas sack onto the desk.

Calebros examined it closely, at the same time attempting to downplay his considerable interest, lest he give Emmett too much satisfaction. The prince sniffed at the sack and the miscellaneous collection of items within. "Get the others."

"They're already waiting."

"Then let's go."

———

There was no mistaking Cranston for a sane individual. His eyes, blue-gray and piercing, seemed to take in something no one else could see. And whatever it was that he did see was, in his eyes, worthy of scorn, hatred, destruction.

They found him in the cellar of the Brooklyn tenement. By the time he realized they were there, Emmett and Mike and

Clubfoot were on him with fists and claws and teeth. Emmett had insisted that Calebros wait upstairs—he was the prince, after all, and shouldn't be directly involved with such rough work any longer. Junior and Albatross had gone down with the others, leaving Pug, of all people, as an honor guard of sorts with the prince. Calebros twisted with impatience, only half-heartedly attempting to stretch the painful crooks of his twisted spine.

When they sounded the all-clear and Calebros made his way down the stairs, he found Cranston beaten into submission. "On your knees for the prince, you ingrate," Emmett told him with a none-too-gentle cuff to the head.

"That won't be necessary," Calebros said. Strange, he thought, that Emmett seemed to enjoy the trappings of royalty more than did the prince himself.

Perhaps it was merely a convenient outlet for his broodmate's mean streak.

Cranston looked quite the worse for wear. There was little enough blood, but he had several gashes on his face and head. At least three hundred stitches' worth, Calebros estimated, if he'd been kine. His stringy black hair hung past his shoulders. He was severely thin, a pale scarecrow dressed in black. Two of his fingers lay on the floor nearby; they looked as if they'd been bitten off and spit out.

"Don't worry," said Mike Tundlight, following Calebros's gaze. "They'll grow back."

From the looks of things, Cranston had moved into the cellar some time ago—that, or he'd been extremely busy in the intervening period. Scattered along the floor were a series of six irregularly dug graves and a discarded Santa suit. Only a fool or a madman brought his dinner home with him. Death was an unfortunate but occasional side effect of feeding, but burying bodies in one's haven was an invitation for some kine to come poking about and take special notice. The graves were not even disguised or hidden.

This one we'll have to put down, Calebros knew. The integrity of the Masquerade demanded as much. But there were other things that they must learn first. He reached out a hand, and Albatross handed him the canvas sack. "This came from here," Calebros said. "You found it somewhere. Where?"

Cranston's blue-gray gaze came to rest vaguely on Calebros, but the prisoner showed no other sign of having heard the question. Emmett drew back a fist, but Calebros stopped him with a curt gesture. The prince very calmly shifted the sack in his taloned grip and dumped the contents onto the floor. There were several small rocks and dented, empty cans, a tangle of metal wire, a broken flashlight, and...*something.* It was like a short length of rope or cord, except...fleshy. Emmett nudged the thing with his toe. Cranston did not look at the items on the floor. Now that he had looked at Calebros, he seemed unwilling to look away.

"Were these in the bag when you found it, or did you put them in it since?" Calebros asked him. *Did you find the sack, or take it from Jeremiah?* he wanted to ask. *Did you destroy him? Like you killed whomever these were?* Calebros glanced at the graves that surrounded them. Cranston had the eyes and manner of a mindless killer; he exhibited the telltale disconnect between action and consequences. There were kine in those graves. Kindred would have crumbled to dust, simply disappeared— as Augustin had disappeared. Cranston had not merely hunted for food; he had hunted and killed—not out of any true necessity, not from a need to defend himself, or friends, or a warren. He had simply killed. Because he could. Because he wanted to. A Kindred isolated often ended up that way, sliding over time into the maw of the Beast. And if he had come upon Jeremiah, he might have destroyed the unfortunate, addled Nosferatu out of hand—for something as simple as a canvas sack, or something even less significant. Cranston did not respond to the prince's questions.

Calebros nudged the fleshy cord much as Emmett had. A trickle of viscous, bloody juice trickled from one end. It was at least partially hollow, like a short section of hose—hose made of skin and meat and blood. "Where did you find the sack?" Calebros asked.

And then a slight smile crept over Cranston's face, a mocking smile. "Not so far from the dragon's belly," he said.

"What did you say?" Calebros snapped, having heard but hoping that his ears had deceived him.

"Not so fan" Cranston's smile grew to a full sneer. "What did you say?" Calebros pressed him. "Before." The other Nosferatu seemed very far away suddenly. There was only himself and the smiling, icy-eyed killer saying words that he should not.

"Hell," Cranston said, relishing the word, caressing it on his tongue. "The dragon's belly. Not far away at all."

The dragon's belly. He *had* said it.

Calebros leaned close to the killer and spoke in a low, hard-edged whisper. "You are a childe of Malkav, then? Have you spoken with Anatole?"

"Spoken?" Cranston found that amusing. "No."

For a moment, Calebros feared that he should not have mentioned the Prophet of Gehenna, because Cranston's fleeting engagement with reality, the brief recognition in his eyes of place and time, suddenly faded. But he spoke again, and his words caused the stolen blood in Calebros's veins to run colder. "An angel must enter the hell of the dragon's belly before this age passes...."

"Lest all ages come to pass," Calebros whispered these last words—the words of the Prophet, given secretly to Jeremiah the messenger but understood by the prince. Or first translated by the prince, if not completely understood. *Do the words come to*

him through his blood? Calebros wondered. Or *through Jeremiah's blood, perhaps?* Had the killer found him and somehow reclaimed Anatole's knowledge for his deranged clan?

"I will take you," Cranston said. Calebros looked at him suspiciously. The Malkavian nodded toward the canvas sack. "I'll take you, if that's what you want."

"To where you found the sack?" Calebros asked. The grinning lunatic nodded. To where he'd found the sack. Hell. The dragon's belly.

One of the graves in the cellar wasn't a grave but rather, when the heaped dirt was pushed aside, revealed itself as a hole that wound down through the cracked foundation of the tenement. Unwilling to risk Cranston squirming through and escaping, Calebros sent Mike ahead first, and then Emmett. Cranston went next, with Calebros on his heels, and Pug, Junior, Clubfoot, and Albatross filing along behind. The false grave led down to a tunnel, and that tunnel to another, and that to another. At every fork or turn, Mike and Emmett paused until Cranston indicated which way they should go.

As they trudged along, Calebros watched the Malkavian's back and tried to divine from his movements and bearing any hint of what had happened to Jeremiah. Did the prisoner appear guilty? Did he hunch his shoulders as if he expected a vengeful deathblow at any moment? Was Cranston *capable of* remorse, guilt, fear? Had he killed Jeremiah? Or was Calebros merely imagining the defensiveness, seeing what he wanted to see? There was no way to be sure. Calebros soon abandoned the task. He thought instead of the last time he'd seen Jeremiah: huddling, a trembling mass crammed back as far as he could go in the most remote crevice of a dead-end tunnel. Jeremiah had always been high-strung, but that night he'd quivered and laughed and sobbed and spoken words of doom. All that after

his time with Anatole. *After I sent him away with the Prophet.*
Calebros thought. But Jeremiah had agreed, had wanted to go,
and in the end his sacrifice—of his sanity? of his unlife?—had
proven vital in the destruction of their enemies, the enemies of
the clan. Leopold. Nickolai. The murder of Petrodon had been
avenged.

That had all been going on still when Calebros had seen
Jeremiah. Calebros had not become prince yet. He had not fully
understood the depth of the other Nosferatu's distress, and had
left him alone. So much had been going on, every person had
been needed. Calebros had sent Pug back to check on Jeremiah
periodically. But Jeremiah had disappeared. Vanished.

There were subterranean dangers aplenty to which a
healthy, lucid Nosferatu might fall victim: *antitribu* angered
over their rough treatment at the hands of the newly ascendant
Camarilla; insane Kindred, like Cranston, who sought refuge or
prey or both beneath ground; old wivestales taken flesh,
Nictuku, or, as Calebros had come to suspect, terrors far, far
worse. Who was to say what danger might have overcome
Jeremiah in his vulnerable state? They might never know; they
might never find him, or evidence of what had happened to
him. But opportunity had presented itself in the person of this
Malkavian, by the looks of his dwelling, a serial killer of kine.
Destruction of Kindred and consumption of vitae would be no
great crime for one such as this. And there were the words of
the Prophet….

So Calebros followed. To find where the lunatic might lead
them, to see what, in the end, the canvas sack would reveal.

Eventually, Cranston's route led them into a much larger
tunnel, a cavern. The Shaft. They were still relatively close to
the surface world, and here the Shaft ran at a fairly gentle angle,
which they followed downward. Other tunnels led away from
the main hollow, some straight down, others from varying
heights along the walls. Shortly, however, the Shaft turned

sharply downward, the angle of descent growing increasingly steep until soon there was no floor or ceiling, only up and down, and vertical walls pock-marked with irregularly radiating tunnels. For the band of Nosferatu and their guest, the going rapidly changed from simple tunnel-crawling to skittering down the steeper slope to difficult climbing, searching for foot and handholds in the darkness.

Insanity. Calebros thought. *Only a childe of Malkav would bring us here.* But he knew that was not true. Back when Jeremiah had first disappeared, Pug had tracked him to this area, and though he'd been unable to find Jeremiah, Pug was seldom wrong about such things. The rest of the Nosferatu had been too busy to join that search, but Hilda had helped Pug. Now she was missing as well.

The Shaft was a forbidding place. The darkness, normally friend to the Nosferatu, clung heavily to them here, as if it were water seeping into their clothes, their flesh, adding weight and pulling them downward. As much as possible, they tried to descend in a spiral, no climber directly beneath another, so that a single misstep, though it could mean the end of one of them, would not take them all. Is *that what Cranston wants?* Calebros wondered of the Malkavian below him. He *couldn't think all of us would fall—but enough so that he could escape?*

Calebros was relieved when the Malkavian finally pointed out one of the side tunnels that they should follow. They waited—far enough in that Cranston, if he did try a desperate attack, couldn't push anyone over the edge—until all of the Nosferatu were out of the Shaft. Calebros could sense the relief of the others at being out of the dark, seemingly bottomless well. He shared their sentiments. As it was, it was a miracle that Clubfoot, at the very least, had not fallen and taken someone with him, like some twisted carnival game of cadaver pinball.

———

"This is the place? You're sure?" Emmett asked.

Cranston turned to look at the Nosferatu—no, to look *through* him. The blue-gray eyes saw some invisible place in the middle distance. The thousand-yard stare, but not a blank stare. Cranston was definitely seeing *something*, something that only he could see. His stare clearly made Emmett want to look back over his shoulder. But the Nosferatu did not; probably didn't want to give the childe of Malkav any satisfaction. Calebros suspected that Cranston wouldn't have noticed either way. He was intent upon his own private vision.

"This is the place?" Calebros echoed his broodmate's question. "Where you found the sack?" The section of tunnel was unremarkable; there was no curve, no outcropping, no prominent feature of any sort that might remind a traveler of the underworld that he'd passed here before. How could Cranston know that this was the spot?

"If you brought us all this way to jerk us around..." Emmett let an ominous, drawn-out silence complete the threat.

Calebros had just begun searching the area—hoping to find any sign of Jeremiah, or a clue about the fleshy cord, anything that would connect Jeremiah to this place—when Pug, nose to the ground, started waving one hand excitedly. "It's him!" he said, sniffing about more enthusiastically. "Jeremiah, his scent!"

"Don't lose it, for Christ's sake," Emmett said.

Calebros moved closer. "Where does it lead?"

"This way." Pug was already moving down the tunnel.

Calebros and Emmett fell in step behind him, and Junior behind them. "Mike," Calebros said, "make sure our guest does not lag behind." Clubfoot and Albatross took up positions behind Cranston, and the entire procession trailed along behind Pug. No light penetrated this far beneath the earth. Only the grossly dilated pupils of the Nosferatu allowed them to maintain the pace they now assumed. The Malkavian, who'd kept up well enough while the group had been dependent upon him for directions, began to have difficulty, stumbling. Clubfoot and Albatross grabbed him by either arm, holding him upright and dragging him along.

Close behind Pug, Calebros was reminded of their recent hunt, when Anatole's riddle and Pug's nose had made the difference in bringing the Tremere *antitribu* Nickolai to justice. Remembering an unexpected attack that had materialized out of the dark that time, Calebros alternately watched Pug and scanned the darkness ahead. And, for the first time this night, the prince felt the stirrings of real hope. If Cranston was not lying or mistaken, if that had been the place he'd found the canvas sack, and the trail led away from that spot, then chances were good that Jeremiah still survived. He hadn't been destroyed—not by the lunatic, at least. Calebros could not speak for the other terrors of the dark.

They continued that way for several hundred yards—this collection of sniffing (Pug), hoping (Calebros), and limping (Clubfoot) Nosferatu, dragging a psychotic Malkavian with them—until Pug grew excited again. The scent had seemed strong from the start, and he'd paused only twice to check his direction; but now he sniffed and wrinkled his flat face with increasing agitation. "It's recent here. Much more recent than before." He backtracked for a moment to confirm what his nose was telling him—and that was when Calebros saw movement ahead. A shape dodging around a sharp curve in the tunnel.

"There's something there." Calebros said in a hoarse whisper.

Emmett must have seen it as well, because he sidestepped Pug and slipped past Calebros like a shot, but the prince was not far behind. They turned the comer in time to see the shape— was it *two* shapes? Calebros thought—duck around another turn. The rest of the Nosferatu had joined in the chase now as well. Calebros turned the second comer and thought again that two shapes were disappearing into the darkness ahead of Emmett down a long straightaway. The prince was well along the tunnel himself when he heard shouting and the sounds of struggle behind him.

He turned, fully expecting to see Cranston attempting escape, but the two raging beasts at each other's throats were Clubfoot and Albatross. They were a mass of savage fangs, flailing limbs, and slashing claws. Reason had fled them—both of them, victim to the cannibalistic hunger that was never far away for the Kindred. And where sanity was not in evidence, neither was the Malkavian.

Calebros looked back the other way, where Emmett was receding into the darkness. "Pug, Junior—Go with Emmett! Hurry!" Calebros shouted, then, "Mike, stay with me!" As Pug and Junior registered what their prince had said and tore themselves from the spectacle of their warring clanmates to follow Emmett, Mike was trying to separate Clubfoot and Albatross. He took as many blows as he prevented, and then for a moment it seemed that he had succeeded in attracting the combatants' attention—and they both turned on him. Mike staggered away from them, sensing the bloodlust that drove them.

Calebros didn't bother with getting their attention. He swooped in with flashing talons and hamstrung Clubfoot. The unsteady Nosferatu crumpled to the ground and, as Albatross turned, the heel of Calebros's hand slammed upward against that frenzied Kindred's chin. Albatross's thin neck whipped up and to the side, and he fell stunned to the ground among a clattering of broken teeth.

For several seconds, Mike stared at his suddenly incapacitated clanmates, then at his prince. Calebros was already stepping past him. "Come on," he said to Mike.

They quickly began retracing their steps toward where Cranston had claimed to have found the canvas sack. Calebros's sense of smell was not nearly that of Pug's, but the Nosferatu prince hoped he'd be able to tell if Cranston had deviated from their earlier route. That would be the best chance the prisoner had; in such total darkness, he couldn't hope to outrun the Nosferatu—but who could guess what path a Malkavian might choose to follow?

Within a very few moments, Calebros didn't have to guess. The prince was covering ground rapidly, Mike struggling to keep up. Calebros's painfully twisted spine did not slow him down when circumstances demanded speed, and shortly past the point to which Cranston had led them, Calebros spotted the Malkavian ahead. Cranston was not moving nearly as slowly as he had been; he was not as disadvantaged by the darkness as he'd led them to believe, but still Calebros and Mike were gaining ground on him.

Although a tiny portion of Calebros's mind continued to ponder the two figures fleeing in the other direction, most of his energy and attention were focused on the Malkavian. Surely Cranston had brought the hunger, the madness, on Clubfoot and Albatross. It was the Malkavian's fault that they had done harm to one another, that one would likely have destroyed the other had Calebros not struck them both down. Calebros felt the cold fury of vengeance rising in his veins, but even as he considered what he would like to do to repay Cranston, the Nosferatu tried to keep the comeuppance within reason. He remembered the blind hatred in Cock Robin's eyes, in his animalistic warble, as they had tracked down Nickolai. And just as de^struction of the Tremere had closed off an avenue of information, a destroyed Malkavian would serve no further purpose. There might be much they could still learn from this lunatic—which wasn't to say that he would not suffer.

As Calebros and Mike closed to within a few yards of Cranston, the racing trio was rapidly approaching the edge of the Shaft, where their tunnel ended abruptly in nothingness. *He'll have to slow down.* Calebros thought. *Whether he plans to climb up or down, he'll have to slow down to grab a handhold—and then we'll have him.* Cranston would never make it as far as the Shaft. Calebros estimated the point at which the Malkavian would have to slacken his pace—several yards shy of the Shaft. The two Nosferatu would be on him the instant he slowed—

But the Malkavian did not slow. He did not pause, but instead ran until the ground ran out beneath him, and without word or scream he plunged headlong into the abyss. Calebros and Mike just did manage to stop at the edge, but the Malkavian was already lost to the deep darkness below.

———

"But who were you with?" Calebros asked.

Jeremiah had not fought being brought back to the warren, and he seemed perfectly content now, smiling up at Calebros. Jeremiah's smile was neither cruel nor mocking, nor was it a particularly insane smile. But this was not the same focused, analytical Nosferatu whom Calebros had sent so many weeks ago to lead and be led by the Prophet of Gehenna. "I was alone until you came for me," Jeremiah said. "Alone with the darkness."

"But I found you only last night," Calebros pointed out. "What you said before—you make it sound like we were together many nights." Calebros had asked the same questions over and over again; sometimes Jeremiah gave slightly different answers, but all were similarly unhelpful.

"You believed me," Jeremiah said gratefully. "You believed me and took me where I'd be safe."

"Of course you're safe here in the warren," Calebros said, but he couldn't help the feeling that they were speaking at cross-purposes. Jeremiah was talking about someone else— someone else who'd believed his mad ravings, someone else who'd taken him *somewhere* else, not to the warren. And Jeremiah's reaction bore out Calebros's suspicion.

For the first time, Jeremiah seemed cognizant of the fact that he *was* in the warren. The stone walls of the small room were solid, but he glanced around suddenly as if countless predators were descending upon him from every direction. Jeremiah pushed himself back into the comer; he pressed his back against the converging walls, but took little comfort in his more easily defensible position. "This place isn't safe!" he screamed. "Especially not this place!"

Calebros recognized both the panic that took hold of Jeremiah and the catatonia that quickly superseded it, seemingly the only way he could cope with the imagined horrors that assailed him.

Imagined, Calebros thought. I *pray that they're imagined.*

There was nothing more to learn from Jeremiah once he entered that state—not that he'd revealed much of substance otherwise. He'd slipped in and out of paranoid paralysis all night. Calebros had had his fill for the time being. It was enough that Jeremiah again was safe among them, the prince told himself, but the consolation was slight.

What of the other shape I saw fleeing in the tunnel? he wondered. Emmett had caught up with and pounced on Jeremiah, but neither Emmett nor the others sent to aid him had seen a second shape. And Jeremiah's answers since then had proven singularly unrevealing. *Then again.* Calebros thought, *Jeremiah's notes about Anatole proved of limited use—until the exact moment when they were the most use.* As if they were meant for a specific purpose and would not be unraveled until that purpose was at hand. Could Jeremiah's ranting be another maddening gift of the Prophet?

Calebros raked his talons across his vein-raddled scalp. His head hurt; his entire body, every bone, and joint, hurt. He'd gotten more exercise running about the city these past few weeks than he had in the past thirty years, and he was convinced it wasn't healthy. An eternity of quiet contemplation was more to his liking, but his responsibilities to the clan, and now to the city, demanded that he act otherwise.

The warren was abuzz with activity. In addition to the ruckus caused by Jeremiah's presence and condition, there was significantly more pressure to gather and digest information from all over the city now that Calebros was prince. The slightest, most seemingly inconsequential bit of news or gossip might reveal a danger toward his person, and the reports that had always flooded his desk now washed over his office like a tidal wave. There was increasing word of paranoid dread of the prince among Kindred loyal and disloyal alike—they seemed to think that Calebros was everywhere, and he tried to foster that impression, that he knew *everything*, by knowing as much as he could. Now that Jeremiah was accounted for, there was more than enough work to get back to.

After a brief stop to make sure that Clubfoot and Albatross were recovering from their Malkavian-induced rage and the injuries Calebros had dealt them, the prince returned to his office and his desk with its comfortably familiar, if overwhelming, stacks of reports, newspaper clippings, and photographs. So preoccupied was he with the latest discussion with Jeremiah that Calebros had almost let himself collapse into his sturdy wooden chair before he realized what was wrong—or *different*, if not exactly wrong.

The tiered candelabra still stood near—but not too near—his desk, but the candles did not bum. Yet the office was not in darkness. The desk lamp that Calebros had buffeted beyond use and then stuffed into the trash was now upright on his desk, nestled in among the stacks of papers and his trusty Smith Corona. It was an irony of unlife in the warren that among the Nosferatu, who so closely watched over and used to their advantage the city's department of sanitation, no one ever emptied the trash with any regularity. In the case of Calebros's office, no one so much as *touched* his rubbish can; he'd long ago boxed bloody the ears of any such do-gooders. For the rare item that Calebros actually brought himself to throw away, his trash can was much more a purgatory than actual banishment. More often than not, he repented of his decision. The scraps of paper or twisted trinkets he'd fished from the bottom of the container were too numerous to count, and so the prince was particularly protective of his seemingly cast-off possessions, which an ignorant clansman might consider fair game. Umberto had made that very mistake just over twelve years ago—it had been a smashed transistor radio, Calebros remembered—but Calebros had promptly set matters aright, and there had been no repeat, by anyone, in the intervening years.

And now the desk lamp, from the sanctity of Calebros's trash, had been restored to functional life. Not only did it illuminate his desk, but the light was bright and strong, without the first hint of a flicker. The light had *always* flickered, from the first night Calebros had liberated the lamp from an abandoned office in Queens.

Calebros did not lower himself into his chair. He looked carefully around the grotto, his office sanctum, which had been violated. Aside from the lamp, all was as he'd left it—all except a certain bookshelf that was several inches farther from the wall than it should have been. The lamp and the bookshelf told him what he needed to know—they told him what he would have thought to be impossible.

The prince of New York left his desk and pulled the bookshelf farther from the wall. He bent down, with a great popping of joints, and crawled into the low, narrow tunnel the shelves concealed. With one foot, he hooked the metal bracket attached to the back of the shelves and pulled the unit to. *There were two shapes,* he told himself as he crawled along the tunnel and down the increasingly steep slope. By the time he emerged into the larger chamber that was home to his own personal lake, Calebros had convinced himself of who he would find.

Nonetheless, he was surprised to see Augustin sitting atop the large bags of salt next to the lake, waiting for him. "It has been a long while," Calebros said.

"Indeed, it has." If looking at Emmett was like gazing at a reflection, then seeing Augustin was like peering into a funhouse mirror: The features were not dissimilar, but they were contracted, shriveled, aged. Calebros didn't know how much older than he Augustin was, but he knew the difference was considerable. In addition to his other talents, the elder Nosferatu was an accomplished tinker; restoring a discarded lamp to life was right up his alley. "I have been watching," Augustin said, "but now the time has come."

"Watching me," Calebros said.

"You...and a great many people and events."

"What time is it that has come?"

"Hasn't Jeremiah told you?"

"His mind is gone," Calebros said, though he felt a dam within his soul crumbling, and walled-away, unfounded fears beginning to seep through. "He is a fearmonger now, little more." *He was broken by his time with Anatole and speaks only of the darkness beneath the earth, and the Final Nights.*

"He is wiser than any of us," Augustin said. "You know it. I've seen your notes. You just won't let yourself believe."

"The *Nictuku* are nothing more than old wives' tales," Calebros said, still trying to convince himself that he could hold the dam intact if he but tried hard enough.

"Oh, they're real," Augustin said nonchalantly, "and they're awakening. But they are the least of our problems."

Calebros was speechless. Mythical creatures of destruction, three steps in blood from Caine himself—and they were the least of the Nosferatu's problems? "You left *years* ago to find the truth about the *Nictuku*," Calebros said. "Now you return saying you've proven your worst nightmares, but you're not concerned?"

"I didn't say I'm not concerned." Augustin worked his way down from the bags of salt. "I am. They are worse than I feared. But they are no longer my *worst* nightmare, nor should they be yours, prince of New York."

"The darkness beneath the earth," Calebros said.

"Nothing that has happened has been by accident," Augustus said. "You know that, don't you? Oh, the war with the Sabbat would have happened regardless, but did it have to go the way it did—the particulars, I mean?"

"How much has been *your* doing?" Calebros asked. "You were with Jeremiah. Near the Shaft."

"Yes. I knew that the Malkavian would come to your attention sooner or later. I'd hoped you'd find the sack, and that it would lead to that place, though I admit I was growing tired of waiting. There were other clues you missed—"

"The *bozzetto*, the one in Atlanta that was different than the rest, the wrong type of clay, more like the ones in Chicago. And the picture."

"Very good." Augustin gave him a dainty golf clap. "I'm not blind to the needs of my clan. I did my part for you and Cock Robin—although mostly I wanted to make sure that he moved on. He's fairly…limited in his perspective, not so much a free thinker, as you are. But don't fool yourself into thinking that all the fingerprints you've imagined are mine."

"You've read my notes," Calebros said sharply. "You say you know what I think."

Augustin scowled at him. "You've begun to ask the right questions, but you won't let yourself go far enough. Imagine the worst-case scenario—and then let yourself believe that reality is as bad tenfold, hundredfold. Yes, your clumsy handling of the Eye of Hazimel might have helped set things in motion, but do you really think that a single Ravnos—even a Methuselah, perhaps the eldest surviving member of that clan—could be the cause of everything that has happened? Do you think it coincidence that New York fell to the Camarilla? An accident that you are prince?"

"Certainly, no Ravnos *caused*—"

Augustin cut him off. "I'm not going to debate free will and determinism with you. You may choose what you're going to wear when you get up. If I know what that will be, *for a certainty*, not just a guess, and I wear the same thing, did you have free will regarding whether we would wear the same thing? Was it coincidence?"

Calebros could see the dots connecting one to another. He had charted the dots for so long now, but he'd been unwilling— *afraid*—to draw the lines.

"That Leopold," Augustin continued, "even with the Eye, should he have been able to do what he did to a small army of Gangrel? Wouldn't he have destroyed all our allies, not to mention half the city, if he'd wielded the same power just a few weeks ago? There was a *reason* for him to destroy the Gangrel. The Gangrel abandon the Camarilla; the Camarilla is forced to abandon valuable territory; their only chance to salvage the situation—take New York from the Sabbat."

"But how—?"

"I'm talking about a consciousness so profoundly greater than ours," Augustin said wagging a finger, "with predictive powers of our actions so extensive, so accurate, as to be able to look into the future, to *shape* the future."

"How can you be so certain?" Calebros asked weakly. He wasn't sure exactly when he'd sat down, but he was sitting now on the shore of the underground lake.

"After a few decades of seeking the *Nictuku*, of searching for signs of the dark, hidden things under the earth," Augustin said, "I began to realize that all that we know, even all that we speculate about, is but the tip of an infinite iceberg, and we are in a very tiny boat on black, black waters."

"If what you say is true, and I've been walking down this predetermined path, why didn't you warn me?" Calebros wanted to know.

"I am a watcher."

Watcher. Inconnu.

"Much of what I've learned," Augustin said, "I've confirmed with others who have watched and searched far longer than I. Why didn't I warn you? It is not our way. We flatter ourselves that we are beyond the reach of the Jyhad, above the maneuverings of the ancients—but it is a lie. We are pawns as surely as you are. Still, to show ourselves is to risk much."

"Then why now?"

"Because *time has run out.* The red star shines in the sky, and the *Nictuku* rise...and because you are blood of my blood."

Time has run out. The words rattled like thunder in Calebros's mind. *The Final Nights are at hand.* "But if the ancients are as powerful as you say, then there is no hope. Our cause is futile."

"You are right that, whatever sleeps beneath us, we cannot surprise it. The behemoth wakes, surveys its surroundings, knows the hearts and minds of all creatures of the blood, sets in motion events that will safeguard it, and returns to its slumber. I believe, though, that there are multiple paths within its plans, differing possibilities, though they all lead to its survival."

"But if it has such pervasive predictive powers," Calebros protested, "there is nothing we can do."

"Nothing we can do that will *surprise* it," Augustin said. "You're right. So, in this case...we do what it wants."

"We defeat it by helping it?"

"Not defeat it. Prolong the struggle. We must assume the ancients do not yet wish to be revealed, else they would be— and that would be the end. So, the ancients' ideal path is to remain hidden. And so, we help them remain hidden. For now.

There are those of my comrades who believe, with time, we will be able to defeat the ancients, or avert their rising altogether."

"Prevent Gehenna," Calebros muttered, shaking his head in stunned disbelief.

"If the Sabbat had secured all of the East Coast," Augustin said, "some among them would have had leisure to begin the search. They claim to wage war against the ancients."

"You fear they would have discovered one?" Calebros asked. "Then it is an ancient that lies beneath us?" *Ancient. Antediluvian.*

"Naming is a way to gain mastery, and I do not pretend to gain mastery over…over *it*. But there is an elder power. And were we to expose it tonight, it would mean our destruction, the destruction of all of our kind. And perhaps of the earth itself."

"And so hiding it," Calebros said, "does not defy its will, and works in our interest as well."

"Exactly," Augustin allowed a mirthless smile to crease his lips. "Unless I am wrong."

Calebros considered that possibility for some time. Even if little of what Augustin said could be *proven* beyond a doubt, much of it dovetailed with Calebros's own suspicions — suspicions he had been denying. And suddenly Jeremiah didn't seem so insane — or rather his insanity had been brought on, thanks to the Prophet, by seeing what no Kindred or kine was meant to see. Calebros wished he could have the old *sane* Jeremiah back. The prince wished that he had never guessed any of this, that Augustin were long dead instead of standing before him. It was *all* insane, the more Calebros thought about it. How many individuals were involved? How many of their actions had been influenced, or predicted? Better not to know at all. Better not even to suspect. "But why — if it is true — why a Nosferatu prince? Who else would be more likely to stumble onto the truth?"

"Who indeed?" Augustin asked.

Who better to see the truth? Who better to play along, to make sure no one else stumbled upon what must remain hidden? "Then it knew you would come to me; it knew you would warn me."

"Perhaps," said Augustin. He sounded less sure of himself than he had earlier, but by now he would know that Calebros had taken the hook. There was no more need to convince the prince of New York.

———

"Colin, this is Emmett. He works for the prince," Gordon said. He'd already gnawed away the patch of perpetually itching hair on his shoulder tonight and was now working on his knee. He chewed his knee only when he was nervous. He and the disconcertingly ugly Nosferatu—as if there were any other kind—were waiting in the apartment.

"So," Colin said, trying to sound more confident than he really was, "I guess the prince got my perdition."

"Your petition," Emmett said. "Perdition is all yours."

"Right," Colin said, not quite understanding. "And so...?"

"The Kindred you told us about has been removed."

"Removed? What do you mean? Like..." he made a gesture with his finger slicing his throat, "...removed, or just, you know, removed?"

Emmett folded his arms. "How badly do you want to know?" Something about the way he asked the question told Colin that he did not want to know, that it might not be healthy to want to know.

"Uh...nevermind. That's not the important thing. Am I right? The important thing is that I..." Colin paused significantly, "have been vindicated. That squatter son of a bitch is gone—wherever and however ain't none of my business, and I don't wanna know, right? Right. The important thing is that my territory—*our* territory—is safe again. That Prince Calebros is a stand-up guy. Am I right?"

"Oh, by the way," Emmett added, "the tenement where that squatter son of a bitch was holed up—it's off limits."

Colin cocked his head. "Huh?"

"You know," Emmett said with a blank expression, "off limits. Stay the hell away. Don't go near it. Probably a good idea to stay away from the whole block. Think of it as a commission. The prince took care of this little problem, and you're so happy that you gladly turn over that territory." He gave Colin a cold, hard stare. "Am I right?"

Colin didn't know what to say. He stared at Emmett, then at Gordon, then at Emmett again. Finally, he recognized that there was only one thing he could say. "Uh...right."

After Emmett left Colin and Gordon, the Nosferatu made his way through the gently falling snow to the cellar where he'd found Jeremiah's canvas sack. Tonight, he found Mike Tundlight there supervising a handful of their clanmates. There was no longer any sign of graves, shallow or otherwise; there was no Santa suit. The floor of the cellar was now smooth, fresh cement, not yet dry. One of Mike's workers was finishing the last corner.

Mike shook his head. "I guess we don't have enough cement to fill in the whole Shaft, so we're going to close off all the tunnels." He let slip a wry laugh. "It'll take years."

Emmett sighed. "Yeah, he's doing the same thing around the warren. Pretty soon all of Manhattan is gonna be a concrete bunker."

"What's Calebros afraid of?" Mike asked.

Emmett just shrugged. "Don't know, but I guess whatever it is, it doesn't hurt to be ready." They stood and watched for a few minutes as the worker smoothed over the final corner.

Five Courses

Justin Achilli

Bad cop.

Preston Marshall sat back in his chair and stuffed the last bit of his Subway sandwich into his mouth. *Bad cop.* Fine security officer, though. Well, not really, but at least it made more money for him to be a crooked security commandant than it had for him to be a high-profile renegade law officer.

Six years ago, Preston had been indicted and convicted for going above and beyond the call when it came to restraining a suspect. Okay, fine; it was two suspects, but at least it wasn't in the same case. The incidents were months apart. The first one, some drunk, snotty college kid, only spent a few weeks in bed recovering. The second one, that crazy nigger bitch who had scratched him and then stabbed him with his own car keys, she wasn't so lucky.

After a brief media circus, Preston found himself out of a job. Damn kangaroo court was what it was, with liberals and spooks in the jury. In the end, though, it worked out all right. He'd answered an ad for the midnight security supervisor over at RJR, and they hired him on the spot. Turns out they wanted someone willing to look the other way and shut the hell up for a few bucks. One of their export companies drove a truck in every now and then and all Preston had to do was water-damage their manifest. Whatever happened with sixty-million-dollars-a-year's worth of cigarettes after that wasn't his problem.

Some of the guys on his shift had had a problem with it. Some of them found themselves unemployed or reassigned to day shifts. No big deal. They learned that it was best to shut your mouth if you wanted to keep working. Preston found out that it was worth an extra thousand dollars a month—hell, an extra fifteen hundred dollars in some months—to acquire a selective blindness. If it wasn't him doing the deed, it would be someone else, so why be a martyr...especially if you don't believe that anything seriously wrong is happening, anyway? The export company was probably just selling the cigs in Mexico or Canada, ducking the duties and taxes that only made those government bastards rich.

Preston Marshall's face opened up like a watermelon dropped from a second-story window. Blood, flesh and less identifiable bits of gore spattered the security dispatch office, marring the windows, the computer, the clipboard, the stack of bills of lading....

Under the sterile darkness of shadows thrown by fluorescent lights, a figure in a navy peacoat walked nonchalantly into the unassuming night, smelling ever so faintly of gunpowder.

Monday, 27 December 1999, 12:04 AM
The villa of Biagio Giovanni
Ombrosa, Italy

"It's quaint. It's almost medieval." Isabel looked to the clock, which proclaimed the time to be just after midnight. 'I'm sure you do it for convenience, though."

"Very true, my dear cousin, very true," replied Biagio. "When the men you work with keep their hours only after dark, you learn to make concessions for them. You take your supper when you can." He smiled. "May I pour you wine?" Biagio waved to a servant but Isabel held up her hand in polite protest. "No? Nothing at all? I know your tastes, but a gracious host never assumes...."

"No, that's fine, Biagio. You have a lovely home and a lovely table. It's a shame that I must decline." Isabel noticed the pleasant warmth emanating from the great fireplace that heated the patio. Without the comfort given off by the great hearth, it would have been far too cold to sit outside on such a cold night.

Isabel watched as the two stewards set the table for their master. In her own haven, Isabel would likely have dispensed with all the pomp, perhaps waving her hand toward a ghostly servant to bring her a snifter of decanted vitae. Then again, no — in these modem nights, such truck with the spirits was frivolous. As fewer and fewer of the departed souls seemed able to answer the call of the Giovanni's deathly magic, the practice was now a luxury, not a convenience.

Biagio Giovanni's wine steward poured him a glass of valpolicella; apparently the meal would be pasta. The other servant brought forth a scalloped bowl, filled to brimming with field greens, a crisscross of sliced ham and cheese, and a few of the black calamata olives Biagio's younger brother grew in Greece. She smelled the bite of vinegar.

"I hope you don't mind," her host continued, his eyes on her and not on the food being set before him. "Battista says it repulses her, but she said it wouldn't be too untoward to eat before you if the invitation specified dinner."

"I don't mind at all. This is what I do." Isabel leaned back in her chair, feeling the satin of her Yves Saint-Laurent gown crush the tender velvet of Biagio's ostentatious patio furniture. She imagined a host of attendants earned their keep only by watching the skies and waiting for the slightest hint of rain before scurrying out and rushing it to some unobtrusive safe place inside their master's loggia. "I have had dinner with diplomats, ambassadors, and heads of state. You'd be surprised what a simple complaint of a delicate constitution or upset stomach can defer. Few of them have been as gracious as you, however, Biagio."

Again, her host smiled. "What is a man, if not the sum of his demeanor?" He picked up a salad fork, speared a leaf and an olive, and raised them to his mouth. "Now I should tell you why I've asked you here, should I not?"

If one chose to look deeply enough, one could find current employment records for Detlev Hrad in over sixteen companies, half of which weren't even in his native Estonia or adopted home in the United States. Detlev's job consisted primarily of receiving large shipments of cigarettes from an American wholesaler attached to RJR, and cycling them as inventory through each of the sixteen companies for which he worked. With many of these companies, Detlev was the sole owner. In others, he was a member of a partnership. Still others were limited-liability offshoots of existing companies, perhaps even with their business documents sent to mail rooms of larger corporations that didn't even know Detlev had paid a mail-room attendant or two to pass on letters addressed to him in weekly bundles.

Cigarettes went to Detlev's warehouse in New York, where they sat and waited to be shipped to distributors after circling the globe three or four times — in principle, if not in practice. It was beautiful: Nobody knew anything was illicit, and even if they did, what were the odds that they'd trace it back to him through *sixteen* fronts?

Someone had, though. Detlev sat stock still in his executive chair, his white-knuckled hand clenched so tightly around his red ledger pencil that he had snapped it in half. Someone had found him, and was making one hell of a racket in the foyer of his for-appearances office. For a long time, Detlev's girlfriends had been complaining that he seemed paranoid and distant. Whenever one brought it up, he dumped her. Half of him wished he could have all those girls there in front of him, so he could slap them, scream at them, "See? See? I was right."

Detlev's other half, though, was scared shitless. Normally anyone who came to the office was either in the wrong place and stepped right back out, or announced their presence at the door, like the FedEx guys and the mailman did. For a moment Detlev had thought that it might be a bum looking for a dry place to spend the night, but the moment he'd seen the light in the foyer flicker out and heard the deadbolt of the front-door lock, he knew he was in trouble.

Who could it be? It didn't seem like a cop—the actions were too ominous. A cop would have arrested him already, or at least announced his presence. Detlev wasn't aware of any enemies. He paid RJR on time, he never short-shipped any of his "independent representatives," and he wasn't aware of anyone else's international claims to territory. Still, a man in his position was bound to upset someone. Maybe it was one of the Cosa Nostra fat tonys, one of the yaks, or even the Russian mob. Maybe it was some activist or the relative of some smoker who died who'd gotten a wild hair up his ass and dug up Detlev's number. Whatever—this was someone who was pissed about something, because no one else ever came calling.

Without warning, the noise stopped utterly. Detlev sat stock still, looking expectantly, fearfully, to the doorway that led from the foyer into his office proper. A long, *long* minute ticked away on the cheap electric clock hanging above the Ansel Adams print to Detlev's right; a pair of flies dueled over the oily Chinese takeout sitting on the comer of the desk.

The desk… ?

Detlev noticed the pen from his desk set had gone missing. Was that what this was all about? Was that all? Someone had broken in while he went to fetch the Chinese food, stolen the utterly unremarkable pen from the matching set in the office, and was awkwardly trying to escape? It couldn't possibly be so innocuous.

Detlev felt his doubt confirmed when a harsh, strong hand grabbed the top of his head and pinned him back in his chair. A piercing sensation pulsed briefly at the back of his neck, and he knew that the missing pen had been driven into the divot between his shoulder blades with unimaginable force. For a flickering moment, it hurt as if a fire had been ignited in the pain center of his mind; his eyes widened involuntarily and bulged forth. Then the pain dulled, and with it dimmed all of Detlev's awareness of the world around him.

Breaking the few protruding inches of the pen off, Detlev's murderer unbuttoned his navy peacoat and left through the front door, leaving it unlocked.

"And what is it that I can do for you, Biagio?" asked Isabel, casually running her finger around the rim of an empty crystal glass.

More servants had entered the room, carrying away her host's antipasto and leaving in its stead a small silver tray of spinach-garnished *crostini* covered in melted mild cheese, and a plate of small bay scallops and orange slices that smelled like they had been pan-seared with a sweet wine.

Biagio sipped from his wine glass and then offered Isabel the plate of bread. Smiling, she declined. "Don't feel as if you have to offer me something each time your staff brings it to the table."

"I'm sorry. It's force of habit." A wisp of steam rose from Biagio's mouth.

"No, it's not," Isabel looked across the table, her eyes meeting Biagio's. "You're trying to change the subject. You know you have to ask me whatever it is you're going to ask me, but you're nervous about it." Isabel crossed her hands in front of her. "Honestly, Biagio, do you think I haven't talked with enough people over my hundreds of years to recognize an uncomfortable gesture or an empty motion?"

"Hundreds of years? You wear it so well!" Biagio joked in reply.

"Now you're being ridiculous."

"I'm sorry; I'm making light of my own fault. But I certainly hope you don't think it was completely disingenuous?"

"Not at all. I'm certain that you honestly were sharing the bounty of your table with me. But that doesn't mean you weren't using the most available avenue to deter the conversation."

"As I'm continuing to do now?"

"Exactly."

"Such psychology! I truly share the table with a master."

"As I said before, it's what I do."

Biagio Giovanni, his eyes never leaving Isabel's, impaled a tender scallop on his fork and raised it to his lips.

Gianfranco switched off the lights of his English truck and wheeled the heavy vehicle from the road into the darkness of the Italian night. Twenty-five gross cartons of "duty-free" cigarettes—over fifty thousand dollars at American retail—rode with him. He stood to make his usual ten percent cut, with maybe a few dollars in "bonus" if Biagio was feeling characteristically generous. A man could get used to the smuggler's life, especially when it paid so well every other week for just a few hours' work and a few minutes of risk. All you had to do was grease a few palms at the airport and watch out for the roadblocks where they searched your car for contraband. Since Gianfranco's brother-in-law worked for the police, he always knew where the roadblocks would be and when, and happily shared his knowledge for a few cartons and a hundred peeled from the roll in Gianfranco's pocket. Kill the lights, coast downhill and hit the road a half a kilometer from the roadblock, and it was practically a free ride from there.

Mama had even packed him a snack to make the trip more comfortable: a small bunch of grapes, a wedge of lemon and a crusty roll. No doubt the farmer over whose field he was currently cutting would have a similar meal for lunch tomorrow, wondering just who in the hell had become so drunk that they decided to take a shortcut through his flock's pasture.

It always occurred to Gianfranco as he crept slowly past the roadblocks that his truck smelled of stale smoke and gunpowder—he knew he had to quit pocketing the odd packs of American cigarettes that broke loose from his bundles because sooner or later Biagio would find out and he'd probably lose his bonus pay. The gunpowder smell came from the *lupare* shotgun he had stashed under his seat. That was another similarity between Gianfranco and the farmer—they both carried the "wolf-gun," albeit for presumably different reasons. While the *lupare* worked well against the wolves who chased down stray sheep from farmers' flocks, it also put the fear of God into fellow marauders who prowled the night, animal or otherwise. Not that Gianfranco had ever used his *lupare* against a man. That would cut the poor victim in half! The few times he'd had to grab for it, the appearance of the thing alone had warded off his antagonists.

And then Gianfranco saw the wolf in his rearview mirror. At the crest of the hill, just before the place where he had turned the truck from the road, stood the unmistakable predator's form. It seemed almost as if the wolf had followed Gianfranco's very path. He felt an odd sensation come over him, perhaps spawned by his musings about his gun and the virtually divine placement of the wolf. Or maybe it was the thrill of being caught that enticed him; smuggling was always more exciting at the cinema or in the books than it was in real life, and he felt no small disappointment at that. On a whim, Gianfranco decided to brake the truck and shoot at the wolf.

It served no purpose at all, of course, this humanly cruel endeavor. Still, Gianfranco reasoned that it could do him no harm. Even if the roadblock police heard the shotgun's report, they would simply think it was a farmer putting an end to some unlucky predator. He probably couldn't even reach the damn thing—it was a scrawny target, probably half-mad from hunger yet wary of untended meals, and likely too far away for the short, brutal scatter of the weapon's shot. But men have never been known for prudence or kindness, and Gianfranco was no exception. He brought the truck to a stop using its parking brake and quietly exited the seat, gathering his gun with him.

Almost half a kilometer away, a candle's light went out at the farmer's cottage, and a door opened briefly, discharged a slight form from inside, and closed quietly.

Gianfranco crept slowly back up the grade, unaware of the silent figure following him. He found a small outcropping of rock and squatted down behind it, using it to hide himself from his oblivious prey. The light of the heavy moon shone down, enabling Gianfranco to draw a bead on his mark with ease.

With similar ease, Gianfranco's hunter closed on his own prey. A change of plan, surely—the smuggler was originally to have been dragged into the farmer's home and the whole thing set ablaze, but this would do. Indeed, this might prove to offer a little more creative freedom....

As Gianfranco slid a shell into the barrel of the gun, his predator made short work of the distance between himself and his victim. Rising slowly, quietly, deliberately above the crouched form of the gunman, the killer announced his presence with a disapproving "Tsk, tsk," and slapped the gun out of Gianfranco's hand as the latter turned in shock.

The killer took up the fumbled weapon and raised it over his head, intent on bludgeoning the man with it. Gianfranco put his own hands over his head, as if his feeble arms could deter the blow that came down. Deftly, the assassin took out a heavy hunting knife and dressed the unconscious body, taking distinct care to leave the victim alive. Blood scattered; flesh parted.

Gianfranco awoke to a dull ache in his head and chest, and cold in his extremities. He could move neither his arms nor his legs.

On the slope above him, the wolf had smelled blood on the wind. The predator would eat well tonight.

And again, the murderer in the peacoat strode away unmolested into the relentless darkness of the Italian countryside.

"It's more complex than a simple favor." Biagio wound a bulge of linguine around the end of his heavy, silver four-tined fork, taking care to include a caper and a sauteed shrimp in the payload. Long shadows emerged from behind him, as if the night had grown as tired of his delays and deferrals as Isabel Giovanni had.

"I'm sorry? What is?" Isabel replied, making less and less effort to hide her increasing frustration. She had volunteered to meet with Biagio as a favor. The man was a financial prodigy, well-versed enough in both American law and Italian to find a not-quite-illegal method of importing tobacco from the United States into Italy without paying the mammoth tariffs and taxes on the product. Through a series of blinds and exchanges among front companies, he kept the paper trail obscure enough to hide his own involvement and further occlude the location of the product itself. Of course, the product never made more than three stops, but to trace its supposed location, one would have to call a dozen different companies before being graciously redirected to the first.

Isabel felt this was not unlike how she was being treated herself. Either Biagio was stupidly unaware of the passions of the Kindred—unlikely—or he was so thrilled and satisfied with himself that he found it pleasurable to test the limits of everyone with whom he came in contact.

"The whole situation. I've broken a few rules, Isabel, and I wanted to talk to you about making amends."

"Amends for what? Not going through the proper channels?"

"So to speak. I know that I haven't paid what's due."

"Don't you think it's a little late for that? Anyone who has a problem with what you're doing has undoubtedly already made up his mind against you. As a matter of fact, if I can indulge in a little of my own psychology, that's what you're really asking me. Someone's jeopardized your business, and you want me to find out who he is."

Biagio put his fork down in the pasta bowl. "Isabel, please don't make me the villain here."

"It's not a question of villains. It's a question of doing what's expected. You know you didn't do what was expected of you—you didn't talk to your don and you refused to pay off the local *gabelotti*. You didn't think it would matter, but the cigarette business grew so quickly that they noticed you before you were wanting them to."

"That's not wholly true, Isabel. I didn't know who to go to. I didn't know who to tell. I figured that they would come to me once I was worth their notice."

"Dammit, Biagio, who do you think you're talking to here? You're a part of one of the most influential and respected families in the world. You were mentored by one of the three biggest drug smugglers running the triangle between Cuba, the United States and here."

"Isabel, please—ᵂ

"No, Biagio, you know it as well as I do, as does everyone in this house, whether they're the person who cooks your dinner or the daughter who plays with toys out by the fountain. These people know what it is to be involved with the Giovanni family. They know who the Giovanni are and what they do. But, before you interrupted me, I was talking. You yourself took the trip between Cuba and Italy several times, and not for the purposes of vacation. You saw an opportunity, you took it, and it broke your heart to think of paying anyone who didn't know that they were due."

"It's not like I've done anything wrong, Isabel. I haven't paid the thieves and racketeers who dip into other businesses because they've scared everyone into accepting their presence."

"You *are* a thief and racketeer, Biagio. Now that you've been caught, you're all upset and claiming that everyone else has done an injustice to *you*. While that may work for adolescents, I don't think it's going to hold much water when the dons really grow frustrated with you and want *your* head on a platter. That's what this is about, isn't it? You understood the message that they sent you by killing your people, and you want me to take care of it before it makes it back to you."

Biagio licked his lips and sipped his wine. "In so many words, yes. But how do you know that some of my associates have turned up dead? Is the information network of the estimable Isabel Giovanni so vast that she knows the movements of the world before they happen?"

"Put aside your snide vanity for a moment and think it through. Yes, I have contacts everywhere, but up until now, who cared about another cigarette smuggler?"

"This is what I'm asking you, Isabel."

"It's someone from your own family, you simpleton." Isabel made a grand point of sighing with this revelation.

Seven more men turned up dead, having been seen by others only the night before. All seven men, it was whispered through the streets of town, had worked as "salesmen" for Biagio Bemando Giovanni, the new and reckless don.

Old Dondi had strangled in his sleep, wound up tightly in his own bedsheets.

Carlo had had too much wine, and was dead before he could make it to the hospital because the blood in his veins couldn't carry enough oxygen.

Peter and Joseph's mother had locked the house, not remembering that her sons had left for the evening. They must have tried to climb in through a second-story window and fallen, because both were found in the bushes in front of their house with broken necks.

Lui's own wife had thought he was a burglar when he returned home, drunk, from the public house and killed him without knowing what she had done. The neighbors remembered her screaming in hysteria hours before he had come home—perhaps a *real* burglar had scared her and driven her to such fear that she'd stabbed her husband, thinking her tormentor had returned.

Gianni's tie had become caught in the belt of his car's engine as he looked to see why it was making some terrible noise. It had pulled his face down into the fan and burned the bloody remains against the hot radiator.

Silvio had been nailed to the underside of the pier with an oil*soaked rag stuffed in his mouth so he couldn't call for help before he drowned.

It was also said that a drifter had left town in the early hours of that morning, before the sun rose. He had nothing with him but the woolen coat on his back and a stray dog that chased him to the horizon but returned shortly thereafter.

"I don't know how you stay so thin, eating like you do. It's enough to stop a man's heart," Isabel commented.

"Not that you have to worry about such things," replied Biagio with all the bile he could muster. In truth, he was growing a bit sleepy, having sated himself with such a luxurious repast. It didn't help that someone in his own family had chosen to work against him; disappointment weighed him down, as did the feeling of having revealed to Isabel that perhaps he wasn't as clever or wise as his success implied he was.

Breaking Biagio from his brief reverie was the servant bringing his final course to the table: tender veal garnished with asparagus and soft*shelled crab caught down by the docks. Children who lived near the villa, the families of the servants and the young Giovanni themselves, brought crabs they had trapped to Biagio's chef, Giuseppe, who paid them a few lira, and rewarded them with a smile. Indeed, everything Giuseppe cooked was fresh; no doubt the lamb was brought in from market this morning and the *crostini* had been baked this very afternoon.

The manservant set the succulent dish before his master and vanished quietly into the kitchen.

Isabel continued her unblinking stare, albeit without any further remark. Another barb would simply add insult to Biagio's injury, and her malevolence was not one of petty spite. Quite the opposite—Isabel was like a wolf or a raptor, a woman for whom "evil" was an utterly inappropriate word. She was a balance of virtues twisted by the Embrace: Her esteem for her family had become tainted by her knowledge of its predatory nature. Her duty to the family name had made her a vicious rival, turning her back on those too weak to preserve the prominence the Giovanni had achieved. The fact that she was a drinker of mortal blood, a "Kindred," also made her a murderess.

A murderess.

Such being the case, Biagio felt his blood grow chill. She had come here to kill *him*. But if that was true, why did she simply sit there at the end of the table, enduring his ever-more-awkward manners and his growing fear of the hideous world of monsters who lurked in the shadows and took their tribute as they took the warm sustenance from their prey? Why had she not simply broken him with the news that he had disappointed whomever it was in the Giovanni who had sent her here? Why did she at all explain to him the true nature of her charge?

Was this a test? Had Isabel been sent to bless or curse him with the same deathlessness that afflicted her? It was a tantalizing possibility—that someone had recognized his "audacity" as ambition and his "temerity" as drive. Like his blood, his bones grew cold with the thought, that he might change into one of those night creatures and know power of which this mortal life was the merest echo. To become a monster! To taste the might of Heaven or Hell and wield it like a feudal lord over the peasants of the sunlit world!

Biagio could practically feel the change already—he no longer wanted the sumptuous spread that had comprised his dinner, could hardly bring himself to place the morsels into his mouth. It was true! She worked the magic right now, bringing him into the family of the dead! His extremities grew numb, his limbs resistant to movement. His eyes drooped. Biagio's joints ached with the coming of his new nature!

"Joseph..." Isabel called. What was this?

From the kitchen emerged a man in a heavy woolen coat of navy-blue hue. This was not Giuseppe, nor a servant. Damn her! She had poisoned him under his own roof and he had taken it all in like a gluttonous fool, the verist embodiment of greed, much the way he had taken his ill-earned money.

"But...why bother? Why...this way?" Biagio croaked, his stiffening lips forcing themselves with terrible exertion to form the words.

"For two reasons," Isabel glared down at her expiring cousin. "First, we have no need even to clean this up. It will appear that your own gluttony did you in. No one will believe it, of course, but the coroners should have no reason to doubt their expedient result.

"The second reason, though, is one after your own heart. You said yourself, 'What is a man, if not the sum of his demeanor? This is true not only of men, but of the Kindred; perhaps even more so. I'm no knife-wielding throat slitter, cousin. Among our kind, subtlety is the surest way to preserve one's own unlife. It's a lesson I'm sure you appreciate.

"But at such a great cost. Good night, cousin."

With dead eyes, Isabel Giovanni watched the ghost of her cousin flow fluidly up from his dead body and fade away into the cold air. Then she accompanied her peacoated associate on the long walk home.

The Dragon's Belly

Stewart Wieck

Friday, 31 December 1999, 11:28 PM
The Shaft
New York City, New York

There is a story of a greedy and cruel king who lived within a castle formed entirely of perfect leaded crystal. He ostensibly demanded this transparent abode so that he could look out upon the lands made lovely by the tireless work of his servants, but in truth it was because he knew those who plotted behind his back were legion. The king was determined that his enemies would never find a comer in which to conspire.

No paramours for his wife. No allies for his advisors. No sleepy guards at the gate.

Of course, the result of this was increasing paranoia. Though virtually omnipresent in his near kingdom and crystal castle, he was not omniscient, and he began to ferret out enemies where likely none existed. He came to distrust his own eyes, so that when he saw his craven uncle speaking with a guardsman, the king could only believe foul intentions were the topic of conversation. He was no fool!

Any sign at all became an ill omen. And that's exactly what I require when my angel descends this so-called Shaft straight to the hell of the dragon's belly.

The point of my story? None that it has not already served. Fire with fire is what's required here. Thankfully, it's not truly fire we're dealing with, as that's just a metaphor for metaphors. Fire versus fire, I would lose. No matter the fact that I no longer possess any real essence. But with metaphors the weak can become mighty. And that is my only hope for saving humanity, for in the shadow of the dragon I am truly nothing.

True, the thing, the dragon I fight may simply exist as a metaphor as well even though it wields tremendous power. For in truth, how seriously can you accept this anthropomorphized evil? The embodiment of the direct blood-spawn of the presumably mythical fourth inhabitant of our planet?

Yet it's against such an implausible reality that I have struggled for centuries. Would you demean me so as to point out the ridiculousness of my battle? Despite ample proof I could offer? Or question so the reasons for which I have continued this struggle in the first place?

I seek to delay—I would not presume to use so strong a word as halt—a terrible event that I have every reason to believe is moments from commencing. But pardon me, now, for I have instructions to dispense. My angel has arrived. And he must See things.

———

A hunchbacked figure approached the entrance of the Shaft. The figure's shambling feet still trailed debris of unknown nature and origin from the slimy and fetid walkways of the sewer tunnels that had brought the figure here. But the Nosferatu Donatello was oblivious of such unpleasantness, much as he disregarded his physical deformities. Especially on this foreboding night when he felt that he was walking into a lion's den.

He was truly a dead man walking, but the strange circumstances that had led to Donatello's being here made the vampire certain that this night even his unlife would end. How else should he feel, informed by Calebros, the new prince of

New York, of the content of a coded message from the mad prophet of Gehenna, the Malkavian Anatole: "An angel must enter the hell of the dragon's belly before this age passes, lest all ages come to pass." To the prince this meant only one thing: Donatello, tattooed as he was on his back by the hand of a gifted mortal with the figure of Uriel, the angel of death, must descend the Shaft before the new year—the new millennium—began.

And so here he was, seeing ominous signs in every shadow, sensing a grave responsibility that was evidently his, yet not knowing what exactly he must do. And here too was Anatole.

The Malkavian appeared to pixilate into soft focus until he was adumbrated by the fragile light that illuminated the Shaft.

Donatello approached the elder Kindred with care, yet in plain view and without the benefit of his shrouding powers, for the Malkavian appeared not to notice him. The Nosferatu did not wish to become a casualty of destructive reflex.

Donatello said, "I am here as you instructed, Prophet."

Despite Donatello's echoing words, Anatole did not budge. The Nosferatu imagined him engaged in some internal dialogue from which his crazed consciousness could not escape.

This was the Nosferatu's second encounter with Anatole, and he felt no more at ease than before. In fact, the prophet's odd, almost impossible lack of movement made him even more uncomfortable, as if there was a pressure here building toward some resolution that could surely only be fiery. Or perhaps it was because Donatello had met Anatole before but could recall nothing of the encounter that he felt uneasy now.

The prophet looked much the same now as he had then when Donatello had spent several evenings with him within the Cathedral of St. John the Divine. His blond hair was dirty and tousled. His eyes stared blankly, not just into Donatello, but through him. In general, Donatello was stunned again as before by the paradox of the mundanity of this man and his seeming saintliness. Perhaps it was a true paradox. Anatole was so ordinary that he seemed something more. And not saintly in a trivial, soup-kitchen kind of way, but in a larger regard, as if the prophet truly did carry a greater Word and was ever at liberty to disseminate it.

Donatello almost laughed out loud then, because he suddenly realized that this was not Anatole at all. Rather, here, on the verge of the dreaded Shaft, the wide tunnel with countless entrances that plunged ah most vertically into the heart of the city and maybe the whole damned Earth itself, where the darkness seemed more intense and where the already clotted blood inside a vampire seemed to grow even heavier — here, Donatello was hallucinating.

Despite being a figment of the Nosferatu's imagination, Anatole's eyes suddenly came into focus, staring directly into Donatello's own. The Nosferatu shuddered. Donatello's senses continued to inform him that this Anatole was an apparition, but it was far more a Holy Ghost than a phantasm to be explained by the Nosferatu's apprehension of the Shaft and his descent therein.

Still staring silently, intently, the vision of the visionary clasped his fingers together high in front of his chest. There was nothing akin to supplication in this display, but only the impression that what he was about to say was indeed more than the mere words of a mortal, or at least one who had been such some time in the past. With a voice like the wind through a hollow reed, Anatole spoke.

"An angel must enter the hell of the dragon's belly before this age passes, lest all ages come to pass."

Despite his trepidation, in spite of his anxiety, Donatello felt a bubble of anger and frustration burst within him. He nearly shouted at Anatole, but held back out of respect and also for shame, for was he as mad as the prophet to be snapping at a specter? Even so, realizing that he was engaging an illusion in conversation, he muttered through clenched teeth, "That much we...I...know already, Prophet. But why? And why me, if indeed any could truly conceive of me as angel? And for what purpose? If there is—"

Anatole cut him off with a slight motion of his hand. "Aisling Sturbridge thought you beautiful. Tremere witches can be wise indeed."

Donatello wondered for a moment at the stories he'd heard of a likeness of the mistress of the razed and overrun Atlanta chantry—what was her name? Hannah—in the cavern in upstate New York where Anatole had last been seen. Had that gargoyle been an advisor to Anatole when the Malkavian had written in blood upon the cavern's walls?

And then Donatello felt an itch upon his back. Not merely an annoying irritation, but more like a scratching that quickly grew to a sense that something within his body was clawing its way out. Then the sensation spread into a lopsided ring across the breadth of his back and Donatello squirmed in discomfort. He knew it was his tattoo, the final masterpiece of the artist Ernst Lohm who was to the mortals much of what Anatole was to the Kindred: someone who seemed to look in all the wrong places yet find all the right things.

The Nosferatu continued to twist about. Suddenly, great fiery wings blossomed from his back and shed light upon the tunnel and the Shaft as if a torch of God had illuminated the firmament. No heat radiated from these great wings onto Donatello's face even though great licks of feathery flames crackled only inches away. But Donatello could not deny the existence of either the prophet or this seeming miracle. He thought it best if he did not too prodigiously apply logic to this mad, mad night, especially now, mere moments from the millennium.

Anatole's crisp voice rose above the popping of the flaming wings, "Now descend to Hell, angel. Follow the trail of the martyr's blood and spread your light to briefly illuminate the infinity of darkness."

With a slow and heavy stroke, Donatello's blazing wings beat the air and lifted the Nosferatu from his feet. His body swayed like a pendulum over the recesses of the abysmal Shaft below. Then he descended into the depths, the light of the great wings pushing the darkness aside.

You think one so old could not be so misled? Then you do not understand the power of metaphor. It has never been applied against you. As in examining the secrets of the mistress of the traitor of a cabal's inner circle, you never know where truth dovetails into falsehood. That is why this is fire against fire in so many ways. What is the truth of this old one? It is his greatest weapon that we cannot answer that question with any degree of certainty. However, like the king (remember him?), he cannot know what we *can in fact* verify.

And only a nudge is required. I know so many secrets. My time in and between the minds of these ancient monsters has revealed much. More than enough reward for centuries of diligent exploration. Perhaps more than enough for an eternity, for what truth matters beyond the one with the power to destroy you?

I know this story: God sent its father away, so perhaps an angel will suffice for it. My own belief in God wavered, was perhaps extinguished centuries ago, but God as metaphor proves ever-strong even in the hands of the infidel.

Why should I go to such lengths? Why have I even gone to any effort at all? Why save mortals from whom I am now two steps removed, or even the Kindred whom I have left behind now as well? It was the blood of this willing martyr—myself!—before Cranston's reluctant blood that set this endgame in motion. Why did I ever embark on this road, this effort to save millions—now billions!—of miserable lives, even if among this sad majority there are a handful of good souls to spare?

Is this a question my adversaries have already addressed? Dismissed? Do they care? Whatever their thoughts, their actions betray them. It falls to me to preserve this trivial existence for a little bit longer. It is without any sense of pride that I complete this task, that I see the angel now stepping into the dragon's belly and dispersing ever so slightly the gathering darkness.

So, my answer? A metaphorical one, of course. Why does a wolf disable its hunting prowess, its means of survival, and chew off its leg to escape the huntsman trap?

Or am I or my mission or my adversary or even the greatest truth I can offer—my story—*only* a metaphor too?

Regardless, there shall be no Gehenna this night.

Curious about other Crossroad Press books? Stop by our
website: http://crossroadpress.com
We offer quality writing
in digital, audio, and print formats.

Subscribe to our newsletter on the website homepage and
receive a free eBook.